Thy Cup Runneth Over

Black Men Fear Love

By Trey Parker

Table of Contents

Psalm 23

23 The LORD is my shepherd; I shall not want.

2 He maketh me to lie down in green pastures: he leadeth me beside the still waters.

3 He restoreth my soul: he leadeth me in the paths of righteousness for his name's sake.

4 Yea, though I walk through the valley of the shadow of death, I will fear no evil: for thou art with me; thy rod and thy staff they comfort me.

5 Thou preparest a table before me in the presence of mine enemies: thou anointest my head with oil; my cup runneth over.

6 Surely goodness and mercy shall follow me all the days of my life: and I will dwell in the house of the LORD forever.

Intro

This is a story about love. Not that Hallmark shit that gets pushed at Valentine's Day either. Real love. Love of self, of circumstances, of material and moral ideals. Even love of other people. In this story, it won't be described in the all-encompassing, heart-beating fast kinda way. Nah, this love involves the way we sacrifice ourselves and our character for that which we claim to love. They say black men either fear, or simply don't know how to love. I say black men show love in the only way they've learned how, and it's an unfortunate fact that the women often follow suit. This is a story of what happens when love, or each person's definition of it, is not quite enough…

Chapter 1: First Base

Something isn't balanced. Something isn't right. A missing piece of a puzzle leaves a void. That's how I feel. If you have a deck of cards, and you're missing one, then the deck is no good. You can't play the game. The hand that I was dealt is missing a card. But this isn't a game at all. This is my life. It's just not fair.

I logged off of Facebook, because I realized that I was sick and tired of seeing everybody post Happy Father's Day pictures with their old, rusty daddies. I didn't care, nor did I feel like anyone else did. People were probably just surprised to see that these people even saw their daddies once or twice a year. Everybody was putting on, acting like they loved their daddy. Well, I don't love mine and his absence over the years showed that he clearly ain't love me. I couldn't find one picture with us together to post. I looked through all the old, dusty ass photo albums around the house and I couldn't find one. Not one! I don't get it. My mama never talked about why he never took the time to come around here, but I was determined to get some information out of her. Straight to the laundry room I went. Mama was washing clothes as usual, rocking back and forth listening to some old folks' music. Luther Vandross. She loved her some Luther.

"Mama, I have a question."

"What you want, Terrance?" Mama asked, not turning around.

"Are you and Daddy married or divorced?"

She turned around. "Why do you ask that?"

"Because I want to know. Y'all don't live together. Are y'all divorced?"

"We're not together. That's all you need to know," Mama said with an eye roll as she turned around.

I looked away, shook my head, and then looked back. "Mama tell the truth! I'm 13 years old now. You can be honest. I'm old enough to know something."

She sighed as she stopped doing laundry and turned around. "Me and your father were never married. I had you when he and I were together, but we never got married."

I nodded and folded my arms. "So why y'all ain't never get married?"

"Because. We just didn't. We were happy being alone."

I raised my eyebrow. "Don't seem like it. You don't look happy taking care of me by yourself."

Mama laughed. "It might not look like it, but I'm just as happy as could be."

"Well I'm not happy not having him around. Why he don't come around much?" I asked.

Another eye roll. "Because he's out being your father."

"He hates me, doesn't he? He's ashamed of me."

"That's not true. I'm the reason why he doesn't want to come around. Him being gone has nothing to do with you," Mama said.

I heard loud knocking coming from the front of the house. "Jay's at the door, Mama. I'm going outside."

"Bye boy," she said, as she turned back around and continued with laundry.

***

I could never understand it. I'm the only child, but my mama is taking care of me by her damn self. I know she's struggling because she's always complaining about everything. Bills, bills, and more bills! Life is hard if you let my mama tell it. And I know my daddy don't pay child support, because she be complaining about that too. But enough about her.

I walked out to the front of the house, opened the door and saw Jay and Omar on their bikes waiting on the porch. They both stood halfway on their bikes, with one foot on the pedal, and the other on the ground. Jay's white shirt was off and around the back of his neck, resting on his shoulders. One hand was on the handle bar and the other held a Capri Sun. Jay was my best friend. Omar was a kid from the neighborhood that occasionally came around to hang. I didn't care for Omar much.

"What up boy!" Jay said with his arms open.

"Nothing much." I closed the door behind me.

6

"Guess where we just came from," Omar butted in.

"Where?"

"Smashing these two chicks! Rhonda and Veronica," Jay said, pretending to hunch the bike.

"Word?"

"Yep. Smell my fingers!" Jay walked up to me with his fingers in the air.

"Eww, stop man! Get back!" I shoved them out of my face. "How was it?"

Omar looked at Jay and looked back at me. "How was it? It was some of the best pussy I ever had. Too bad you wouldn't know how that feels. Ain't you still a virgin?"

"Don't worry about that."

"Hey, hey! Leave my boy Terrance alone. So what if he's a virgin! It ain't his fault. Mama Tammy ain't having that; she won't even let him out the house. He a good boy, a church boy," Jay said, looking back at me.

"Ain't nobody no damn church boy! I'm just not tryna get no diseases and I ain't trying to get nobody pregnant."

Omar rolled his eyes and looked at Jay. "Here he go. That's why you put on a rubber, stupid." Omar shook his head.

"Ay, it's cool, Terrance. But ain't you 'bout to smash that one chick?" Jay looked up and snapped his fingers as he tried to remember. "What's her name? Rebecca, right?"

I nodded. "Yea that's her. We been talking a little bit."

"Oh yea, man she look like a freak. She fine. I know she ain't no virgin, so that should make it easier for you."

"How you know she ain't a virgin?" I asked.

"'Cause Leroy from around the corner hit it," Jay said, pointing behind him.

"Oh. Well, we'll see what happens. Her mama be at work a lot so I should have a chance to slide over there soon."

"That's what I'm talking about! I'm rooting for you." Jay smiled and held his hand out for a high five. Omar grinned and nudged Jay with his elbow.

"He look like he scared of some pussy. Make sure you put it in the right hole." Jay smirked a little, trying to hide his laugh.

7

"Shut up, Omar! Terrance, go get your bike man. Let's ride up to the park."

I held my middle finger up at Omar and walked to the left side of the house to get my bicycle. I lifted my knees as I lunged through the high grass full of weeds. The grass looked as if it hadn't been cut in years. I popped open the fence and walked into my backyard. My bicycle was leaning on the side of the house. I stood for a second before grabbing it. I could still hear Jay and Omar laughing.

Being a virgin in my group of friends sucks ass. Jay and Omar always have something slick to say about me. Jay is 14, but he's having sex with a lot of girls. He comes to my house with so many sex stories. He's light-skinned with white teeth, so the girls love him. They say he looks like Chris Brown. I disagree, but whatever. And Omar is 15, and he always talked about hitting chicks, too. But to be honest, I have no idea how he gets chicks. He has a big ass forehead and a gap the size of Texas between his two front teeth. I think girls just like him because he's popular and he can dress nice. And plus he's a bad boy- a wanna be thug. Girls love the bad boys at school. I know that if Omar can get girls to lay in bed with him, then I have a chance. I'm chocolate. Some girls say I look like a young Denzel Washington. And my mama said I'm going to be tall like my dad, so that helps too. I'm going to lose my virginity soon though. I can feel it. Me and Rebecca been texting. I know she will let me hit it. She likes me. She's had a crush on me for a while now. She's cute enough for me, so we're bound to do it, very soon.

I head to the backyard to get my bike. It's hot as hell out here. The summer heat is real. The sun is in my eye. I can barely see my text messages. Plus, there's no telling what's back here. The grass is super high. There might be snakes. I hate snakes. They creep me out. If my daddy lived here, this wouldn't be the case. He would cut the grass just like all the other men around the neighborhood. My mama isn't going to cut this grass, and I'm damn sure not going to cut it. I'm sweating already and I just walked out the house. Man, it's hot enough to be in the pool, but the pool is the last thing on my mind. I want to do a cannon ball inside

8

Rebecca. I finally got the text that I've been waiting for. Rebecca said that I could finally come over. Her mama is at work and she has the house all to herself. It's about time. We've been talking about this day for a month now.

When I finally got to her house it felt like it took an eternity. I checked my phone and noticed that Rebecca had sent me directions to put the bike on the side of the house and come to the back door. I did just that. As I walked up to the back door it reminded me of the entrance to a haunted house- an old, rusty, brown house. I didn't like how her house looked from the outside; it wasn't very welcoming. I hoped it looked better on the inside. I needed to stay as calm as possible.

The back door made a clicking sound as it unlocked. I jumped a bit. The door slowly swung open and Rebecca was standing in the doorway. She had little bedroom shorts on and a tank top. The gloss on her lips made them shiny. Her skin was glowing like she had just put on two full palms of cocoa butter. Yep, she was looking good and was ready to do the nasty.

"Um. Are you going to come in?" Rebecca asked with her hands up.

"Oh. Yea, I'm coming," I said, approaching the door.

I followed Rebecca to her bedroom. The air was scented with candy, burnt hair, and perfume. Mirrors were placed randomly around the room. We sat for a couple minutes without saying anything.

"Why you ain't saying nothing?" Rebecca asked.

"Because you ain't saying nothing to me!"

I sat awkwardly trying to figure out what to say. I didn't want to say the wrong thing. I decided that I was going to have to speak up. I could feel my chest pounding from the inside.

"You must be scared," I said, looking away.

"Scared of what?"

"Scared of me. And scared to do what we talked about."

"No, you scared! You're the one that's just sitting there."

I got excited. "Come here then, you sittin' so far away. As a matter of fact, come sit on my lap." I pointed at my thigh.

Rebecca hesitated, but then got up and walked towards me. My heart was beating through my chest like Mike Tyson pounding a punching bag.

My imagination began to run wild. I was finally about to become a man. I thought about Jay and Omar and how they would finally respect me. The sex conversations would now have to include me. Rebecca sat on my lap. I hadn't planned on what to do next. I then wondered what Jay or Omar would do.

A car door slammed outside. Rebecca jerked as if she'd just gotten shocked by lightning. She jumped so hard that she sent shock waves through to me. She ran towards her window and peeped outside. She turned back as if she'd just seen a serial killer.

"My mama is here! Hide!" My eyes got big. My body was stiff, almost like I was paralyzed. I looked at her as if she was talking Japanese.

"Hide!" Rebecca yelled as if her life depended on it.

She can't be serious, I thought. How did this happen? Does she not know her mama's work schedule? Shit! I didn't know what to do. My horniness turned into fear in the blink of an eye. I ran into the closet and almost tripped over her whack ass shoe collection before closing the doors behind me.

"No, stupid! That's the first place that she's going to look! Get under the bed."

I felt like an idiot. This was insane. I jumped out of the closet and crawled under the bed fast. It was a super tight fit. Much tighter than I thought. It was dark under there too. I couldn't see a thing and could barely breathe. It was dusty, hot and smelled like old gym socks and perfume. I was sweating and lying on top of something. Whatever it was, it was poking the hell out of me and piercing through my skin. Ugh! I couldn't believe she told me to go under there. What was she thinking? I'd rather hide in the closet where I could at least breathe. It was torture and dark, but I did recognize something. I saw a size 11 Jordan shoe to the left of me. Yep. She was a hoe. I knew it. She's the only child, and it was just her and her mama that lived here. It was Reggie's shoe; he lived two doors down from me. I knew his shoes from anywhere because he decorated all of his shoes to make them look like they were custom made. Disgusting.

The front door closed and keys jingled. The sound of heels tapping the floor became louder and louder as they approached Rebecca's room.

"Rebecca! Rebecca, I know you hear me."

Her mama sounded mean. From what Rebecca told me, she was like the grim reaper. I was shaking. Boy did I wish to be somewhere else at that moment. I felt so out of place, so I just closed my eyes. If I could disappear, I would have. If that was what it took to try to lose my virginity, I figured I'd rather keep it forever. *God, forgive me for coming over here*, I said to myself. I knew better. I learned my lesson. *Never again God, never again.*

Chapter 2: Moving On

"Snap out of it, Terrance!" Fred clapped while looking at me. You've been sitting there for a couple minutes now. Who you daydreaming 'bout?" he asked.

I had blanked out for a second. I was with my best friends, Jay and Fred, at Gladys Knight's Signature Chicken & Waffles off Cascade Road. Jay, Fred, and I would have Sunday brunch occasionally. We enjoyed it because it was a time to relax and fellowship before the start of a hectic week at work.

"Damn, I was reminiscing. My bad. Ay Jay, you remember Rebecca?"

"Rebecca who? I don't know a Rebecca," Jay said, looking down at his plate while cutting his waffle with a knife and fork.

"Rebecca! Back when we were kids man, in middle school. You don't remember?"

Jay stopped cutting and looked up. "Oh! The one that you lost your virginity to?"

"Yes, her."

"Ahhh man, you took it way back! I think she has like five kids now and is shaped like a pregnant seal. What made you think about her?" Jay asked, looking back down and continuing to cut his waffle.

I smiled, and shook my head. "Just thinking, man. I wanted to lose my virginity so bad. I was so jealous of you back in the day. You made me want to have sex so bad. You used to pick on me. According to you and Omar, I was late losing my virginity at age 13."

Jay laughed. "Looks like you weren't too bad, especially compared to our good friend, Fred, who lost his virginity in college." Jay turned and patted Fred on the back.

"Don't touch me." Fred pushed Jay's hand off of him. "Unlike Terrance, I was fine with losing mine at 21. I was never in a rush," he insisted.

"Obviously," Jay said as he smiled and took a bite of his pancake.

"Right after I did it, I felt like I was finally a man. You couldn't tell me anything. Damn, I've come a long way."

"While you're sitting here and reflecting on the glory days, did you check the time to see when you need to be home to meet with your cable guy?" Fred asked.

I looked at my watch. "Damn! It's 1:00 p.m. already? I'm out of here. See y'all later." I hopped out of my chair and headed towards the door.

The Atlanta traffic was backed up, like it always was this time on a Sunday. For what reason, I don't know. While waiting in it, I busted out laughing. Fred really caught me daydreaming. But, it's okay to glance at your past, to see how far God has brought you. Boy was I a knucklehead. All I wanted was to get into a little something. I was always running the streets, but it was really to impress my friends, of course. Thank God I got out of that follower's mentality. I'll admit that I was lost. Now I'm a leader. I'm a twenty-five-year-old Black man working in Corporate America making $75,000 a year. Not bad. Not bad at all. Especially since I had no father figure to look up to. That's why I was so lost. I had to find my own way. But now I understand. I understand why some Black men struggle. I understand why a young Black man can get lost, because without a father he lacks that compass to direct him towards manhood.

It wasn't that I had any disdain for my father, or that I even considered him particularly necessary; I just lacked understanding as to why a person would choose not to be a part of their child's life. No father figure in a household will lead to a void. I had no man to emulate. No man to admire. No man to listen to. No man to fear. I had a lot of questions I wanted to ask my father. I didn't feel comfortable asking my mother… so I held it all in.

Thank God Jay and I managed to become successful without father figures in our lives. Omar didn't have a father figure either. As a matter of fact, he ended up going to prison for life for armed robbery. His father was in prison for the same thing. Like father, like son. But not me; I made the decision to be nothing like him, especially since I know he was a womanizer.

I admit that I felt myself becoming that. When I was in college, I grew into my sexiness. I'd become a tall, dark, handsome, clean-cut gentleman. I was a girl's nightmare and a nightmare for a girl's father. I was the guy they were warned about. When those girls fell for me, they fell hard. They

13

threw themselves into the arms of someone that just wanted to catch a nut. They ended up dropping everything for someone who wouldn't even pick them up if they'd fallen. They held it down for someone that didn't want to be held accountable for their feelings. I would create a false sense of love and appreciation, only to get them into their vulnerable state, where they lowered their invisible wall of suspicion. That wall originated when they were younger, when their parents told them to keep their legs closed. The same wall of suspicion created when their pastor preached to them to save themselves for their husband. This wall protected their hearts. The old me loved lowering that wall. Lust, paired with bragging rights between my friends and I, was the bridge that led to me becoming a professional heartbreaker. At that time, I thought that was what it meant to be a man.

I'm happy to say that I'm a changed man now. When I met my ex-fiancée, Lisa, my actions changed. My thought process changed. I finally cared about the feelings of women. Lisa introduced me to love. That's when I finally realized that women were caring and loving human beings that were not created to be exploited. Lisa reminded me so much of my mother. They had similar loving spirits. And of course, my mother was a victim of a rolling stone: my father. God rest her soul. She was exploited. Left to raise a child by herself with no help. No financial help. No moral help. He didn't lift a finger. I refused to go down the same path as my so-called father.

Monday Morning 7:30 a.m.

I tried not to spill my coffee on my suit. I sipped slowly as I pulled out of the Starbucks driveway. Lord knows I spend too much money at Starbucks. It was Monday morning and I was headed to work. Pulling up to a four-way stop, I watched as a man held his hand up to make sure I had his eye contact so that he could cross the street. The man then walked by while holding hands with his son. The child skipped joyfully as he crossed the street holding his father's hand. His backpack bounced loosely up and down. Seeing that made me smile. It had been thirteen years since I asked my mom about my dad. I still wondered how things would've been different, if he happened to be in my life.

14

The office got loud at times due to the printer going off continuously. The cubicle next to me played classical music all the time. I liked it. It helped me focus. My fingers moved swiftly across the keyboard with my eyes on my screen. Right before I submitted my work, an envelope fell over my shoulder and onto my desk. I stood up to see who dropped it. My co-worker was throwing mail to recipients. I sat down and picked it up. It was from Lisa. Lisa Smith. My heart dropped for a minute. I broke the seal and opened it.

Terrance,

Thank you for the letter and the donation! It really means a lot and I am very appreciative. I am so glad to know that you're doing well. I want you to know that I love you to death and I always will. But as of now, I am on a spiritual journey that is truly liberating to say the least. Honestly, I don't think God wants me to venture off of my path. So in other words, I'm still finding myself. And if you're wondering if I'm with someone right now, I am not. I'm just seeking God's Kingdom and following my dream. My organization is doing awesome and I'm praying that it continues to flourish. So many people have been blessed because of this organization. However, we most definitely can keep in touch.

Love,

Lisa

I crumbled the letter and tossed it right into the trashcan next to my desk. I sat still for 20 seconds and then hopped up to go to the bathroom. As soon as I entered, I pulled out my iPhone to call Fred.

"Hello," Fred answered.

"You won't believe this shit man... You will not believe what I'm about to tell you."

"Wait, what? Why are you cursing?"

"You remember the letter? The letter I wrote to Lisa, trying to reach out to her to get back with her."

"Yea, I remember. What happened?"

"She basically just wrote back and said that she doesn't want to be with me. I called her my fiancée and everything, Fred. I don't understand!"

"Well, what did you expect? It's probably going to take a while man. She's been through a lot and she's not the same person."

"This shit is making me feel some type of way. I feel numb. This is my baby we're talking about, Fred, the love of my life. She's the one who I would kill for. How can she not want me back? This is not how I envisioned it."

"Relax, brother. Relax and just give her some time. I'm sure she has a lot on her mind."

"The hell with that! She's had plenty of time to think about it. We've been separated for a year now. This is me giving her another chance. How can she not want me back, Fred? I feel like a little bitch in this situation."

"You're not, man. You're not a little bitch. If you say you are, then you are. You are a man, and you will learn from this, alright?"

"I don't know, Fred. I don't know."

"How about this, let's meet up tonight at the bar. Let's talk this over with Jay and have some beer. You know Jay knows how to cheer you up."

"You're right. You're right. I'll see you tonight, brother."

I ended the call and paced around the office bathroom. Thoughts were running wild. I walked up to the sink and turned the knob to splash water on my face. I looked in the mirror, dried my face with a brown paper towel and proceeded out the door. As soon as I walked out, my boss saw me.

"Mr. Hill, you okay?"

"Yes sir, I am fine."

"Okay, just making sure. We can't have our top Financial Analyst down and out."

"No sir, Mr. Hinson, I am fine."

I couldn't let Mr. Hinson see me pouting. He was a man I respected. I respected him because he respected me. He was about 42 years old and very successful; a tall white guy that had style. All of the receptionists had a crush on him. He reminded me of David Beckham. He always had on tailored suits. He looked out for me and wanted me to be great. He always said that I reminded him of himself when he was in my shoes: young,

16

ambitious, and talented. I could tell that he wanted the best for me. Usually, in the corporate workspace, you don't get that type of genuine leadership where someone really wants you to be elite to the point where they can even be surpassed, especially across two different races. I appreciated that. It made me want to work harder and not let him down.

Twin Peaks, Buckhead Atlanta

The bar was loud. Everyone was laughing hysterically and yelling at the football games on the televisions. The waitress's dress code consisted of short shorts and a low cut top. Jay looked at every waitress's backside as they walked by. We all sat around the circular table with large cups filled with beer and foam at the top.

"I thought you had more balls than this man," Jay said with his hand gripping my shoulder, shaking me.

"I thought I did too. I never figured that I would be sprung over a woman. Not me, the Terrance that could get any girl he wanted. Never in a million years."

"I think we all grow out of that phase. Once we find the one we want to love, then all of that playa stuff goes out the window." Fred offered his input.

Jay looked at Fred, then at me. "See all of this sad and lonely shit is y'all problem. I'm single, successful, and happy. Y'all know it's okay to be single and happy, right?" He waited for us to agree.

"For how long, Jay? How long will that last?" Fred asked.

"However long I want it to last. My life is exciting as shit; I don't have a leash around my neck! Terrance, your life can be exciting too. Get money, have fun, live life, and stop worrying about one female," Jay advised.

Fred looked at me. "Man, it's okay to love someone unconditionally. It's okay for it to hurt. I think you should get some sleep, pray about it, and I think after a while she'll come back to you, man."

"Terrance, I want the old you back, the Terrance that was live. The Terrance that would tag team these bitches with me in college. Now you're all sad and crying over one chick. Get over it!" Jay yelled.

"Easier said than done," I said, taking a sip of beer.

17

Jay shook his head. "Bruh! This is the same chick that had a sex tape with a professional basketball player on camera."

I banged on the table with two fists and pointed at Jay. "Watch your damn mouth!"

"Chill, Jay! Why do you have to say that man?" Fred intervened.

"Nah, y'all chill! I ain't the bad guy here. I'm your frat brother. I knew you before this chick. I'm just stating facts. We are all young. We're all successful. There should be no reason why you can't find another chick that is successful and just as good looking, if not better looking than Lisa. Am I right or am I right?"

Fred looked at me. I looked back at him, then at his cup.

"Where is he going to find his new wife, Jay? The club? Instagram? BlackPeopleMeet.com? ChristianMingle.com? Tinder? It's not that simple, man."

"Shut up, Fred! The world is huge with beautiful women everywhere."

"You got a point, Jay. I think I forgot my worth for a second."

"You damn right you forgot your worth!" Jay leaned in closer to me. "Listen, you're a successful Financial Analyst at one of the biggest banks in the world and you're only 25. The sky is the limit."

"Jay, maybe he just wants to share his success with someone else, bruh. You ever thought of that?"

"Fred, you can't give this man any advice on women. You and your girl, Michelle, have been together for four years and you lost your virginity to her. You ain't have no hoes before then. So you can't relate, and you don't know what the hell you're talking about," Jay said.

"Correction. We've been together for five years, and stop calling women hoes. And so what, am I any less of a man since I lost my virginity a little later in life?"

"I didn't say you were. I'm just saying that you, Terrance, and I have different outlooks on women. We've seen more and done more; you're an amateur when it comes to women."

"Whatever man," Fred replied while taking a sip.

"Look bro," Jay said, putting his arm back on my shoulder, "we're going to this nice hang-out spot tomorrow and I'm going to get you to know your worth, because obviously you don't know how much power you have anymore."

18

I hesitated for a moment, then nodded. "I'm down to go."

"I'm not going," Fred replied.

Jay frowned. "You weren't invited anyway. It's just me and Terrance, the single men," Jay said, smiling at me.

"Well, y'all enjoy." Fred took another sip of his beer.

Fred and Jay bumped heads all the time. It was mainly because they're like polar opposites. Fred was super sensitive. Jay can oftentimes be an asshole that has no filter or no feelings. But we got along just fine. But see, Fred came a long way. We met back in college. I would always see him around, hanging out in the student union. He was pretty much to himself. Heavy guy. Didn't seem like he had many friends. But it did seem like he wanted to hang out with us, the cool kids. I think I was like the only guy that would actually speak to him. I was a junior, and he was a freshman. For some reason, I somewhat felt sorry for him. One day, I was driving around campus and I saw Fred walking home from class. Dark clouds came out of nowhere and it began to storm. Fred had no umbrella. He began to jog as the hail started splashing down. He was getting soaked. There was no telling how far he had to run to get wherever he was going. And a guy his size wasn't going to get that far that fast anyway. So I pulled over and stopped.

"Yo, hop in man, you getting soaked!" I yelled. He looked at me like I was Jesus coming back to save his people. At first he did hesitate, as if he was surprised that a person like me would show an act of kindness. But he hopped in. That was when our friendship began. I always wanted to look out for him. I was one of the reasons why he lost a lot of weight. I motivated him to be healthier. He went from 260 to 220. He's like a little brother to me, even though we're close to the same age. Once we started hanging out, I eventually introduced him to Jay. We've all been close friends ever since, even though Fred is not my Frat brother.

Suite Lounge - 12:30 a.m.

I walked in and saw beautiful women everywhere. Now I love all types of women, but there was just something about a beautiful black woman. Jay caught my attention as he was in the back waving his hand for me to join.

"Boy it's some hoes in here!" Jay said as he sat down.

"Come on man, stop calling women hoes." I hated that. "But where'd you find this place? Never heard of it." I looked around.

"A good friend of mine," Jay said, taking a sip of his drink. He motioned the waitress over to the table. "Can you bring two Hen and Cokes over please? Thank you."

"Drinks on you tonight?" I asked.

"Of course, I got you. I needed to get you away from Fred. I feel like his pathetic attitude towards women was rubbing off on you," Jay said, patting me on the back.

"Nah he wasn't, man. Y'all both think differently that's all. I see what both of y'all are saying. I'm just in the middle."

Three girls walked by. Two were gorgeous. One was unattractive.

Jay looked at me. "Let's talk to those three chicks over there."

"Seriously?"

"Yea. The two in the black dresses are fine as hell. You must not have seen them. Both of them had ass!"

I looked at the girls and looked back. "You can say something to them. I'm good."

"Come on, man! We have to tag team them. Like the old days. I need your support," Jay begged.

I shook my head. "Nah man, I'm good. I'm just chilling right now."

"Whatever! If they walk this way again, I'm going to say something to them," Jay said before finishing his beer.

Just as Jay wished, the three women walked our way. I was looking at the taller of the three. She had a nice figure and she was brown skinned. Pretty face, that's my type.

"Excuse me." Jay approached the three women.

They stopped and looked at us.

"Sorry to bother y'all, but ummm, I wanted to give y'all a compliment. Y'all look absolutely stunning tonight," Jay said. The three girls smiled and thanked him.

He pointed towards me. "This is my friend, Terrance. He's had a very rough day. His dog got hit by a car, so I'm trying to cheer him up."

20

I looked at him like he was crazy. I don't even have a dog. He kicked me under the table and looked back.

"Aww, I'm sorry to hear that. That's so sad," one of the girls said.

"I know. He is so down and out." Jay pointed to the tall girl that I preferred. "Can you help me cheer him up?" He winked at her.

One of the girls came over and took a seat by me. Jay turned to the girl that he liked and started conversing with her. She eventually took a seat while they talked. I realized the unattractive chick looked restless. She started fidgeting and fanning herself as if she was hot. Then she pulled her purse out of her phone and began to scroll through it. She looked around for a second, then she spoke.

"Ummm, I'm about to leave y'all. Y'all tripping. I need to go to the bathroom," she said.

The other two girls agreed. They looked at Jay and I. "I'm sorry we have to go, nice meeting y'all. We'll be back."

"Okay. Y'all better come back too!" Jay said as the girls held hands and walked away.

"See! The ugly bitch is the one that always has to block. I was so close to getting her number," Jay complained.

I laughed. "She ain't have no one to talk to."

"She hangs out with them because she thinks that shit will make her look better. With her ugly ass."

I chuckled.

"You know it's the truth! She just jealous that she ain't getting no play. She need to find some miserable and ugly friends like herself so she won't feel so out of place," Jay continued.

"You and these women. Why are you so cutthroat?"

Jay leaned in. "You want to know my story, bruh? You want to know why I think the way I think about women?"

"Talk to me."

Jay cleared his throat. "I used to be that innocent guy. My sophomore year in high school, I was in love with this girl, right. Man, I thought we would get married. I was so crazy about her that I had the butterflies in my stomach every time I would see her."

"Hold on, let me guess, she cheated on you?" I assumed.

21

"Sure did! With a damn football player. But the worst part about it was how I found out. A good friend of mine told me that the football player had pictures of them kissing, having sex, and all." Jay shook his head.

"Damn. Yea that's messed up. Sounds familiar."

"Was it? That shit changed my life! I went home and cried like a little bitch. I told her mama and her daddy and everything. I didn't know how to respond."

"That's kind of funny."

"You're right. It is funny, but I'm glad it happened. Since then, I have never trusted women and I never will," Jay said, sitting back and taking a sip.

"Come on man, all women aren't like that. You can't let that one girl mess up your whole perception about women."

"Oh no! There's not just one bad apple. Come on, bruh, what about all the women that I've slept with that had boyfriends and fiancés and all that? I know women! They are sneaky. I ain't got time for it."

"Yea, I feel you, but there are good women out there too. You're just attracting those types of women based off your actions."

"How do you know, Terrance? Because of Lisa?"

"Jay..." I gave him that look to watch his words.

"Terrance, I'm just trying to be real. You know I'm going to speak my mind, man. I don't know what you and Lisa had, but all I know is that she wasn't an angel like you thought she was." I took a sip and nodded in agreement.

"I just want you to live life, man. I want to make sure you exhaust all of your resources before you settle down again. That's all."

"I guess I'm down to have a little fun, man."

"Now we're talking!" The waiter came and sat our drinks on the table.

"Take this cup to the head. Let's celebrate the single life and being young, educated, powerful black men!" Jay directed, grabbing the cup and holding it in the air.

I grabbed my cup and put it up to his. "What are we toasting to?"

"I just said it! To being young, educated, powerful black men! I pray that God will let our cups runneth over with blessings, because we deserve it."

We tapped glasses and drank until they were empty. My throat was hot from the strong taste of the liquor.

"Woooo!" Jay said, putting his cup down. "That's my boy! I got you for the rest of the night. This will be a night to remember."

"Oh boy."

Chapter 3:

One Night Stranded

The alarm on my phone went off. I hated that alarm. It was so annoying. Mainly because it usually meant that I had to get up to go to work. *How dare you interrupt my dream, alarm.*

I could never remember my dreams. I'm sure it was a good one though. I needed fifteen more minutes of sleep. I reached for my alarm to turn it off. I shifted my position, opened my eyes a little, and closed them again. I immediately opened them. *Where the hell am I?* I jumped up and looked around the room to see a very decorative lavender setting that had a sweet smell. Shocked, I looked over to see a woman lying down next me, facing the opposite direction. Terrified, I had to wonder, *Who the hell is this chick? What did I do last night?* I couldn't remember a thing. *Was I drugged?* While lying still attempting to retrace steps, the girl began to move. I got more nervous as she prepared to get up and tried my hardest not to move. I didn't want her to know that I was up. The girl got up and sat on the side of the bed, then made her way to the bathroom. First noticing her pink lace bra and thong, my eyes were also drawn to her slim waist complimented with a nice butt. Her face was gorgeous. She was fine as hell. I felt a bit relieved. But I was still lost.

"Damn," I said under my breath.

The woman stopped while walking to the bathroom and looked towards me.

"What's wrong?"

I shook my head and blinked twice. "Uhhh... my head hurts. I had too much to drink and I don't remember anything from last night. And I damn sure don't remember talking to someone like you. What time is it?"

The girl blushed and rolled her eyes. "It's 5 a.m."

"Seriously, how did we end up in the bed together?"

The girl spoke from the bathroom. "Your friend, Jay, introduced me to you and he told me that you were a nice guy. He told me about your dog dying. And then you took over. We talked the whole night about life and we just clicked. I'd never met such a gentleman and I guess the liquor got the best of me. So I invited you over. I drove here."

I rolled my eyes. That damn Jay. "Damn, did we do something? Because I don't remember anything," I said, rubbing my eyes while sitting up.

The girl laughed. "Wow, you were really that drunk?"

"I guess so."

"Unfortunately, yes. I just wish you would've remembered. I don't know how I feel about that. I was drunk, but I remember."

"Hell, I wish I did too." I wanted to go home, but I tried to speak as nicely as possible without making her upset. "Um, is my car still at the club?"

"Yea, I think so."

"How am I going to get there? Should I call Jay?"

"Damn. You don't want to talk or nothing, huh? You just want to straight up leave? Bye then," she said, disappointed.

"Sorry, I just need to find out where my car is and stuff. We can still talk."

"You don't even know my name, huh?"

"You didn't tell me. I told you I don't remember anything from last night."

The girl shook her head. "It's Sarah."

"Sorry, Sarah. It's the liquor. Don't shoot me."

"I swear all of y'all men are the same."

I stopped putting on my pants, looked at her and responded, "Huh, why do you say that?"

"Because y'all are," she said while looking in her bedroom mirror fixing herself.

"What if I said all women are the same?"

"Then you would be lying to yourself."

"Exactly! That's how I feel about what you said."

Sarah sighed. "I'm just so stupid! I don't know why I did this. Talking to you last night had me thinking that you were different."

25

"What did I say last night that had you so into me? I'm curious."

"Maybe that you know how to love, and that you are ready to settle down. I don't know, I just thought you were different."

After she said that, I sped up the process of putting on my clothes. I picked up my phone to text Jay. *Please come get me bro.*

Jay texted back, *What's the address?*

"Excuse me, Sarah, what's the address to your place?"

"3200 Lenox Road NE."

I sent the address. Although I was ready to go, I still felt bad for her, so I started a conversation.

"So where are you from? Are you from Atlanta?"

"Yes, I am. Born and raised, a Grady baby," Sarah replied, looking away.

"That's what's up."

Sarah sighed.

"All men aren't the same; some of us are just still trying to find ourselves. We don't know what we want." I tried to reassure her.

"Whatever."

My phone buzzed. It was a text from Jay saying that he was outside.

"Nice meeting you, Sarah. Keep in touch." I was out.

The bright sun shone and made me squint as I ran outside. I hopped into Jay's car. Jay's face was lit up in excitement. Eyes big, ready for a story.

"Bruh, you are the man! Damn! I am so jealous," Jay said as he pulled out of the driveway. I looked out the window and said nothing.

Jay nudged me on the shoulder. "How was it, bro? That ass was phat! She was so sexy, bruh. You're the only person I know who can pull off a one night stand with a girl that bad... sheesh!"

"Man how the hell did I get that drunk? I woke up scared as hell. I didn't know where I was."

"Come on man! You know damn well I was going to take care of you! If you're with me, you're in good hands. I wasn't gon' have you talking to no busted chicks!"

I nodded in agreement. "True. Well, she was fine."

"Did you smash her right?"

26

"Yea, I did."

Jay smiled and looked at me. "That's my boy! The old Terrance is back! Ha! How was it?" he asked again.

"I don't remember. I was too drunk last night."

"What? Try to remember! I need details," Jay said, looking at the road and looking back at me.

"Man, I don't like waking up like that, bro. It wasn't a good feeling at all."

Jay looked at me with an upset face and looked back at the road. "I would love waking up with a woman like that in my bed any day. You crazy!"

"Yea. It's obvious that she was trying to fill a void with me. She wanted me to stay and talk. She was kind of upset that I wanted to leave."

"What that got to do with you? That's her problem! Let her deal with that," Jay replied.

"I don't know. I kind of felt sorry for her. Maybe I could've had breakfast with her or something to get to know more about her. I mean, we did just have sex."

Jay looked at me confused. "Bruh. What the fuck is wrong with you? Have you lost your mind? You okay?"

I laughed. "Whatever man, I'm good. I'm just messing with you."

"So what the hell are you talking about then?"

"Nothing man. You can just tell that she was regretting last night. Since I didn't want to talk."

"So what! She knew what she was doing. That's not your problem. You know these chicks are emotional. Full of estrogen and shit."

"Yea man. I was just ready to get out after that."

"Stop caring about these hoes, man! You're too dark skinned to be worried about these women."

I nudged him. "Shut up!"

Chapter 4: Love Birds

Watching the Falcons on Sunday afternoons usually gave me high blood pressure. I was on the couch relaxing and my phone lit up. It was Fred calling.

"Talk to me."

"You got some time to talk?" Fred asked.

"Of course, what's up?"

"Well, I wanted to tell you that I'm thinking about proposing."

"For real man? That's huge! I'm proud of you! What made you want to put the ring on her finger?"

"You know, she's just the one who has been there for me. I wouldn't have it any other way."

"She definitely seems like a good girl."

"Yea man. You know I have to lead by example. There are still some good men out here that aren't afraid to take care of a good woman. I'm pretty sure Jay isn't going to agree with this."

"Fred, this is about you. Other people's opinions don't matter. You do what you have to do, man. Jay is going to talk mess, but I'm sure he'll support you regardless."

"Hope so, but what about you? Have you written Lisa back?"

"Not yet."

"Didn't she say that y'all should keep in touch? You're not even trying?"

"We'll see, man. I will write her back soon. I'm just weighing out my options right now. I'm trying to see if there's something out there for me. You never know. There are a lot of women in Atlanta, you know."

"I'm worried about you. I don't want you to end up like Jay. Jay ain't never getting married. He's going to be that old and lonely 60 year old still trying to holler at chicks at the club. I don't want to be the only one married out of our crew."

I laughed. "Believe me, I'm not Jay. I'll be okay man."

I was so happy for Fred. Seeing how far he'd come just amazed me. I could tell that he was really in love. I knew that he'd make a great husband. I can admit that he put me in my feelings with that call. Marriage is a beautiful thing, but unfortunately it made me think about Lisa. I'm man enough to confess that seeing Lisa walk down that aisle with that white gown would bring tears to my eyes. I would cry knowing that God had somehow miraculously answered my prayers, placing the woman of my dreams right by my side. Hell, I might even catch the Holy Ghost and shout out loud.

I missed that girl so damn much; it was ridiculous. Any person would say that I should move on. Easier said than done. I could only imagine how hard it would be to find a girl that has the chemistry I had with Lisa. I knew Lisa in and out. I favored her flaws; she was imperfectly perfect. I loved everything about my chick. I loved her lame jokes that she would tell. I loved her clumsiness; how she would trip over her own two feet sometimes. I could sense when she was upset. She didn't have to say a word. When I was upset, she could sense it too. I loved how she would try to console me, even if the consoling didn't work. I just loved that she cared. She would bring the kid out of me.

When we were together, time wasn't a factor. I loved when she would get into bed and she would wrap her legs around me. Her caramel legs were always warm and soft. When her legs were around me, I was home. Any problems and worries that happened that day subsided. I was at peace. Life's battles seemed easier when she was by my side, because I knew that she was a soldier that was willing to put her life on the line to protect me from harm's way. And I would do the same for her. I honestly don't know if there's a woman on this earth that can come and match that happiness that I had with Lisa, other than my mama. After experiencing a love so strong, a love so real, it's hard to put up with any type of relationship that's subpar. She spoiled me with love and care. I know how it feels to truly be in love. So when some people talk about their relationships, I can tell when it's a fraud. I know when it's phony. I see through the bullshit. Unfortunately, I know how it feels to let it slip right between my fingers as well. Nonetheless, if Lisa wouldn't come back sooner or later, I understand that I have no choice but to be open to consider my options. No matter how much I love her.

Fun Friday

29

Buffalo Wild Wings was packed. We ordered 30 wings and fries. It was Fun Friday, time to sum up our hard-working week with drinks, laughter, and deep conversation. Well, shallow and deep conversations. The football games played on the flat screens around the restaurant.

"Ahem, I have an announcement to make." Fred grabbed our attention.

"Let me guess, your girl is pregnant?" Jay blurted out.

"Nah man, she's not pregnant. But I'm going to propose to her next week."

"Congrats man! That's great to hear," I responded as if I didn't already know.

"Word? Finally!" Jay chimed in.

"Yea, it's been a long time coming. I want y'all to be in the wedding."

"Of course. You know we're there," I agreed.

"Ditto. I will support anyone else's marriage, just not my own. Now when is the bachelor party?"

"Jay, one day you're going to put the pimping shoes away."

"Nah man, I love women too much to be limited to only one. I'll go crazy!"

"Sounds like you're going to be paying a lot of child support too," I rebutted.

"Nah, never that. I'm a professional at pulling out," Jay assured me.

"Hold on. So you don't use a condom?" Fred asked.

"Nope. I need to feel everything!"

"You're going to be feeling more than what you can handle if you keep that up. Your dick is going to be itching, or it just might fall off," Fred informed him.

"I'm just playing, I don't do it with every girl, just the special ones." Jay corrected himself.

"Yea, whatever," I replied.

"The marriage thing is overrated, man. I just see things differently. Most of my other friends are miserable in marriages. Why would I want to put myself in a situation like that? I would rather just stay single and free. All these women want is my dick and my money, that's all. And after we divorce then they just want my money while they replace my dick with someone else's." Jay continued adding his two cents.

Fred shook his head in disagreement. "Marriage is a beautiful thing, man. It excites me to even think about proposing to Michelle. Especially when you know 100% that she's the one."

Jay offered a rebuttal. "And I'm pretty sure 100% of the men I knew thought that they were marrying the right girl until they were thinking about divorce too. Especially when they get married strictly due to circumstances. For example, having kids together."

"Come on, Jay, why are you bringing all of that negative energy to the situation? Just let Fred enjoy the moment. I'm sure it's going to be a beautiful wedding, and a beautiful marriage. " I tried my best to play mediator.

"I'm sure it will too. I'm just scared of the marriage thing. Once these women get married, they get comfortable, they get fat, and they just let go. I would divorce a woman so quick if she pulls something like that. She better stay appealing to the eye or I'm out. Fred, I suggest that you set the record straight right now and tell Michelle that she better not get fat and ugly on you."

Fred and I looked at each other and shook our heads.

"Why y'all shaking y'all heads? It's the truth. The women these days are more in love with the idea of marriage rather than actually getting married. They want the glitter and glam of the proposal, and the wedding rather than being connected with the person forever. They want fireworks and shit for a proposal. They want it to be magical. They want their proposal and wedding to go viral. They want their wedding ring to be a certain size so they can show their friends to make them jealous. They are full of it and it's all fake to me," he elaborated.

"To an extent I agree, but I don't think Michelle is like those women thou, so enough with the negative talk. Let's focus on the positive and the good. Like the fact that my friend is about to marry the girl of his dreams," I said, tapping Fred on the shoulder. "I'm proud of you. This is a big step in the right direction. So what's the plan? How are you going to propose?"

Fred smiled, ready to share the details. "Since she was a child, Michelle loved to skate; she's almost like a professional, even though I suck at it. There's this skating rink that she grew up skating at. On

31

Thursdays, there's an adult skate night and usually it's a lot of people. I'm going to propose in the middle of the floor. She'll love it."

"Sounds cheesy, but I like it." Jay shrugged before sipping on his cup.

"If you feel it's the perfect place, then there it is. I'm happy for you man."

"Y'all this is the most exciting day of my life. There's nothing like having your best friend for your wife. I just want to have babies and raise a beautiful family. I'm ready."

"Okay, enough with the mushy stuff, I'm about to throw up, but congratulations man. I know you'll be a great husband," Jay said.

"I want to see this! Can we sneak in or something? What time will you do it?" I asked.

"Well, actually everything is already set up. I already contacted the skating rink. All you have to do is invite people, Terrance. I'm going to make it seem like you put it together. I'm going to tell her to invite her friends too."

"Well there it is. Let's make history!"

I held up my glass. "Let's make a toast to Fred stepping up to the plate to make it official with his woman."

Fred and Jay held up their cups and we all said together, "Let thy cups runneth over with blessings." We tapped our glasses and downed our drinks.

***

I could envision Fred and Michelle having a miniature chubby-cheeked Fred running around with a diaper on. I knew that Fred's life would be changed forever after that moment. I remembered the feeling that I had when I proposed to Lisa. My heart was beating like crazy. Back then, the thought of committing myself to the person that I loved was scary, but it seemed worth it. What sucks the most is the fact that the moment, the moment of truth, the moment that I had proposed to her, the moment where Lisa would mutually agree to tie our souls together, will forever be tarnished… because our agreement was broken. And she's not here now.

Cascade Skating Rink

The skating rink was packed. Everyone skated while listening to old school music, which included artists like Dru Hill, Mary J. Blige, and Jodeci. The crowd was 21 and up. It was grown folks night. Michelle and two of her friends had gotten to the rink late. Jay, Fred and I sat on the benches in the corner by the lockers and the snack machines. Fred was sweating like he had just run eight miles.

"You okay?" I asked.

"I'm fine. Just thinking too much." Fred wiped his face with a white rag.

"Just relax, man. This is your time to shine. Own it!" I wanted him to relax.

Jay stared at Fred. "Damn, Worried Willie! Pull it together man! You sweating like a stripper during altar call. Just tell me what the plan is. I got the camera, so I need to be ready to snap."

"They're going to play Michelle's favorite song, which is *Dangerously in Love* by Beyoncé. So that's when I'm going to find her and try to skate with her. And I'm going to take her to the middle of the skating floor and I'm going to fall on purpose. That's when the music is going to cut off and the DJ is going to tell everyone to look towards the middle. Then that's when the magic happens."

"Good! We're going to put this on YouTube and hopefully it goes viral. Y'all going to be on Oprah thanks to me," Jay joked.

Fred laughed and looked towards the door.

"There they are. Come on y'all."

We all got acquainted with each other. Then went to pick up the skates at the front counter. Ten minutes passed and everyone was on the floor skating.

Michelle was the first one on the floor. Damn, that's about to be officially Fred's. Forever. Mrs. Michelle Brown. I must admit that Michelle is attractive. Fred is a lucky guy. He knows it too. Her tall and slender frame graciously skated past everyone as if she was practicing for the Olympics. She looked like a talented skater. Her short jean shorts allowed her glistening, long, brown legs to show. I could see why she caught most of the men's attention.

33

Michelle was headed to exit the skating floor when the DJ changed the song to Beyoncé's *Dangerously in Love*. That was the cue. It was time.

"This is my song!" Michelle screamed as she made a 180-degree turn and headed back onto the floor. Fred skated up to Michelle before she could reach her full stride.

"Can I have this skate?" he asked with a smile.

"Of course!" Michelle smiled, and then grabbed his hand.

They started skating off together. Fred skated slowly and recklessly as Michelle held his hand and laughed. Fred pulled her to the middle of the floor as he continued to skate. His skates pounded the wooden floor and he waved his arm as if he was trying to keep his balance.

Michelle began to appear aggravated. "Boy, where are you going?"

"I don't know. You know I'm terrible at skating," Fred said as he approached the middle of the floor. Jay and I skated slowly but discreetly closer to the couple as they made it to the front. Seconds later, Fred fell on the floor, hard. Michelle shook her head and bended over to help Fred up. As planned, the music shut off and Michelle looked up while she bent down.

"Whoever that is that fell in the middle of the floor, damn you need some skating lessons son!" the DJ said over the mic.

Michelle shook her head and continued to help Fred up. "It's okay baby."

The DJ continued, "But thank God he has a beautiful woman like Michelle that can teach him how to skate." Michelle immediately looked up at the DJ, perplexed.

"As a matter of fact, Fred wants to know if you can help him learn how to skate for the rest of your life," he said.

Michelle then looked down at Fred to see him on one knee with a ring in his hand, smiling nervously. Women in the crowd gasped, pointed and yelled, "Oh my God! Oh my God! Look!"

Jay and I stopped about fifteen feet from them with the camera recording. Michelle covered her mouth with both hands as tears rolled down her cheeks.

Fred smiled and his hands were shaking while holding up the ring. "I love you, Michelle, will you marry me?"

"Say yes! Say yes!" the women in the crowd yelled.

Michelle stood there, with hands covering her eyes. Tears continued to flow. She looked around and saw everyone locked in on the moment. Phones were in their hands, capturing the experience like they were shooting a movie.

"Will you say yes?" the DJ asked. He then softly played *Let's Get Married* by Jagged Edge.

"Can you say yes?" Fred repeated, looking up and shivering, trying not to become emotional. In slow motion, Michelle's head moved from left to right. With a weak and struggling voice, almost as low as a whisper she said, "No. No I can't, Fred... I'm sorry." Still shaking her head, but faster this time, Michelle slowly skated backwards, away from Fred. She then sped off towards the exit and began to cry. Her friends met her at the door and wiped her tears as they left the building.

The whole building was silent for about five seconds. A couple of people from the crowd tried to hide their chuckles, but failed. Others didn't hide that they were amused at all.

They yelled, "It's okay! Don't get discouraged brother!"

The DJ eventually returned to the mic. "Fred, we love you brother. She's going to say yes sooner or later. Keep your head up." He turned on UGK's *International Players Anthem*.

Fred got up off of his knee and sat Indian style in the middle of the floor. His eyes were wide in awe as he blinked continuously. Jay and I skated over to him in a hurry.

"Fred, you okay brother? You know we're here for you," I said.

Fred sat lifeless.

"Talk to us, Fred. Don't do this," Jay said.

Fred still didn't respond.

The DJ came back on the mic. "Ay Fred, I know you hurt man, but you're going to have to move from the middle of the floor. We can't have you out there. It's dangerous and someone can get hurt. Get up and keep skating. The show must go on."

"You heard him, Fred. You have to get up. Be strong for us, brother. I know it's hard, but you got to get up and move on," I told him.

Fred didn't move. Jay and I looked at each other and shook our heads.

"Fred, come on! We're not picking your heavy ass up," Jay yelled, looking down at him.

35

The DJ came back on the mic again and the music stopped. "Ay Fred, security is going to have to remove you if can't follow directions."

I looked up and saw a security guard slowly approaching. I turned to Jay. "Let's just get him up."

We both grabbed Fred and were each on one side, holding him up by our shoulders. We left the skating rink and put Fred in the back seat. Jay and I sat in the front and occasionally looked back at Fred to check on him. His expression didn't change. He stared into the back of the front passenger's seat, as if he was trying to recollect what had just happened. We were all silent.

Once we got home, Fred finally moved on his own and sat on my couch.

"You know you ain't light Fred! I'm not carrying your ass no more, man. Never again! Next time, I'm going to let someone skate on your face. Shit. I'm still sweating," Jay said while wiping his forehead and plopping onto the couch.

With his eyes watering, Fred finally opened his mouth to speak. "Five," he mumbled.

"What?' Jay asked.

Fred shook his head and tears rolled down his cheeks. "Five years... nearly five years of supposed love and happiness."

"Hey man, she's probably just shaken up by what happened. I know she was probably surprised. That's a lot of pressure for anyone," Jay said while pouring a glass of Hennessy.

"This was supposed to be it. Where did I go wrong? I asked God for guidance and this is what happens," Fred ranted, looking straight with tears flowing.

"Stop jumping to conclusions. I'm sure she has a legit reason why she couldn't say yes right now," I said.

"She embarrassed me in front of all those people. She doesn't want to marry me, period. Was I in love by myself? I still can't believe this," Fred mumbled, looking lost.

"You know what, Jay and I are going to go see Michelle and get down to the bottom of everything. I want to know what's on her mind. I just want you to relax, take a nap or something, alright?" Fred nodded and continued sniffling, with tears running down his cheeks.

Chapter 5: Second Place

Jay and I watched Fred. We waited until he sniffled himself into a nap. Then we hopped in my car to go check on Michelle. The ride was quiet for a while.

"So, what do you think is Michelle's problem?" Jay asked, breaking the silence.

I kept my eye on the road. "Hell, I don't know."

"I think I know," Jay said. "Fred is too boring for her."

"Shut up, Jay!"

"No, seriously! I think Fred wants to do everything right and he's too nice to her, and I think Michelle is disgusted by it. It's like he's too perfect for her."

"That's not it, Jay. All women love to be flattered."

"Correction, *some* women love to be flattered! I'm telling you how it went. Michelle was probably getting dogged out by some dude before her and Fred got together. Then, Fred appears into her life with a halo around his head and treats her like a queen." I shook my head in disagreement. Jay shifted his position in the passenger's seat and faced me.

"Come on, Terrance. You and I know Fred is shaped like a short, black ninja turtle. Michelle is a nice-looking chick. She would have never looked his way. Michelle liked him because he was a super nice guy. Then after she was over his flattery, the relationship got bland and boring. That's why she doesn't want to marry him."

"Whatever, Jay. Just say whatever makes sense to you," I said, looking at the road. We made it to Michelle's house and pulled into the driveway behind her car. I knocked on the door.

The door was opened by a 6'1" tall, dark-skinned man. He had a muscular shirt on with his neck and arms filled with tattoos.

"Can I help you?" he asked.

Jay looked at me and I looked at Jay. Then we looked back at the guy. "Umm. We're looking for Michelle. Is she here?"

"Yea, she is. What do y'all need?"

"We want to speak to her. We're Fred's friends. Fred is Michelle's boyfriend and possible fiancé-elect," Jay said.

The guy laughed. "Oh okay. Hold on… Shelly, Fred's friends are at the door, let them in?"

Jay looked at me confused. "Who the hell is Shelly?" he asked under his breath.

"They can come in," Michelle yelled from inside. We walked in. The guy took a seat on the couch comfortably and picked up the television remote and his bowl of cereal from the living room table. He had on grey bedroom slippers. Michelle eventually came out of the back room with a bathrobe on and her hair tied up.

"Did we come at a bad time?" I asked.

"Nope, y'all good." The guy answered for her, while crunching on a bowl of Fruity Pebbles with his eyes on the television.

"Umm, we just wanted to talk about what happened earlier. Fred is really hurting right now and we just wanted to make sure everything was okay with you and him."

"That really ain't none of y'all business," the guy said as he continued to crunch on his cereal.

Michelle looked at the guy and rolled her eyes. "Don't pay any attention to him. But thank you both for coming to check on me. Fred told me a lot about you both and I really appreciate your concern. But Fred and I are no longer together."

I looked at the guy, and then looked at Michelle. "Well is it okay if I ask what happened? I mean, y'all were together for five years, right? According to Fred, y'all were planning on starting a family and getting married. Hell, I'm like really lost."

Michelle looked down and shook her head. "Y'all should have a seat."

"Nah, we're cool with standing," Jay said, glancing at me.

"See, I really like y'all and I want to be completely honest with y'all. I don't think Fred has been 100% truthful about our relationship."

"So what exactly went wrong? Because we know our friend and we know he really loves you and he wouldn't hurt a fly," Jay said.

"Y'all are right. He is a very sweet and genuine person, but I just know that he isn't who I want to spend the rest of my life with."

39

"And why is that?" Jay asked with a raised eyebrow while folding his arms.

"Because your friend is lame as hell," the guy said, interrupting the conversation.

"Be quiet, Keith!" Michelle snapped at him.

"Nah, tell them the truth! You're over here trying to sugarcoat everything with them. Tell them exactly what you told me," Keith said, turning to Jay and I. "Y'all friend is lame. She don't want to be with him because he sorry in bed and she don't love him. She ain't never love him," Keith confessed, leaning back on the couch.

Michelle rolled her eyes at Keith. "I did love him," she said while looking back at Jay and I. "He's just too much for me. When I started to tell him that I didn't think things were working out, he started acting like he was in denial. He started ignoring the fact that I wasn't attracted to him anymore. That's when he started talking about the marriage thing, when clearly I didn't want to be with him. In my head, we were done about a couple weeks ago. I guess that's why he pushed for marriage."

Jay nodded. "Okay, well excuse me if I'm wrong, but you didn't introduce us to him," Jay said, directing his attention to Keith.

Keith looked at Michelle. "Tell them who I am."

"This is my friend, Keith."

Keith laughed. "She don't want to tell y'all the truth. I'm going to keep it real with y'all. I'm her ex-boyfriend. Michelle and I used to date before your friend Fred. I was locked up for a few years, but she realized that she really loved me and she was using your friend just to take up some time. Your fat-ass friend, Fred, was warming her up for me while I was in prison. Don't worry, I been waxing that ass right since I been home. I had to make up for all that lost time. It was only a matter of time before he was going to find out the truth anyway."

Michelle picked up a shoe and threw it at Keith. He blocked it with his arm and continued eating his cereal with a smirk on his face.

I turned to Michelle. "So basically, Keith is telling us that you were cheating on Fred. Is he telling the truth?"

Michelle rolled her eyes. "If you're asking if we have had sex, yes we have. But that means nothing. Fred and I were technically done. I'm just letting Keith stay here until he gets back on his feet. It's nothing serious.

40

We are not back together." Keith chuckled and continued to crunch on his cereal.

"Okay, makes sense. I'm glad this happened. You don't deserve a person like Fred anyway. Our work is done here. Let's go," I said, motioning for Jay to leave.

We were on our way to the car when Michelle hurried out the house to catch our attention.

"Hey, Terrance, you're right. I know I was in the wrong. Fred is a good man; he's just not the man for me. I'm not ready for any type of commitment right now. "

"That's great to know," I said, not looking back at her. We got in the car. Jay stared at me as I pulled out of the driveway.

"So, are you going to apologize to me now or what?" Jay asked.

"I don't want to hear it man. I'm pissed."

"I told you! I told you! I told you! When will y'all take me seriously? That woman is trifling! She didn't want Fred because he can't please her physically and emotionally! It's just that simple."

"And she wants this dude Keith over Fred? This guy just got out of prison and you pick him over someone who is genuine with a secure job?"

"Terrance, when will you get it in your head that these women are stupid? They don't know what they want! The guy Keith probably treated her like shit, went to prison, and came back and she still wants him. She thought she wanted Fred, but she don't want no damn Fred; she want somebody that's going to give her a thrill- somebody with sex appeal. Fred ain't got sex appeal."

"Stop putting women in a box. All women ain't like that. Michelle just doesn't know what she's missing out on. She doesn't deserve Fred. Hopefully Fred realizes that and moves on from her."

"And that's exactly why I can't get married. This proves my point! I can't trust these women! They crazy as hell."

I shook my head. "Honestly Jay, this just makes me want Lisa more. Although she did what she did, I know her heart and I know she wouldn't do anything to hurt me. I trust Lisa."

"Yea, yea, yea. I'm sure you do."

"I'm serious, man. Yea she had sex with a basketball player; somebody recorded her and exploited her. I understand that. She's been

41

through something. However, I know she didn't do anything else. She's a good girl. That's why I still want her. I know she's been through a lot."

"You don't know what else that girl is capable of. You'll never know. You'll only know what she tells you," Jay warned.

"I believe that intuition is God's nudge into the right direction. And every time I think about Lisa, even after all she has went through, I still believe that she's supposed to be with me."

Jay chuckled. "Whatever you say, Romeo."

"You know what I'm going to do? I'm going to get in touch with Wanda, Lisa's old friend. She may know something that I don't about getting back with Lisa."

"Is it that serious? You mean you want to talk to her friend to try to get some type of inside scoop to get back with her?"

"Yep."

We pulled up to my house. We both looked at each other.

"So what are we telling Fred about our visit to Michelle's house?" Jay asked.

"Just tell him that he needs to move on. He and Michelle are over. He can do better."

"We're not telling him about this guy, Keith?"

"Tell him that Keith was there. But that's all. Don't mention any details."

Jay agreed. We walked in the house and Fred was in a cradle position.

"Get up, Fred!" Jay yelled while slapping him on the side of the head.

Fred woke up with a confused face and looked around.

"We gotta talk man." I took a seat on the couch across from Fred.

"Was she there?" Fred asked.

"She was there alright," Jay said.

"So what happened? What did she say?" Fred asked, anxiously staring at us.

Jay and I looked at each other.

"I'm going to break this down in the simplest way possible. Michelle is not the one for you."

"Why would you say that?"

"She's just not," I replied.

42

"What do you mean? I been with this girl for five years; she is the one. She loves me and I love her."

"The girl doesn't love you anymore, Fred. She's with some ex-convict named Keith. He's in your house as we speak."

"Wait, what? Her ex-boyfriend?" Fred was instantly upset.

"Yea, that guy," Jay replied.

Fred got up and paced around the room. "Why would she do such a thing? I thought he had 10 years in prison? I didn't know he was out!"

"Why does that matter, Fred? Your relationship with her is over man. You don't want a girl like her. You deserve better," I said, watching him as he paced back and forth.

"No, no you don't understand. She loves me. She just can't handle the marriage thing. I just have to slow down." Fred was still pacing.

Jay nodded. "Okay, this is what she meant about him being in denial." He shook his head in disappointment.

"Fred, this girl left you for a convict. That should be a red flag right there!" I was trying to get through to him.

"I hate Keith. I swear I hate him. He's the one who hurt her before we were together. He used to beat her and he almost had her go to prison with him when he went down for selling cocaine."

"So he's a dope boy? Michelle likes dope boys. Makes sense," Jay concluded.

"But I don't get it, Fred. Do you not understand that you and her are done? This guy Keith is walking around your house like he lives there! There's a woman out there for you that would appreciate you. Michelle does not," I said.

Fred sat on the couch and was silent.

"I'm cool with this guy that works at this leasing office for these nice apartments. I'm going to hit him up to get you settled somewhere. It's time for you to move on," I continued.

Fred's face frowned with anger, and then he turned and punched a hole in the wall.

"Damn, Fred! I know you're mad but you have to control yourself!" I jumped up and walked over to inspect the hole. "And you're going to pay for that immediately!

43

Fred looked at his bloody fist and shook his hand. "I apologize, Terrance. I'll take care of it."

Jay looked at him. "Who the hell do you think you are? A fake ass Hulk?"

Fred inhaled, then exhaled, holding his tongue. He looked at Jay again with a snarled lip.

"I said I'll take care of it."

Chapter 6:

Saint is Just a Sinner

Jay and Fred finally left my house. The day had been an emotional rollercoaster... just too much drama for me to handle. I sat on the couch and flipped through the channels. Nothing good was on, so I turned it off. I figured I was tired and went to lay down for about an hour. Of course I couldn't go to sleep. I just sat there with my eyes open. My mind was on what happened. I felt so bad for Fred. I just hoped he could bounce back. He lost his virginity to this chick! I mean, his one and only. Fred's situation with Michelle made me even more cautious about finding another woman. I was mad enough for the both of us. See, although Lisa and I weren't together, I knew she would never do such a thing. There was just a certain level of respect that we had for each other. Speaking of her, I remember when we would lay together and she would hog all the damn covers, and my legs would get so cold. I hated that. I remember when we would try to cuddle before going to sleep, but we would always wake up as far apart as possible. It never failed.

Another thirty minutes had passed and I was still up... still thinking about Lisa. Dammit, I really couldn't fall asleep! I was wide-awake. I picked up my phone and saw that it was only 11:30 p.m. I got up. I needed a drink to get my mind off of Lisa. Hennessy would do the trick. I had some in my freezer. I walked straight to the refrigerator, poured up a cup of Hennessy on the rocks. I turned on an R&B playlist and downed a couple of cups. It made me feel a little better. My mind was off of Lisa. Now it was on living; living fast to be exact. I pulled out my phone and went to texting.

Hey Sarah, how are you?
I'm good.
What are you doing?
Nothing. You?
I was hoping to see you again.

For what?
I don't know. I just want to talk.
Only if that's all you want to do.
It is. I promise.

I was a little drunk, but Sarah didn't need to know that. I hid the liquor so she wouldn't know I was drinking. I wanted to appear as sober as possible. I was in my feelings. This was a way to cope with that I guess. *Mind is off of Lisa, and I can stop thinking about Fred's situation. Just kick back and relax.* I really did want someone to talk to. I needed company. I wasn't trying to do anything sexual with this chick. As a matter of fact, a man should be able to control himself. I'm a man. Self-control is key.

Sarah got to my house at 12:30 a.m. But the problem is that once she arrived, she had on black tights and a crop top, showing her flat stomach and her belly button ring. She had a sweet vanilla smell like she had just gotten out of the shower. She had to be trying to test me! Why did she come over looking so sexy? I knew this would be hard.

"How have you been?" I asked.

"I been alright. Just working and stuff," she said while sitting on the couch.

"Okay. Well, yea, I wanted you to come over because I wanted to apologize for the last time we met. I want to kind of... start over."

"Mmm hmmm."

"No seriously, I'm sorry. I'm a really nice guy. I'm not like everyone else."

Sarah busted out laughing.

"What's so funny?" I tried to act as sober as possible.

"All men say that! What makes you so different?"

I looked up as if I was thinking. "Umm, I don't know. I'm just different."

"Exactly! You're just like everybody else. Ain't none of y'all no good," she said as she folded her arms.

"What's your story? Why are you so salty about men?"

"All y'all want is sex; it's simple."

"Why do you think that all we want is sex?" I folded my arms too.

"I don't know. Y'all just do. You tell me why."

46

"Women have the power. Women can usually get sex any time they want. Men can't. Women are in control. So whenever men think that they have a chance, we try to take it, because we never know if the opportunity will ever come again."

"Oh really? So that's all you want to do? That's why you called me over? To have sex, huh?"

"I didn't say that! I was just speaking in general."

"So why am I over here then?"

"I said I just wanted to talk. Sheesh! I already told you that."

She shook her head. "You don't have to lie, Terrance. I've been in this situation enough times to know a man's real intentions. I can't believe I even came here." She folded her arms and looked away. I said nothing, then looked up to the roof.

"Sarah, I'm sorry. I'm going through a lot right now. I've been drinking a little bit. I'm a little in my feelings."

"So what do you want? Do you want to really talk about us being together or was this a booty call?"

"It was neither, Sarah. I told you I have a lot on my mind, that's all." We both sat in silence as the light from the TV brightened the room.

"I've been going through some things too. You know women are really emotional. We just want someone there that is loyal and trustworthy. I've been broken so many times. Usually we give up sex because we're tricked into thinking the guy really cares, when most of the time, he doesn't," Sarah explained.

"Well, men are emotional too. Just like women, we don't know exactly what we want sometimes. That's why we search and try different things, sexually and mentally. And oftentimes we're scolded for it."

"I'll never understand men, I guess."

"You won't. Get over it. We won't understand y'all either."

Sarah sighed and looked up to the sky. "Damn, God, please just send me a real man. That's all I ask."

I laughed. "Real man, huh? What's a real man to you, Sarah?"

"A man that appreciates me… a man that's faithful… a man that's financially stable… a man that isn't all about sex… A man of God! Need I say more?"

"Before you go asking God for a real man, look in the mirror. Are you a real woman? Are you financially stable? Are you a true woman of God? Are you not all about sex? Hell, we had sex on the first night, so you're not as holy as you think. Stop wishing for a man that has standards that you can barely live up to yourself. You attract men that are just like you and you don't even know it."

"Wait, did you just call me a hoe?"

"No!"

Sarah popped up and stormed towards the door.

"Wait!" I blocked the door so she couldn't leave. Sarah tried moving me out of the way.

"Please, Sarah! I didn't call you a hoe! I just meant that I think you should be the girl version of the man that you want, meaning you should be spiritually, mentally and financially grounded just like the man you desire," I explained, holding her shoulders. Sarah looked away, trying not to look into my eyes. "Do you understand now?"

Sarah nodded. "You're right. I have to be a better person first."

"I'm glad you understand. I couldn't have you leave on that note."

"You might have a little bit of sense, Terrance. Why do you have to be such an asshole though?"

"Oh you definitely don't know me. I'm the opposite of an asshole. I care about people and their feelings. To be honest, I may care a little too much. I might've come off a little blunt, but that's just the liquor talking."

"What are you drinking?"

I was hesitant. "Well, I was drinking Hennessy. That's my favorite drink. Why?"

"Can I have some? You got me all in my feelings now too."

"Um, yea. I don't have any chaser though. I was just sipping it straight."

Sarah shrugged. "I don't care."

I walked to the kitchen and fixed her a glass of Hennessy on the rocks. I fixed myself another cup as well. I brought it back to the room and gave it to her as she sat on the bed while watching television. She began sipping.

"I'm glad you decided to stay. I apologize again if I rubbed you the wrong way."

48

"It's okay. I'm fine now. Just trying to get my life together. That's why I'm so emotional."

"How is your life not together?" I asked taking a sip.

Sarah took another sip too before sharing. "Long story. My long-time boyfriend since high school broke up with me a year ago. And since then I've been trying to cope."

"Why did y'all separate?" I probed for more information.

"What do you think? It's the reason why I don't trust men. It started with him. He's an athlete and we were doing well as a couple until he made it to the NFL. I mean, we had our ups and downs with the groupies in college, but I managed to put up with it. But after he signed his NFL contract, he just started treating me like the scum of the earth. He barely even wanted to touch me."

"Oh my," I said, taking another sip.

"I mean, Terrance, look at me! How could anyone not want this? It was the groupies!" Sarah said, looking at her body.

"I'm speechless," I replied.

"And listen to this… after I officially said that I was done, I was an emotional wreck. I couldn't sleep for anything. I thought he would come running back, but he didn't. He didn't care. Then two months after we broke up, I see him with some skank on Instagram all hugged up! He's taking her out to eat, giving her flowers and doing everything that he didn't do with me!"

I was silent.

"And since then I been waiting for a man to step up to the plate, but I've had no luck."

I still said nothing.

"So what is it, Terrance? Why aren't you saying anything?"

"There's nothing to say, Sarah. All I can say is to work on yourself and the right man will show up for you. In due season, when you are ready."

"That's boring advice," Sarah rebutted, taking a sip. "So what's your story?"

I smiled. "The girl that I love is traveling the world and promoting self-growth, self-love and perseverance. She's so caught up in her work that she's not too interested in what I have going on right now. She started her own non-profit and she hasn't looked back since."

49

Sarah nodded. "So it's time for you to move on as well."

"It's not that simple. Something tells me that we'll be together in the near future, so I should be a good man and handle my business and wait for her to come back to Daddy. However, another part of me says that she's never coming back and that I'm a free man and I should explore."

"Explore?"

"Yes, explore. Meet new women. Mingle. But the problem with exploring is that I used to be a ladies' man in college. I used to have lots of sex and I loved it. I did a lot of exploring in college. I'm afraid I'll turn into the old Terrance. My friend Jay wants me to go back to that version of me."

"I just don't understand. Why be a man that just wants to be reckless and exploit women?"

"I don't like to make up excuses, but I didn't have a father growing up. He left my mom when I was three. My father wasn't there to teach me how to treat a woman. My father wasn't there to teach me how to be a man. So I had to grow up learning from the world. I'm still learning today."

Sarah shook her head and drank the last portion of Hennessy in her cup. "That's the story of a lot of Black kids."

"I told myself that I was going to be a wonderful father, and an awesome husband. I have to be the opposite of him."

"You will be. I see it in you." There was a moment of silence. Sarah scooted over closer to me, but I kept my eye on the television, not paying attention to her. She then leaned on me and began to kiss on my neck. I couldn't believe it. After all the talking we did, she still wanted to be scandalous. I thought to throw her off, but it felt so good that I didn't want her to stop. I contemplated on what to do, but couldn't think straight. She then began to unbuckle my pants. At that point, I couldn't resist. I reached for her blouse and then started feeling on her as well. I took all of her clothes off and then I looked to the top drawer for a Magnum. I ripped it quickly and put it on. Sarah laid on her back, naked on the bed. Ready.

I looked at her spread out on my bed. *Damn she is fine.* Her body was like a masterpiece, a coke bottle shape with beautiful titties. And she was as bald as an eagle down there. Not a hint of hair. *God forgive me. Please forgive me because I knew exactly what I was doing when I invited her over.*

I was on top and slowly went inside of her. I felt like a welcomed visitor, because it most definitely wasn't home. She grabbed my waist and pulled me deeper as if she wanted every inch of me inside of her. She began to moan my name, like her body was mine to keep, but I didn't claim it. She grabbed my face with both hands and kissed me as I went in and out. I hated kissing, but I was too nice to hide my lips. Her tongue caressed my neck. Eventually, I could feel her juices running down my thigh like a river flowing downstream. Our sex began to feel right after a couple of seconds. But after 15 minutes, I was finished. I slowed down my stroke. My body became weak as I ejaculated with an abrupt finish. I was reminded that lust had grabbed ahold and took control of me, again. I rolled to the side of the bed.

"What are we doing?" Sarah asked.

I rolled my eyes. "What do you mean what are we doing?"

"Why did we just do that?"

"It was the liquor, we weren't thinking."

"So what are we now?"

"What? What are you asking, Sarah?"

"What am I to you?"

"We're good friends."

"Good friends? Really!"

Sarah hopped up and began to put her clothes on. She sniffled and her eyes became watery. Once she was fully dressed, she walked out of the house. I just sat there and watched her get dressed. Why would I stop her? It was best if she left anyway. Not because of her doing anything wrong, but because of me. I had again used her body as a motel, to check in then check out without having any thoughts of staying there for the long term. Plus, I didn't have the energy to even chase her. I was miserable. I regretted inviting her over. I loved her body, but I didn't love her. I admit that. That was a problem. I felt like the old me. I tried to do this to get my mind off Lisa, but it only made me feel worse. I wanted Lisa even more. Lisa wouldn't have to leave after we made love. She belonged here. See, when Lisa and I did our business together, I made love to her, not just her body. There was a huge difference. *I have to stop doing this. It's counterproductive. This is my last time.* I needed to make a promise to myself. No more senseless sex.

I rolled over to pick up my phone from the dresser. The room was dark so the phone light shined brightly in my face as I held it up. I saw that the time was 3:20 a.m. I dialed Fred, hoping that he would answer the phone.

"Fred, you got a minute?"

"You know what time it is?"

"I know it's late. I have to vent again, man. You're the only person that I can talk to about this. You got a sec?"

"I'm listening."

"I have to get Lisa back."

"Ah man! What happened now?"

"Nothing. I'm just over here having senseless sex."

"Senseless sex?"

"Yes! Remember the sexy girl Sarah that Jay introduced me to that one night at the club? The one I had a one night stand with?"

"You did her again?"

"Yep! I got drunk and invited her over around 12:30. I feel myself trying to fill that void of Lisa physically and mentally and it's killing me man. Sarah's trying to fill a void too and it's sad to see her do it to herself."

"Why would you even invite her over that late? You and I know that she was a booty call. It was the liquor. You wouldn't have done that if you were sober."

"You're right."

"Maybe you should just reach out to Lisa again. Just let her know how you're truly feeling."

"I agree. I need to."

"You have her email address, right? Send her a nice email or something."

"No. I need to just chill right now. I got some soul searching that I need to do before I go messaging her again."

"Whatever you say."

Sunday Brunch at Boogalou Lounge 12:30 p.m.

52

Sunday brunch was refreshing. The food was always good. Today, I ordered a steak omelet. I loved these days because our conversations didn't include heavy libations. The most that Fred, Jay, and I would have was a couple of mimosas. The mimosas were mixed with some cheap concoction that included a lot of orange juice, but not much liquor. To me, our conversations made a little more sense. Liquor would make our discusions a bit more entertaining, but with entertainment came emotions. Then our pride would take over.

"Terrance, when was the last time you went to church?" Fred asked as we ate.

"Man. Ummm... I haven't been in a while. I can't even remember the last time I went."

"Shame on you!" Jay yelled.

"You been going, Jay?"

"You know I'm playing. I don't remember the last time I was in a church pew either."

"I think we should go to church next Sunday. Let's all go together," Fred suggested.

"I'm down to go," I replied.

"Nope. You know I don't do them church folks. All they do is sit around and judge," Jay mentioned, shaking his head.

"Let's not be negative, Jay," I replied.

"Nah. I know this because my uncle was a deacon and my aunt was a deaconess at a church. All they used to do was come over and gossip about what was going on at the church. Who was stealing money? Who's sleeping with the pastor? Who cursed who out? Who can't sing? Who was a crackhead? Then they went back to church and acted like they were sanctified and filled with the Holy Spirit. Them church people are all fake to me," Jay further explained.

"Wait, what church did you go to? Please let me know so I know not to go there," Fred inquired.

"Jay, for one, we ain't going for the people; we're going for ourselves. We're overdue for a church visit. Plus, all church folk ain't like your aunt and uncle. Let's go for some cleansing. Let's just go to give thanks. God's been blessing us, the least we can do is go into His house and praise Him."

"I guess. Since you put it that way. I am blessed to be breathing. Yea, and plus, we need to go because that's where the freaks be at," Jay stated.

Fred responded with a face palm.

"I'm serious! Y'all know it's the truth. Most of the time they be in church on Sunday because they be praying for God to forgive them for all the freakiness that they were involved with during the week. That's the perfect place to find a woman. She's a freak and she loves Jesus! You can't go wrong with that." Jay picked up his mimosa.

"Do you actually think about what you say before you say it? This is a serious question," Fred asked.

"I just say what y'all are scared to say. I keep it real."

"Jay, we ain't going to pick up no chicks. Not our intentions man. We're just going to praise the Lord."

Fred looked at me. "Well, Jay needs to go to repent for all the sinning he been doing. Hopefully this will change his life."

"Yea and maybe you can catch the Holy Ghost and do laps around the church so that you can lose some more weight," Jay rebutted.

"I guess you can make a joke, but you can't take one. I was just playing but you want to get personal," Fred responded.

"With every joke there's a bit of sincerity, Sir," Jay said.

"Hey, hey, hey, chill out. Both of y'all are sensitive. We're going to church next Sunday because we all need it."

Chapter 7:

Easter Sunday Fresh

Elizabeth Baptist Church 11:00 a.m.

I wasn't going to church to meet any women. I know the church is not some hook-up spot for singles. However, that didn't mean that I was going to show up not looking good. Just in case there was a special someone there worth my time, I was going to look good. First impressions are everything. I mean think about it, would it be such a bad thing if I found my wife at a church? Two people searching and yearning for God's glory, meet in God's house, and fall in love. It made sense.

I stood in front of my closet and sorted through my hangers. I wanted to wear a suit that I wouldn't wear to work, a suit that was relatively clean, that I never really wore anywhere else because the color combination never really fit the occasion. I paused and chuckled. I felt as if I was just as bad as the typical people that went to church only on Easter Sunday. They would come into church with some of their best outfits with loud and crazy colors; they looked like they hadn't been in church for ages. That was me today. My outfit was Easter Sunday fresh, even though it wasn't Easter Sunday.

The ushers of the church opened up the double doors. I walked in and immediately looked around. I spotted Jay and Fred and pointed to them. An usher then walked me to my seat. Jay and Fred were to the right, close to the back of the church. I told them I was running late so they had to save me a seat. I sat with them. My eyes panned the church; it was a decent crowd. It felt good to be in a place of worship. The choir was singing great songs. They did something to me, I don't know, but they did something. It was ironic that the preacher's sermon was about being thankful for God's blessings; not only the big blessings, but also the small things that we take for granted, like the gift of life, breath, and being able

55

to wake up in the morning and have a roof over our head. I feel guilty of that a lot. I forget about the simple things in life.

I was locked in on the preacher's sermon when Jay nudged me with his elbow. I turned to him. He leaned over and whispered softly, "Man I been looking around the church all morning and as big as this church is, I don't see any bitches."

"Ouch," Jay said after I elbowed him in his ribs.

I whispered back, "Come on, man. Be respectful in the Lord's house. Listen to the Word. You might learn something." I pointed towards the preacher. I was angered and disgusted. I had to remind myself that as smart and successful as Jay was, he was still ignorant.

The preacher finished his sermon. Emotions flared in the congregation. People were crying, hugging each other, and clapping. I couldn't help but reminisce on how God had blessed me with so many opportunities. I thought about how far I had come in growing into the man that I dreamed of. I began connecting the dots of my life and I knew that it was all God's work. I could feel myself becoming emotional. I tried my best to keep my emotions in check. I admit that I didn't want to look soft in front of my friends. I looked over at both of them. Jay had his phone out and was scrolling through his Instagram page. Fred was standing up, with his eyes closed and a tear rolled down the side of his puffy cheek. It made me smile. I was thankful for my friends, flaws and all. I was glad I went to church.

The service was ending. The choir had one last song to sing before we were officially dismissed. I looked to Jay. He was still on his phone. I know him. I could see that he had mentally checked out of church a long time ago. He was ready to leave. Fred was on his phone, too.

The choir began to sing their last song. It was called, "Now Behold the Lamb" and was led by a soft and heavenly voice. The whole congregation yelled and chanted in excitement. The singer's voice got the attention of all of us. We stood up so that we could see who it was.

Jay nudged me. "I guess I spoke too soon." I looked to the choir to see what Jay was talking about. The lady that was singing the song was beautiful. She had appeared out of nowhere. She sang with so much passion, as if she put her soul into it. Her voice was spectacular. The song hit me hard. This time, I couldn't hold my emotions. My eyes got watery.

Her voice gave me a certain joy that I just couldn't explain. It was as if God had let the church borrow one of his angels from his own personal church in heaven. She had on all white, so it seemed even more believable. I couldn't tell if my heart was touched by the song, or by the woman singing the song, or both. But either way, she had my full attention.

"Man, I have to get her! Damn she fine!" Jay said.

Fred frowned at Jay. "Ay, watch your mouth in church!"

"Damn is in the Bible, stupid. Leave me alone," Jay snapped.

"Seriously, Jay, please leave that girl alone. You're too much for a chick like that. You will contaminate her. She looks pure. She looks like she's God's niece, literally. I'm usually against trying to hook up with someone at church, but this time, Terrance, I feel like she has your name all over her. That's your type," Fred suggested.

I said nothing; I was just watching her.

Jay looked at me. "You know what, I agree. That's all Terrance right there. Are you going to barbecue or mildew?" Jay asked.

While Jay was turned to me waiting for an answer, the song ended. The congregation stood up and gave the woman a standing ovation. She put the microphone on the stand and smiled. She then went over and hugged another woman. They rocked back and forth.

I turned to Jay and Fred. "Keep your eye on her. I want to make sure I fellowship with that sister before I leave."

They smiled. "I knew you had it in you!" Jay exclaimed, patting me on the back. "The bible wants you to find a woman, a wholesome woman of God like that one anyway. Let's go introduce ourselves."

We waited after church outside of the church's front doors until she was by herself to approach her. She spoke with a lot of people as she slowly made her way out to the parking lot.

As we gravitated closer towards her, I began to sweat. I turned to Jay.

"How can I make sure that this isn't awkward? I'm really about to ask a girl out on church grounds. A church that I'm not even a member of at that," I said.

"The only way it would be awkward is if you make it awkward. Just tell her you're a visitor of the church and that you loved her performance. Then slowly transition into getting her number," Jay advised.

"Okay, she's walking out to the parking lot now," Fred informed us. We waited until she was ahead of us walking to her car. I took a deep sigh and proceeded towards her.

"Go get her tiger," Jay said.

As I walked up, I saw that she was even prettier up close. She was hands down a 10 out of 10. Light skinned with long, thick hair that came down to the middle of her back. I had to be careful with my words. I knew that even saying, "excuse me beautiful" to a girl like her wouldn't flatter her much, because stating the obvious wasn't enough.

"Excuse me. Excuse me," I said, walking behind her.

The woman turned around. Her long hair swung in the wind; some of it got in her face and she moved it.

"Yes, Sir?"

"Hi, my name is Terrance. I'm a visitor of the church. I wanted to catch up with you to let you know that you absolutely blew me away with your voice."

She blushed. "Thank you, I try. What church are you from?"

"Excuse me?"

"You said that you were a visitor. What church are you visiting from? Where's your home church?" she asked.

"Oh! I'm sorry, I thought I heard you say something different," I said, chuckling. I was stumped. I had no idea of what to say. I had no church home. Nor did I know of any church names off the top of my head. I didn't want to lie. I thought that if I said that I didn't go to church that she would be turned off immediately. Plus, I didn't want to say that I was looking for a church, because I felt like she would try to get me to join hers. The last thing I wanted to do was lie on church grounds. So I said what came to my mind.

"Um, honestly, I don't have a church home. I just like visiting different churches here and there. I like to listen to different pastors and their different styles of preaching. I also like to witness different choirs. I'm not trying to commit to one church yet. It's a lot to choose from."

She said nothing and looked at me. She then busted out laughing. I felt like an idiot. I was uncomfortable. I knew that my answer sounded stupid. I smiled anyway.

"What's so funny?" I asked.

58

"I'm so sorry! That was rude of me, but what you said sounded like something that my ex-boyfriend would say."

"Is that a good thing or bad thing?"

"No, it's cute! It's not bad. Y'all are just so indecisive," she said, smiling and still giggling. I knew that I had her where I wanted her after that response.

"Well, yea I'm guilty of that. But I will know when it's time to commit. I don't make many decisions without God's permission. He will let me know which one is the right fit for me."

She nodded in agreement and stopped giggling. "Amen."

"By the way, I didn't get your name."

"Grace."

"You have to be kidding me! That's not your government name."

"That's my government name. The name on my birth certificate. That's what my mama named me," she confirmed.

"Wow, talk about a name that fits a person! Your mama knew at birth the impact that you would have on people. That's crazy."

"I guess she did."

"Well, Grace, I don't want to hold you up any longer, but I would love to stay in contact with you."

"You sure you can't stay in contact with me by coming to visit me here? I mean, I'm pretty much here every Wednesday and Sunday."

"If that's really what it takes to stay connected, I would, but to be honest I would like to stay connected with you outside of the church's perimeter. If that's okay with you."

Grace said nothing at first. She was hesitant. "Okay, where's your phone?"

I handed her my phone. She put her number in and handed it back to me.

"Nice meeting you, Terrance," Grace said before walking away.

"Nice meeting you too, Grace! I'll keep in touch," I said, waving. I walked back to Fred and Jay.

"Took you long enough! I thought y'all were going to place a quilt on the ground and grab bologna sandwiches out of the car for an afternoon picnic. Sheesh! Please tell me you got her number." Jay was impatient.

"I did. It was tough though. I felt like she had her guard up. I had to ask twice."

"Well at least you got it. Let's go because this heat is killing me, I need to get out of this suit," Fred stated.

I got home and immediately changed out of my church clothes and hung them up. I was still thinking about how it was such a coincidence for that woman's name to be Grace, and grace was exactly what I felt when I heard her voice. She truly had a voice from God. She had a voice that can bring anyone to his or her knees. Whether it was to beg God for forgiveness, or to beg her for a date; she had the power to make anyone kneel. I mean she was drop-dead gorgeous. To be honest, judging off of looks alone she was wifey material. She was on my mind, so I decided to text her. It wouldn't hurt to start getting to know her as early as possible.

Hey Grace. This is Terrance. Again, it was nice meeting you today! I sent the text and then turned on the television.

Two and a half hours had passed. I checked my phone at least twelve times, but I wasn't actually counting. I made sure that my phone wasn't on silent. Hell, I even turned my phone off and back on to make sure there wasn't some type of glitch that stopped me from getting text messages. *Did she give me the wrong number?* Maybe she gave me the wrong number on accident. But either way, the anticipation of waiting was eating me alive. What the hell was taking her so long? I'm not a fan of texting someone more than once if they don't respond the first time. It's almost like spamming them. I wasn't trying to seem desperate. Maybe she didn't receive it. There's a small chance that she may not have, so I texted her again.

Hey Grace. I just wanted to make sure that I had the right number. Did you get my first text?

I put the phone face down on the table after texting her. If she didn't respond this time, that was it. I'd leave her alone. I'm naturally an optimistic person, but I'd be damned if I get my hopes up for nothing.

My phone beeped. A sigh of relief came to me. I turned it over. It was a text from Fred. *Damn!* Talk about disappointment. What the hell did he want?

Are you watching the Buccaneers play? Man they suck!

I placed my phone back face down and didn't respond. Five minutes later, I received another text message notification. I didn't pick it up for a second because I didn't want to be disappointed. I eventually turned it over. It was Grace. Thank God. I had the right number.

Hey Terrance! I'm sorry, I took my regularly scheduled Sunday nap and I didn't hear my phone. And yes you have the right number! If I didn't want you to have my number, I just wouldn't have given it to you. No need to waste time and mislead you with a fake number.

I liked her answer. It was acceptable. However, I could tell that she would be a possible handful to deal with it. Well, nothing worth having comes easy.

Grace and I continued to text each other throughout the next couple of days. She was a terrible texter. I mean terrible. It took her forever to text me back. I hated it. I don't know if she was just naturally a bad communicator, if I was too anxious and impatient for my own good, or both, but I knew how to solve the problem. I needed to ask her out on a date so we could establish a real, face-to-face connection because through text messages it was merely impossible. Plus, she told me that she wasn't fond of talking on the phone anyway.

Hey. I would love to have lunch with you sometime soon. When are you most likely free?

I sent that text at 5:30 p.m. on Tuesday and waited patiently for a response. I never got one. I was pissed off the whole night. She could've just told me that she didn't want to go instead of just ignoring me. No one denies an offer to just have lunch. What was holding her back from at least saying yes or no? Was she in a relationship? Did she not respond on accident? I sat on my couch a bit frustrated. I was in front of the television, but my mind was somewhere else. I knew that she saw the text because it said that it had been seen at 5:40 p.m. that day. But I was more disappointed in myself. Why did I even care? Why was I even stressing over this chick? Why was my mind so locked on her anyway? I'm sure she wasn't thinking about me like I was thinking about her. That's exactly why I was about to leave her ass alone and not text her again. See, a person like me needs clarity. No response from Grace might've actually been a message in the first place; a message that she wasn't interested in me. That's why I was falling back.

Wednesday was a great day at work. There were rumors going around the office that certain people were going to get pay increases. I didn't want to jump to conclusions, but I believed I was in that number. I had a very strong feeling about it. I was called into my manager's office around 11:00 a.m. I knew it had to be the good news that I was waiting to hear. I slowly opened my manager's office door, hoping that my intuition was right.

"Mr. Hill, good to see you!" Mr. Hinson said, not looking up from his desk.

"Pleasure to see you too, sir. How's your day going thus far?" I asked smiling.

"Every day above ground is a great day," Mr. Hinson replied finally looking up.

"Amen to that."

"Terrance, I'm going to be really brief, but I just want to commend you for the work you do for this firm. People like you make our firm one of the best in the industry. You represent the backbone of this company."

"I appreciate that, Mr. Hinson. That means the world to me."

"I've seen your progress in this company since you arrived here, and I am impressed. So with that being said, we've decided to bump your salary from $75,000 to $80,000 starting the next pay period."

"Wow! I don't know what to say. I'm speechless, Mr. Hinson."

"You don't have to say anything. You earned it. Just get your butt out there and continue to work like a champion."

"You bet, Mr. Hinson."

I opened Mr. Hinson's office door and walked out. If no one was watching, I would've screamed at the top of my lungs and did the Harlem Shake, but I calmly walked to my desk like nothing happened. I was proud of myself. I deserved it. I loved the fact that my efforts were being recognized by the administration.

Although I was ecstatic, there was still something lingering on my mind. It shouldn't have been, but it was: this damn girl, Grace. How could she not recognize greatness when she saw it? Now I'm modest as could be, but I'm still a young, black man that's successful and ambitious. Was I not at least worthy enough to receive a text back? I would appreciate her honesty more than anything. Simply ignoring me was unacceptable. I decided to follow up by sending her another text message.

Hey! I'm guessing you weren't interested in my offer to take you to lunch yesterday?

This time, I wasn't worried if she wouldn't text back. If she didn't respond this time, it was her loss, not mine. I was just giving her another opportunity to accept it.

Five minutes after my text, my phone lit up.

Hey Terrance! I'm sorry for not responding yesterday. I was just too busy.

I knew she was lying, but I wasn't going to combat her statement, so I just rolled with it. I was still a bit relieved that she responded.

Okay. Soooo when is the best time for you?

I'm off tomorrow. So I guess we can do something then.

There it is! Meet me at Panera Bread on Roswell Rd at 12:15!

I put my phone face down on my desk and regained focus on my work.

It was now Thursday and I was fresh at work. I had on one of my better suits. I got a couple of compliments. I smelled good too. Before I left the house, I sprayed on a little more of my favorite cologne Versace Eros. While sitting at my desk, my belly rumbled. It surprised me and scared the hell out of me at the same time. I placed my hand on my stomach and remembered that I hadn't eaten breakfast. I looked at my watch. It was 11:20 a.m. and I looked around hoping no one noticed the weird growling sound coming from my stomach. I wasn't going to eat anything, because I was looking forward to having lunch with Grace. Speaking of her, something told me to text her to let her know that I was looking forward to seeing her. I didn't want any excuses, because I know she's good for them. I grabbed my phone and wrote her.

See you soon!

As soon as I sent the text, my stomach let out another loud bellow, even louder than before.

"You alright over there, man?" a co-worker in the cubicle next to me asked.

I chuckled. "Yea, I apologize. I didn't eat breakfast this morning. I'm starving." I was a tad bit embarrassed.

My phone lit up. It was a message from Grace.

OMG. I'm glad you texted me... I almost forgot! But I will be there!

I knew it! What a slap in the face! Was I really not that memorable? This lunch had been on my mind since yesterday. I was convinced that there was no way that she had so many things going on to almost forget about our plans. Now I was even more determined to show her that I'm not the forgettable person that she was making me out to be.

I arrived at Panera Bread at 12:15 on the dot. To my surprise, I saw that Grace was already seated. I went straight to the table.

"Well hello there," I said, walking up.

"Hey, Terrance! You look nice," Grace said, getting up to give me a hug. My memory was refreshed. It dawned on me why she was so hard to communicate with. It made more sense. This damn girl was so fine! Sheesh! Her beauty made her unresponsiveness acceptable. She had a reason to be conceited. Grace reminded me of the girl that always got awarded "best looking" in the school yearbook. She had the kind of beauty that made other women question God and ask what she had done to deserve such flawlessness.

She had on a sleeveless white dress that exposed a tattoo from her shoulder down to her forearm. I didn't notice it when I met her at church. It was sexy! But it also had me curious about what she did for a living, because I knew that Corporate America wasn't as accepting to such visual body art.

"Thank you for coming. Did you order something to eat already?" I asked, pointing towards the front counter.

"Nope! I'm not really hungry."

"You sure?"

"Yea, I am fine, but thanks for asking."

"Okay. Well I'm starving. I'm about to order something really quick. I'll be right back," I said before getting up. I was thrown off immediately. I could tell that she was a difficult individual. I knew that I would feel awkward eating in front of her while she sat empty-handed. I again felt as if she wasn't interested. I stood in the line wondering why I was still entertaining her if she wouldn't show any signs of interest. I eventually returned to my seat with my meal.

"So, Ms. Grace, thank you again for coming. How's your day so far?" I asked, while looking down at my plate to cut my sandwich with a knife and fork.

"Umm, it was whatever. Just glad to have a day off! Thank God," Grace responded.

"I feel you on that! I wish! Where do you work?" I asked, taking a bite.

"I work at Burger King."

I almost choked on my food. Did I hear her correctly? I immediately coughed to clear my throat. I couldn't believe her statement. I tried not to look or act surprised. I was scared to ask if she was joking.

"You okay?" Grace asked.

"Yea, I'm sorry. A piece of the sandwich went down the wrong pipe. What position?"

"Cashier really, but they have me doing pretty much everything. I'm looking for another job now though. I need a job that pays more. But at least I have a job. I'm grateful. I'm not ashamed. So many people are unemployed."

I was in awe. I was confused about where to take the conversation, but tried to be as casual as possible.

"So, how is the job search going?"

"Um, it's going. It's tough to look for a job while having a job. Plus, when I'm off work I have to take care of my daughter, because I'm not paying a babysitter when I'm off work to take care of my child."

I had no idea how I was able to keep it together. I'd never done a better job of acting. My ability to control my facial expressions and to act like I was not flabbergasted by what was coming out of Grace's mouth deserved an Oscar. Inside, my jaw dropped to the ground. I had no idea that there was such a disparity between her and I in regards to our careers. My perception of her changed drastically. It was obvious. She wasn't on my level. I mean that in the humblest way. The lunch turned from me wanting to show that I was worthy of her time to me feeling sorry for this chick. She was gorgeous, but her looks alone weren't good enough to bring her up to my standards. I had to take the lunch in a different direction.

"So what do you like to do for fun? What's your passion?"

"I don't have time for fun. I just have time to take care of my daughter and that's it. Everything that I do is for me to be able to provide for her."

"Okay. Question. If money didn't exist, what would you do for a living?"

Grace shifted in her seat. She looked away from the table as if she didn't hear my question. She licked her lips as she stared away momentarily. She didn't mean to be sexy, but I thought it was the sexiest shit ever.

"Hello?" I asked as I turned to see what she was looking at.

She looked back at me. "Sorry, I was thinking about something. What was your question?"

I chuckled and shook my head. "I said if money didn't exist, what would you do for a living?"

"I would sing."

"Hmmm. That's what I thought. Do you sing a lot? How often do you sing at church?"

"Once or twice a year. You got lucky last Sunday."

"What? Why don't you sing more?"

"Because I choose not to," Grace blatantly stated.

"Well, there has to be a reason. It's hard to believe that you don't sing much with a voice like yours."

"I actually don't like talking about it." She was sterner this time.

"Okay. Well, I'm sorry. I just can't help but to think that you were put on earth to sing. When I heard your voice, it was like I heard an angel singing. It was scary good. Never heard anything like it. You have a true God-given talent."

"Thank you."

The conversation fell silent. I finished the last bite of my sandwich. Grace picked up her phone and looked at the time.

"How long were you planning on the lunch going until?" she asked.

I wiped my mouth with my napkin. "If you have to leave, you can go. I didn't want to keep you long. Just wanted to have a friendly lunch."

66

"Okay, because I have to be somewhere in a little bit, but I really thank you for inviting me out. It was nice seeing you again," she said, grabbing her purse.

"No, thank you for coming out. Make sure you keep in touch," I responded, getting up from the table.

She flashed a slight grin and got up from table. We walked out of Panera Bread and went to our cars.

I returned back to my desk to finish my shift. The second half of the day usually went by fast. Today, it would go by even faster. I was sitting there still trying to figure out what the hell just happened. That lunch date was the most uncomfortable date that I had ever been on. My vibe had been ruined for the rest of the day. I was ready to vent to Fred and Jay on Fun Friday.

Blu Cantina – Peters Street, Atlanta GA

I was dying laughing listening to Jay. He is a fool. Especially when the liquor is pouring. He was acting crazy and telling Fred and I about his crazy week at work. I glanced at Fred and watched him frown and shake his head. I laughed at Fred too, because he just doesn't understand Jay's thought process, ever. I was all smiles though.

It's just amazing how far we'd come as friends from college to the present. It feels good to know that I have friends to turn to when times get rough. These two guys are all I need. See in college, I had too many friends. My life consisted of some seasonal friends, and like a tree in the fall, I had to shake off all the dead leaves in order to grow. I didn't need a huge number of fake friends that pretended to like me; friends that would pretend to want the best for me, but in their gut hate my success; friends that wanted me to be stationary and not strive for greatness because they'd feel inadequate. I needed friends that add value, not envy. I needed friends that are just as ambitious as I am. I'm glad I have friends to laugh with and to laugh at. These two guys understand me, and they support me. If I didn't have these two guys when I separated from Lisa, I have no idea how I would've recovered.

67

"So, I have to tell y'all about Grace, the chick from church."

"Oh yea! Her fine ass! What's up with that?" Jay pressed for details.

"Man, Grace in a nutshell, that chick is weird. I had lunch with her this week and it was a disaster. She was so difficult to talk to. I didn't like her vibe at all. Her energy was off."

"Really? It looked like y'all were on the same page on Sunday," Fred stated.

"Nah, man. I don't know what was up with her, but it was definitely not what I expected. I'm not feeling like I can get anywhere with her at all. There was zero chemistry."

"That sounds like the typical light-skinned chick. Hard to get her to text you back, hard to get her out the house, and extremely difficult to get in her bed. She probably was texting three different guys while she was with you. Then she was probably upset with one of her side niggas. That's all. You'll be fine. Light-skinned chicks are like onions; there are so many layers to them. Once you start getting through those layers, she'll be begging you to come see her."

"But that's not all. Check this, y'all aren't going to believe it... this chick works at Burger King."

Jay had his cup to his mouth drinking his beer, but after he heard me, he spit it all on the table. He couldn't hold in his laugh. Fred and I backed up from the table trying not to get anything on our clothes.

Fred looked at me. "You can't be serious."

"If I'm lying, I'm flying. And she has a child."

"That bitch works at Burger King? Oh hell nah!" Jay yelled. "She is too damn fine to be flipping burgers!"

"Who you telling! I couldn't believe it either. I felt so bad while I was talking to her because I felt like we weren't even on the same level. Why would I even waste her time or mine? Am I wrong for feeling like that?"

"No, you're not wrong. Men have standards too. You can do better than that man," Fred encouraged.

"Hell yea, you can do better! I wouldn't even let you take her serious. But you should still fuck her. She too fine not to. I know I would," Jay said, taking a sip of his drink again.

"Yea, I'm not going to entertain her anymore. We didn't have chemistry anyway. But I still was trying to understand why she wasn't

68

feeling me like that. Did she not realize that I'm actually a good man? A college-educated, black man with a great career as a Financial Analyst that is actually ready to settle down and find a wife. I'm not conceited, but I thought about writing her a message on our lunch napkin, 'Do you know that I can save you?' I'm still scratching my head in disbelief."

"Don't feel bad. She ain't used to dudes like you. Dressed nice and talking all proper. She probably mess with straight ball players and drug dealers. She probably wouldn't recognize a good man if she saw one. Plus, you don't want to play step daddy anyway!"

I disagreed. "Drug dealers, I don't think so. Athletes, maybe. And no kids for me anytime soon."

"That just goes to show that looks can only get you so far. Yea, delete her number man. That's a downgrade for you," Fred shared.

"Before you delete it, send it to me. I can take it from here," Jay said, reaching for my phone.

"Move!" I said, jokingly pushing Jay away.

Jay smiled. "It just amazes me how these chicks be so basic. Then they have the nerve to tell you what they want in a man. I want a man with good credit. I want a man that loves The Lord. I want a man that can provide for me and my family. I want a man that knows how to treat a woman. I prefer a man over 6 feet. Shut the hell up! Don't feed me that bullshit on what you want or deserve in a man! Stop lying about how high your standards are. Show me your last three relationships and I'll show you your true standards. That's what you attracted, that's what you accepted, and that's what you deserved. You are what you date. If you think you deserve better, then stop accepting worse. Upgrade yourself first, invest in yourself, then you'll increase your net worth."

Fred laughed. "You got a point."

Chapter 8:

Cupcakes for Days

I hate cooking. I can cook, but I hate doing it. Lisa was a beast in the kitchen. I miss coming home to a delicious meal. Even though she worked all day, she still came home to cook dinner. She didn't mind it. She loved cooking. She was a true chef. She spoiled me. I took it for granted sometimes. Silly me. Let's just say that I lost a little weight since then.

I was sitting here on the couch thinking of what I should eat. It didn't help that I was watching the food channel at 8:30 p.m. *What fast food place is closest to me?* I didn't want McDonald's. Chick-Fil-A sounded good. *Those waffle fries are scrumptious. Chick-Fil-A it is!*

As I got up to head to Chick-Fil-A, my phone beeped from an incoming text message. It was Grace. I saw her name and did a double take. She must've texted me on accident. The text simply said *Hey.* I was skeptical. Either she was super bored, drunk texting me, or she was upset with one of her three "boyfriends" as Jay would say.

I texted her back, *Hey what's up.* I was really curious to see what this chick wanted.

Two minutes later, she texted me back, *What are you up to?*

Interesting... She actually wanted to know my whereabouts. I responded, *Nothing, at home watching a little TV. Why what's up?*

Five minutes later she responded, *My daughter and I just got done making cupcakes. We made a whole bunch and now we have cupcakes for days. I was inviting you over to see if you wanted any to take home. If not we will probably just throw them out.*

What? Cupcakes with her daughter? Something was definitely up. What was she trying to do? Was she setting a trap? All I could think about was being a stepfather, which was scary! There I was overthinking everything, as usual. It was probably not even that deep. Regardless, I knew that she wasn't girlfriend worthy. So whatever trap she had under her sleeve wouldn't work on me, because I have boundaries. I was simply going to pick up cupcakes. That's all. As long as I was aware of what I was doing, I'd be fine.

So I replied to her, *Don't throw them out! I'll come get some.*

I was on my way to her place, but I remembered something crucial. Grace works at Burger King, so I wouldn't be surprised if she lived in some type of low-income housing. *Damn man! I'm not thinking. What am I doing? I can't believe that I'm probably about to end up in some broke down projects at night, for some damn cupcakes.* I was halfway there, so I wasn't turning around. But whatever happened, I'd learn my lesson from making these bonehead decisions.

I arrived to the address she sent me. It was a luxury apartment complex in Midtown, Atlanta, which was odd. How could she afford this on a Burger King income? That made no sense but I just left it alone. I got on the phone and she directed me to her unit number. I reached the door and knocked twice. She answered.

"Hey you! Welcome to our dwelling," Grace said, waving her hand for me to come inside.

I walked in slowly and began looking around. The apartment was clean. I walked towards the coffee table and saw many pictures of Grace and her daughter. I picked up one of the pictures and looked closely.

"Your daughter is so cute! Where is she?"

"She was in the back talking to her god mama on the phone. I'm about to go check on her now. Hold on... Destiny!" She walked towards the back room.

I was convinced that she was trying to set me up to be a stepdad. *Look at what she has on!* Grey tight jogging pants with a grey sports bra. She had tattoos down the side of her arm and on her back. Her body was banging! And my goodness she had a nice ass! A nice ass is my kryptonite. Sexy is an understatement. Man if Jay saw her like this, he would go crazy.

Grace's daughter ran out of the room. She had on a pink pajama outfit. She was full of energy. Her hair was big and natural. She looked like a miniature version of Grace. They looked so much alike that it was almost creepy. This little girl was the cutest thing ever, and I don't even like kids! I couldn't help but smile when I saw her.

71

"Awww! What's your name?"

"Destiny," she said, as if she was shy.

"Don't act shy now." Grace looked at Destiny and smiled.

"My name is Terrance."

"Say hey, Terrance," Grace said, looking down at Destiny.

Destiny waved her hand then ran into the back room.

Grace shook her head smiling. "That girl is something else."

I had the biggest smile on my face. I couldn't stop smiling watching her. Like I said, I don't like kids at all, but if I were ever to have a daughter, I would want her to be just like Destiny. "Your little girl is too cute. How could you discipline her? I feel like I would never get mad at her; I would let her get away with murder."

"Oh she knows not to act up. But thankfully she's a pretty good baby."

"Can she sing like you?"

Grace looked at me and grinned. "She's learning. We might do a mother and daughter duet for you soon."

"Nice! I would love that."

She looked in the kitchen. "Oh! Come get some of these cupcakes before I forget. I have eight in a pack for you. Is that enough?"

"That's fine."

She was in the kitchen getting the cupcakes together for me. She then chuckled to herself and shook her head.

"What are you in there laughing at? I want to laugh too."

"Nothing. Talking about my daughter and I singing brought back memories."

"Memories?"

"Yep memories…"

"Memories of what? I know I'm being nosey."

She said nothing for a second. She then let out a big sigh. "When I was a child, my mom and I used to sing duets together."

"So it's a tradition? That's cute. Why were you so hesitant to share that?"

"Because my mother is the reason why I don't sing anymore. It's a long story."

"Seriously? Well I have time. I have to hear why you don't want to use that God-given talent of yours." I leaned forward in my chair.

72

Destiny ran out of the room with a colored notebook and marker.

"Mr. Terrance! Look at my picture! Look at my drawing!" she yelled, holding up her notebook.

I took a look at the notebook and saw a stick man and scribbly lines. I couldn't help but smile.

"Hold on," Grace said. "Destiny, it's bed time. Go color in your room and I'll be in there to read to you in a second. Okay, baby?" Destiny skipped to the back room.

"My mother was a very talented singer. She loved singing. She's actually sung with people like Patti LaBelle, Diana Ross, and others. She sung for a living. She was a single mother just like me. She used to sing to me all the time, ever since I was born. She took me everywhere with her. When I was three, we started singing together. We would sing together in the tub, and we performed in our living room as if we were in a stadium full of hundreds of people. My mama was superwoman to me. Her voice was so amazing."

"I'm sure she was good looking like you too," I interrupted.

"She was gorgeous. Men would do anything for her. She could sing any man out of his wallet and have him on his knees begging to marry her. But that's what tore her apart."

"Oh no. I'm scared to ask what went wrong."

"Drug abuse and partying began to affect my mama's voice. So of course, no voice means that we were losing money, which meant we couldn't pay our bills. So one day... I will never forget this day. My mother had a random man in her room. I was 13 years old. She called me into the room. Of course she was high on drugs, her and the guy. They both were wrapped in the covers. I believe they were both naked. She told me that her voice was hoarse and she wanted me to sing happy birthday to the man. I felt weird about it, but I sang it anyway. I always obeyed my mama. Afterwards, I asked her if I could leave. She told me to hold on. The man whispered in her ear. My mother shook her head no to him at first. The man kept talking in her ear. Her eyes began to water. Then she looked up at me and said that he wanted me to sing a sexy song next. But I had to go in the bathroom and come out with just a bra and panties on. I said no at first. She yelled at me and told me to follow directions. I went into the bathroom and cried on the floor in my underwear, for like ten

73

minutes. I could hear the man telling my mom to tell me to hurry up. Then I heard her moaning from sex. I got up and ran out of the bathroom with just my underwear on. I left the house, and I never saw my mother again. That's why I said I would never sing again."

I was speechless. "That is a crazy story. Wow. So where did you go?"

"I lived with one of my girlfriends throughout high school. I was fine."

"I'm sorry that you had to go through that. That's so sad."

"Terrance, my mother was like a God to me. She introduced me to the world, and she introduced me to the art of music. To watch her crumble was the hardest thing that I ever had to do."

"So I have a question. Do you still love singing?"

Grace nodded. "I love it. But there's no way that I can go back to it. It reminds me too much of my mama. She worked so hard, but music tore her apart. That life is not for me."

"But you are not your mama! You are Grace! Did I tell you that I cried when I heard you sing? I hadn't cried in years. It did something to my soul. It gave me joy."

Grace closed her eyes as she blushed.

"What you went through with your mama in the past shouldn't hinder your future. That's your story. Your voice touches people's souls. So why would you hold that back from the world? That's what God put you here for."

Grace began to tear up. She tried to look away from me. She said nothing, but sniffled.

"Deep down inside, you know that you're supposed to be singing. You're happiest when you sing, aren't you? Don't you want your daughter to be all that she can be too? You have to lead by example to show her that she can. Especially since you know she will have a voice like yours."

She wiped her tears, still looking away. "I think it's time for you to go, Mr. Terrance," Grace said.

I nodded. "Okay. I'm sorry for anything I said. I didn't mean for it to be negative, but I'm on my way out."

Grace said nothing. She got up and walked me out. She gave me a hug, thanked me for coming, and closed the door. I walked out of her place and headed to the car, and then it dawned on me. Something was missing... something. I felt empty-handed. I rubbed my palms together, itching to grasp some understanding. I didn't understand why I was entertaining this chick. What was the purpose of this visit again? Cupcakes! That explained my empty hands. I forgot the cupcakes! Or she forgot to give them to me. It was probably because she didn't invite me over for cupcakes in the first place. The cupcakes were an excuse. She wanted me. But I'd be lying if I said that I cared about the cupcakes. I don't even like cupcakes like that. I wanted to see her. Her daughter, Destiny, is a little princess. What lousy father would leave a beautiful woman like Grace to raise a little princess like Destiny alone? If I were Destiny's father, I would do everything in my power to be a part of that little girl's life. I wouldn't care what type of relationship I had with her mother. If I was ever having a terrible day, I know that her little smile would transform my frown in a heartbeat.

Chapter 9:

Sing to My Soul

She was actually calling me. Grace's name popping up on my phone was always a bit of a shock. Especially since I would text her and she would always take forever to text me back, and that's if I was lucky enough to get her to respond. I learned to never get my hopes up with her. I would be so much happier if she just came clean and said that she wasn't interested. I don't like wasting my time.

I hadn't heard from Grace ever since I went to see her and her daughter many weeks before. It had been a while. I reached out to her numerous times since then, but she either never responded, or responded so late acting as if she was so busy. To be honest, I was actually kind of glad that I didn't hear from her. It made it easier for me to stay away. Out of sight, out of mind. But today was different. I should treat her like she treats me, and ignore the hell out of the call, but I'm too nice. Why do we worry about people that aren't worrying about us? Hell, I wouldn't be surprised if it was a dude calling me and telling me to leave her alone. *Let me see what she wants.*

"What you doing, boy?"

"Nothing. Don't talk to me like we talk on the regular. You do me so wrong. You are a horrible communicator."

"I'm so sorry, Terrance! I really am. I'll do better; I promise. I've just been busy."

Here she goes with these lies! I hate liars. She's so full of it! I'll let her continue anyway. "I guess. What's up?"

"You're going to be proud of me. I'm singing at this wedding reception. I have a plus-one invite, so I figured that I should invite you since you kind of motivated me to sing more."

"Look at you. I am proud. And yes, I'll go."

"Good! I'll see you there! Wear black and white."

I didn't have anything to do, so I was going. I admit that I didn't mind seeing her though. I got to the reception at 9:35 p.m. It was 20 minutes before Grace was up to sing. I called her to get the exact instructions on where to find her. Once we saw each other, we hung up the phone. She had on all white. Her hair was did up. She looked fine as hell like always, but she seemed as if she was nervous.

"Hey you! You look nice!" Grace said.

"I ain't got nothing on you though," I said reaching out for a hug.

"I'm so nervous. I don't know if I practiced enough."

"Grace, you got this. You were made for this. The couple picked you to sing at their wedding because they believe in you. I believe in you too." I winked at her.

She smiled. "Thank you!" She reached up to give me a kiss on the cheek then grabbed my hand. "Come on! I'm about to go on now."

I followed her inside. We both walked over to the empty seating that was reserved for her. I scanned the room and saw everyone dressed up in black and white. The groom and the bride were sitting together at their own table holding hands. The bride was a beautiful brown-skinned chick. She looked like a 26-year-old Diana Ross. Short. Long hair. Petite. Gorgeous. The groom was a handsome, clean-cut, light-skinned brother. He stood about 6'2". Clean brush cut. They looked like a nice Black couple straight out of a Tyler Perry Film. They all looked genuinely happy. Everyone was dapper with big smiles. Loud, random outbursts of laughs filled the room. Great music. I loved it. Seeing all those people gathered to celebrate two people making a commitment to adjoin forever in the name of love. It was a good feeling to be amongst them.

The host of the reception got on the stage and announced that Grace was next on the program. When she said that, I was just as nervous as her, and I wasn't singing a single note. Grace got up from our table and walked up to the microphone. I could hear brothers whispering amongst each other as she walked up. I looked around and saw their eyes locked on her, like a pack of hyenas preying on a baby zebra lost and alone in the wilderness.

Grace grabbed the microphone. She held it for a moment and said nothing. She slowly rocked back and forth. Her eyes were closed. She made me even more nervous. It felt like she was taking forever to sing. She took a deep breath, put the microphone to her face and began singing.

As soon as the first note was out, the crowd started clapping. Chicks around the room got out of their seats. Some had to get tissue to wipe their eyes. Some guys jokingly pretended to fan themselves as if she was making them melt. Man, I forgot that she was singing for the wedding couple. I felt like she was singing directly to me. As if she was singing to my soul. Once she opened her eyes, she even made eye contact with me. It was only for a second, but it felt like an eternity. It had me weak. Powerless. She had gained control. She grabbed my heart without my permission, like the big bully that stole the kids' lunch money. If this was a strategy to win my heart over, it was working. I shifted in my seat, trying to break away from her hypnosis. Someone tapped me on the shoulder. I turned around and saw a guy sitting at the table behind me, leaning over.

"What's that chick's name up there?" He whispered.

"Grace," I replied.

"Oh okay. Is that your girl?"

"Oh, no. Just a friend of mine."

"Damn, she fine! You hitting that? Or trying to at least?"

"Nah man, we're just friends, for real. I'm not trying to."

"Riiiggght... I believe you," said the guy with a wink as he leaned back in his seat.

I turned my attention back to her. I then heard the guy say to his table, "Oh she's free game. That's not her man." I chuckled to myself. Those guys either thought I was lying or gay.

Grace finished her song and everyone stood up and clapped relentlessly. They cheered and whistled as if they were at a football game. The DJ then put on slow music, so that all of the couples could dance.

She returned to me smiling. "I need a drink!"

"See, I told you! You killed it! That was amazing!"

"I did alright," she said, grinning. "Let's go take some shots! It's an open bar."

She grabbed my wrist and pulled me through the crowd. I followed her and watched everyone watching me. The men looked at her like a pack of hungry lions, but then looked at me wondering if I had marked my

78

territory. The women sized up Grace trying to figure out how all of the men's attention had shifted towards her so easily.

We got to the bar and decided to take two shots of tequila. We both held up our shot glasses. She waited on me to give the toast.

"Let thy cup runneth over with blessings."

"Ummm. Wait a minute, ain't that from the Bible? We quoting Bible scriptures to take shots now? When was that ever cool?" Grace asked, lowering her cup.

"Yea it sort of is. Me and my friends came up with it; it's a ritual. Psalm 23:5. It's just about asking that God continues to bless us with everything we ever strive for. Plus, they drank wine in the Bible, so relax! Jesus turned water into wine."

She shrugged. "Whatever. I guess. Let thy cups runneth over with blessings!" We tapped our glasses together and swallowed our shots.

The New Edition song *Can You Stand the Rain* came on. Grace's eyes widened. "Oh my God, come on! This is my favorite song! We have to dance." She immediately grabbed my hand and escorted me to the dance floor.

We both got to the floor and stopped. She turned towards me, then I turned her way. She reached around my neck. I softly put my hands around her waist. I could feel her curves through her dress. I was a lucky man. We moved slowly back and forth to the music. As close as we were, I still hadn't looked into her eyes. I couldn't. I knew that if I did, I would be in trouble.

"What's wrong?" Grace asked.

"Nothing, why?"

"You're looking down at the floor."

"Okay. I won't anymore." I looked up at her.

"You're funny," she said, and then smiled.

Looking into her eyes was a trap. We finally saw each other face-to-face. I now saw her as my equal. She was no longer below my standards. She'd won. I couldn't help licking my lips. This was the closest that we had ever been before. I felt like I understood her. She meant something to me. I still couldn't figure it out though. I accidently envisioned her in a wedding gown, just like the bride. I closed my eyes to remove the vision.

79

Stop being stupid... Damn! The liquor was already getting to me. She's done nothing to deserve that gown! To this day, that gown only belonged to Lisa. Grace hadn't earned anything.

See, that's my problem; I'm giving this chick too much credit. Grace shouldn't even be considered for such a title, to be called my wife. Maybe, just maybe, one day she can earn that right, but she has to earn it. And she has a long way to go.

I gripped her waist tighter. She licked her lips and her eyes shifted down to mine. Then, she looked up and we were back looking at each other, eye-to-eye, right before she started biting her lip. Damn! All of her little tricks were working on me. That was a signal that I needed to make our lips meet. I pulled her closer, with faith that she would agree. She did. She grabbed the back of my head and pulled me in. Our lips met, as if they were overdue. Her lips were soft and inviting. Our tongues touched, just enough to keep the scene from becoming X-Rated. We kissed as if there was a new beginning. She rubbed the back of my ears. The kiss ended with her pulling herself away. We both licked our lips to catch the aftertaste. I had almost forgotten where I was. *Shit!* I snapped out of my trance and looked around. Everyone's eyes were locked on me. Some quickly looked away. I even saw the guy that asked me about Grace earlier. He was shaking his head in disappointment. I guess I had let him down. The married couple was even watching us. I didn't know if they were envious, or excited, but they kept looking. Either way, I was ready to go; we'd attracted too much attention for my comfort.

"You ready to leave?" she asked.

"It's up to you. I'm on your time," I replied.

We left the building. I was ready to leave the reception, however, I wasn't ready to leave Grace. This night needed to continue.

"So what's the plan? It's still early," I asked hoping for the right answer.

"I'm not sure. Destiny is with a babysitter for tonight so I'm free to do whatever. What did you have in mind?"

"Ummm... I'm bad when it comes to these things. I'm so indecisive."

"Well let's go to my house for a second until we figure out what we're going to do. It's right around the corner. I think I want to change out of these heels."

"Sounds good."

I trailed her all the way to her house. We hopped out of our vehicles, and then we went inside. As soon as we walked in, she put her hand on the wall and moved it up to turn on the light switch. The pitch-black room brightened. She went to her room. I was hesitant and stopped outside her room door. She motioned me to come in. I walked behind her into her room. She bent down to take her heels off, and then through threw them into the closet, which made a thud.

"Ouch. Those things were killing my feet!" Grace complained as she jumped in her bed. She then hopped back up. "Oh, wait a minute! I have some wine in my fridge! You want some?" she asked me.

"Oh no, I'm fine."

"Well I'm getting some," she said walking to the kitchen.

I stood up and began looking around her room. She poured herself a glass of red wine, took a sip, and then returned.

"Sit down somewhere! You look lost. You're making me uncomfortable," she said.

"Sheesh, sorry." I took a seat on the edge of her bed.

"Did you have fun tonight?" she asked.

"I had a great time."

"Me too. The bride was so pretty, wasn't she?"

"Yea she was."

"Too bad her groom was watching me the whole time that I was there."

"Really?"

"I caught him looking a couple of times. The men in there were all over me before you got there. They were nice, but they were like vultures."

"Yea I saw that when we were dancing. All eyes were on us."

"I kept telling them that my date was on his way."

"Date? I didn't know that I was your date. I told some dude that you were just my friend. He looked mad when he saw us later on."

81

She walked in front of me, and then took a seat on my lap. "So, I'm not good enough to be your date, huh?"

I didn't know how to answer. I just looked into her eyes, knowing that at that point I was down for whatever she had in store. She bit her bottom lip again and gently touched the back of my head. My attention was on her lips. I was ready to finish what we had started at the reception. Our lips touched again as if they weren't supposed to be separated in the first place. This time, our tongues were let loose. I put both of my hands on her backside and held it firmly. She didn't resist. I had been waiting to do that since I first laid eyes on her. It was firm but as soft as cotton, just as I'd imagined it to be.

Pre-marital sex? Shit Grace was so fine; she's worth a sin or two. It was time to mark some territory; time to claim what had been avoiding me for the longest. I began to unzip her dress. She assisted and pulled it off for me. She grabbed my shirt and unbuttoned it. We slowly unclothed each other. I laid her on her back, naked. I didn't want any sheets to cover her; I needed to see everything. I took a good look at the masterpiece. Impressive. Who would leave such a precious jewel like her alone? She had two tattoos on her that I hadn't seen before and they made her even sexier. I positioned myself between her legs and grabbed the side of her waist. Her skin was soft and moist; I felt all of what the dress had been hiding from me when we danced. I kissed and licked on her neck, but I was careful not to bruise her light skin. I entered her gently. She winced. She was tight, but I was ready to loosen her up. I gripped her moist skin as if I had finally redeemed my stolen property. I felt her soft hands on my back.

"Uhh, Terrance," she moaned. I had to think about things other than her, because I knew that I would give in too quickly. I needed to savor the moment as much as possible. Plus, this may be the first and last time. I needed to make it worth it. I went back and forth slowly like the rhythm of waves in the ocean. Her body motion responded like she was riding the surf. Side to side, back and forth. All on one accord. When the tide got rough and choppy, I sped up and she held on to my waist as tight as she could. She felt every inch of me as she groaned my name.

"Terrance! Yes, Terrance!"

Thirty minutes had passed and I was finished. We were sweating like we had just completed an intense workout session. I was exhausted. I flipped over and laid on my back. My heart was pounding. She turned towards me.

"You okay?" she asked.

"Yea. Are you?"

She smiled. "I'm better than ever," she said before kissing me on the lips. "Do you want some water?"

"Yes, please."

She wrapped the sheet around her body and went to the kitchen. She walked back in with two full glass cups. Both cups were filled to the top and spilled a little as she walked. She handed me a cup. I sat up and began drinking.

"I cannot believe what just happened," she confessed, shaking her head.

"Uh oh," I uttered.

"Seriously. If you really knew me, you would know that I don't deal with men at all."

"I'm confused. Are you bi-sexual or something?"

"No! I just don't deal with guys. Men have only led me to disappointment and sadness."

I knew that I was in for another story. I remembered Jay saying that light-skinned girls were like onions, full of layers. I felt like I was about to witness another layer, but I was willing to listen. "So what have you experienced that has led to this?" I asked.

"Well, my first boyfriend was in high school. His name was Cory. He was the guy that I lost my virginity to. We had that puppy love. We were voted cutest couple. The day before prom, we had an argument and broke up, so we didn't go together. He went with his friends instead. That night after prom, his friends were driving drunk and got into a car accident. Cory was the only one that didn't survive."

"I'm sorry to hear that. That's crazy!"

"Yep. I was torn apart for a very long time. I have his initials tatted on me." She pointed to the letters C.R. on her shoulder.

83

"But that's not the whole reason why I tried to stay away from men. My child's father is probably the biggest reason."

"So what's his story?"

"Well, again when I was young and stupid, I met my child's father. I was feeling myself then. I knew I looked good and I knew that all the guys wanted me. But of course I didn't give them the time of day because I was still a bit emotional about Cory's death. At least not until I met him."

"What's his name?" I asked.

"Ummm. It's private. I don't tell anyone who my child's father is."

"And why is that?"

"Because I don't want to. Plus, he is well known and is considered to be wealthy. I'd just rather not talk about it with anyone because it brings too much unwanted attention to the both of us."

"Oh, wow. Well, continue with your story."

"Well like I said, I thought I was untouchable at the time, until I met him at this private party at a club. He was famous, he was fine, he was my age and he wanted me. He approached me numerous times at the party, but I kept turning him down. I guess I was like the first girl to ever turn him down because he was persistent. He had the smoothest talk game. It got to the point where I figured that if I was going to date someone, I wouldn't mind it being someone who was rich, famous, and fine."

"Oh, Lord," I said as I did a face palm.

"Yep. Immature. So of course once I fell for him, I fell hard. He was a star that all the girls wanted. But I was that special someone; that's what I thought. I was his ride or die. I would kill for him and do anything that he wanted. If he said crawl, I would crawl like a puppet. It got to the point where he begged me to have a threesome with him and another girl. I refused at first, but he threatened to leave me, so I did it. Then he said he wanted an open relationship, where he could have sex with anyone he wanted, whenever he wanted."

"Oh! That's why you said that I reminded you of your ex-boyfriend, when I said that I wanted to witness different churches?"

"Yep! He said that he wanted to experience different things, and that commitment for him was hard. I told him that he needed to be faithful and do right by me. That's when he changed his number without letting me know. I called everyone from his entourage to get in touch with him. All of them acted like they were unaware of what was going on. Then, I finally talked to someone that told me that he no longer wanted anything to do with me."

"So was this before or after the baby?"

"Before. I later found out that I was pregnant with Destiny and was able to get in touch with him just to let him know. He didn't want anything to do with her. I didn't really want her to have anything to do with him either, so we came to a cash settlement. I haven't heard from him since."

"Your life is a damn movie! My goodness."

"That's why I'm surprised that I just did that with you. You are the third guy that I've had sex with. I never let men get close to me. It's always been me and my daughter against the world."

"Well I'm not the bad guy for sure."

"I like you, Terrance. You're harmless to me. I'm comfortable with you. Plus, you uncovered some things that I had hidden deep down inside for a long time."

"And what is that?"

"My love for music."

"Well that's good to know. I'm glad I had a positive effect on you."

"What you were preaching to me about singing made me so mad because I knew you were right, but I didn't want to accept it. I was miserable. I would watch my idols Beyoncé, Alicia Keys, and Mariah Carey on television and become so jealous."

"It's time to turn your idols into your rivals!"

"I have something to look forward to now. I'm going to chase my dream. I'm excited to work on my craft and to be the best that I can be. I want to do it not only for me, but for my daughter as well. I'm happier this way."

She leaned over and gave me a kiss.

Chapter 10:

You are Who You Date

I had to stop scrolling through her pictures. I was on Grace's Instagram page for too long and liked a couple of her pictures from more than thirty-two weeks ago. I wasn't stalking; I was trying to get a full idea of who she was. Yeah I know social media is only a representation of what people want you to see, but at least I could get a peek. She took some great pictures- some professional, some casual. She's made for the naked eye and the eye of the camera. Her pictures were classy. And of course she had some random guys commenting and telling her how beautiful she is. That was a given. Jay was right, there were definitely layers to this chick. But I finally found out that there was a priceless pearl hidden under all of those layers. I was glad that she was a part of my life. I admit that Grace could be the spark that I had yearned for; however, I know there will be an issue relaying that message to Fred and Jay. Jay was going to be pissed at me. Fred was probably just going to ask a bunch of questions. Nonetheless, I knew they were not going to approve of her. Fun Friday was going to be interesting.

Twist Restaurant at Phipps Plaza

Another fun night of drinks and entertainment with the guys was always needed. Good drinks, good music, and laughter are great for the soul. These times were priceless. See, I love music because it has a way of changing your mood without your permission. I was sitting there trying to figure out how to explain my feelings for Grace to Fred and Jay. How the hell could I bring up the fact that I was about to start taking her more serious? I mean I would have to tell them eventually anyway. I was brainstorming on all of my rebuttals that I would have to come up with when they both threw out their negative comments.

86

"People just have a broke mentality! They complain about being broke, but usually they don't do shit about it!" Jay said while we sat at the bar. Fred and I nodded in agreement.

"If you broke, do something about it! You just have to be able to turn one dollar into two dollars and repeat. We have to do that by any means necessary, instead of just complaining about it all the time. People just ain't willing to cross that line of comfort into that realm of the unknown," Jay continued.

"You preaching to the choir," I said.

"Just like that light-skinned chick! Her ass works at Burger King! I bet you she complains about her job every day and how they don't pay her enough."

"Wait, wait, wait, her situation is a little different. That was just a temporary fix," I rebutted.

As expected, Jay and Fred looked at each other confused, then looked at me with a raised eyebrow.

"What you mean? Why are you sticking up for her? Like that's your girl or something! Terrance you have to stop loving these hoes man," Jay blurted, shaking his head.

"No man, we talked and I have a better understanding of her now. She is doing what she needs to do; she is finally going to do what it takes to make a better situation. She is really gifted," I responded.

"Oh! So you still talk to her? I thought you stopped entertaining her." Fred jumped in.

"Terrance ain't stop talking to that girl. He's still trying to hit that. I don't blame him, she fine. Hell, I don't care if she works at Burger King. I would love to get a piece of that ass. Ain't that right, Terrance?" Jay nudged me.

"Nah man, I ain't trying to just hit that. She's a good girl; she's just misunderstood. And yes we still talk from time to time. I didn't cut her off."

"Okay. See now I'm confused. What are you trying to tell us, Terrance? If you're not trying to hit that, then why are you still entertaining her?" Jay asked.

"I'm guessing you just like her as a friend or something, because you're not trying to wife that. Are you?" Fred inquired.

I thought about responding, but there was nothing to say. I had no words. I didn't know how to answer the questions. I felt like I didn't have to explain myself. So I just chuckled, and then took a sip of my drink.

"Ahh hell nah! What the hell did she do to you? You can't be serious. You are who you date. Remember that? If you trying to date a basic, uneducated chick that works at Burger King, that makes you basic, Terrance!" Jay yelled.

"There's no use of me explaining it to y'all because y'all won't understand. It will fall on deaf ears because you both already have your minds made up."

Fred leaned forward. "Come on, Terrance. This is me. Look at me. If there was ever someone to understand where someone was coming from, it's me. I just want to know what happened for you to change your mind about her all of a sudden. You see something in her that we can't see. What is it? We know your standards are high, so what makes this girl worth your time?"

"Please tell us! Other than the fact that she is just a fine light-skinned broad that can sing really good, what the hell does she bring to the table?" Jay asked, leaning forward as well.

"Well, there's more to her than that. She has a very unique story that makes her different. I'm not going to tell her personal business, but just know that she's been through some things in life. At first I did think I was better than her, just because I made more money than her and because she worked at a fast-food joint, but I was wrong. As a matter of fact I won't ever think like that for anyone ever again. You can never judge a book by its cover, because you'll never know the story. And her story isn't over. I feel like she's a diamond in the rough that just needs to be refined a little. Then she'll shine."

Fred shrugged and nodded. Jay still had a raised eyebrow.

"I'm not convinced. Answer me this, and don't lie to me, Terrance. Did y'all have sex?"

"We did, but that has nothing to do with how I feel."

Jay slapped his knee. "I knew it! That explains it all. That has everything to do with what you're saying right now! She put it on your ass and now you feel like you're obligated to save her. Terrance put on your cape, because you are the ultimate superhero. Stop saving these hoes man!

We don't love these hoes. She works at Burger King, Terrance. Burger King! Take your super-save-a-hoe goggles off and come back down to reality. You are losing and she is winning. She sees you as a way out; you're her meal ticket! Next thing you know her daughter is going to be calling you Daddy. Think! You're better than this."

I said nothing; I just sipped on my drink and looked away.

Fred leaned in. "All I have to say is, if you see value bro, then that's all that matters. I support your decisions, because I know how picky you are when it comes to women. That girl is freaking drop-dead gorgeous. Plus, she has the most amazing voice that I have ever heard; that's all I really know about her. I get it. I would love to meet her too bro."

"And Terrance if you're with her just because you think she's going to blow up because she can sing, think again! You know how many people can sing? That's just a pipe dream! You're just in love with what you believe she can be. You ain't in love with her," Jay continued.

"First off, did I ever say that me and Grace were officially together? No! I was just letting y'all know that she is worth more than what y'all think. That Burger King reference just made her seem worse than what she really is. But if I did say that I wanted to take her serious, so what! That's my decision and I would hope that y'all would support me, but if not then I would be fine regardless."

Fred placed his hand on my shoulder. "You know we support you brother. We just want you to be happy, that's all. I don't care if it's Beyoncé or a bum on these Atlanta streets. If you're happy, then we're happy. That's all that matters."

"You're right, but the happiest person out of the whole picture is Grace. She found a sucker to take care of her and her baby while she quits her lousy Burger King job to chase her pipe dream of becoming a famous singer," Jay inferred.

I grinned. "I'm done with this conversation."

I didn't say a word for the rest of the night. I couldn't explain shit to them when they already had their minds made up. More talking and more of me trying to explain myself would just make me more upset. I expected this though. Jay was purposely trying to get under my skin. I know him. But I know he sincerely wants the best for me, so I understood his frustration. All he was trying to do is make me second-guess myself, but my mind was made up already. They won't ever see the value in her, especially since I told them that she worked at Burger King. But it's not their job to see her value; it's mine. When you judge people based off of one or two characteristics, you'll never see the true value; you have to look at the whole picture. One man's trash is another man's treasure. Yeah, there's plenty of fish in the sea, but when you're going deep-sea fishing and you think you've uncovered a hidden treasure chest, you have to claim it, or someone else will. Besides, nothing is official; I'm just playing it by ear.

At the office

I hate being backed up. I was neck deep in my work, focused on getting ahead rather than staying behind. That was before I received a text from Grace. Whenever I saw her name pop up on my phone, I started daydreaming. It was a great feeling. I read her message.

Hey! I just wanted to let you know that I really appreciate you. I'm super motivated now! I just created my own YouTube page and I will upload songs every day. And I'm singing like crazy now. I'm so much happier and my daughter recognizes it. I'm going to start singing at more events now too. Thank you, Terrance. :)

That text made me smile. She made my day that much better. A woman is supposed to bring you joy and put a smile on your face. I responded quickly.

No problem. Your text just brightened my day. Just know that I believe in you when no one else does. I want the best for you.

Thank you! I won't let you down, Terrance... ;)

I was genuinely happy to know that I had a positive effect on this chick. I would pay to see Fred and Jay's face if she actually accomplishes her goals. She was a dreamer; I believe in dreamers. This was the perfect example of people not realizing what someone is truly capable of.

Chapter 11:

Keeping a She-cret

Jay went to the club by himself. It was the type of night where he just wanted to hang out alone. He pulled up at 11:45 p.m., walked around and didn't see anything appealing. So he sat at his own booth. He was on his third drink and contemplated leaving. After 45 minutes, he saw someone appealing. It was someone familiar, Sarah. He decided to go speak to her.

"Hey, do you remember me?" Jay asked.

"You look familiar! Where do I know you from?"

"I introduced you to, Terrance."

"Oh, hey! I remember now," Sarah said, reaching out to hug him. "It's my birthday! I'm so drunk!" Her eyes were halfway closed.

"Happy birthday!" Jay responded.

Sarah looked at the girl next to her. "I'm sorry, I'm rude! This is my sister, Melissa. Melissa, this is Jay."

"Nice to meet you." Jay and Melissa shook hands.

"She is taking care of me tonight."

Jay nodded. "I'm sure she will take good care of you."

"Where's your big head friend at?" Sarah asked.

"Terrance? Oh he's probably at home or something."

"Oh. You look good by the way. If you weren't Terrance's friend, I would've had to scoop you up."

Melissa slapped Sarah on the butt. "Watch your mouth," she said, shaking her head and laughing.

"You look good too! Y'all have fun tonight," Jay said, right before they walked off towards the other side of the club.

Jay walked back to his booth and ordered another drink from the server. He sat there, on his fourth drink, looking at Sarah. The more he looked at her, the sexier she appeared. After ten minutes, he got back up out of his seat. He saw Sarah and Melissa walking through the club's crowd holding hands. Melissa held Sarah tight as if she was her guardian.

Sarah looked even more intoxicatd. He started walking through the crowd so that his path would run into them. Once they bumped into each other, he put on his sexy face.

"You having fun?" Jay asked.

"Of course I am!" Sarah said, smiling.

"That's good! So what you got planned after this?" Jay yelled in Sarah's ear.

"My bed! Why?"

Melissa stepped in between them. "What's going on?"

"Nothing. She's fine, we're just talking." Jay focused back on Sarah's ear. "I'm just asking. I'm going to my bed too, but I wanted to get your number before I left. I meant to get it from you a long time ago."

"What do you need my number for? I can't talk to you. Terrance would think I was so flaw."

"Sweetheart, I wanted you way before I hooked you and Terrance up. I even felt bad after I did. Plus, Terrance has a fiancé or something right now. He's about to get married I believe."

Sarah looked at Jay surprised. "Really?"

"Yeah! I thought you knew about that. But that's why I wished that you and me would've talked rather than you and Terrance. Because I didn't like how he just used you and moved on, especially knowing that he wasn't going to take you serious."

"I know. I thought he was different. But he's just like the rest of y'all." Sarah shook her head.

"That's why I wanted you to give me the opportunity to show you that I was different. I wouldn't dare approach you if I knew that Terrance cared for you. As a matter of fact, Terrance and I aren't that close. You don't deserve to be treated like just any other chick; you deserve better than that."

"I just don't feel right. What if Terrance found out? He would be mad at me and you."

"Sarah, Terrance is somewhere with his fiancé right now. You are the last thing on his mind. But you're the first thing on mine. Can I show you how serious I am?"

"How?"

Jay grabbed her chin and pulled it closer to his. Their lips touched, softly. Sarah started to pull away, but Jay wouldn't let her. He grabbed her bottom lip with his, leaving her no room to escape. She felt weak, so she gave in. Her lips accepted his and greeted them even though they were unfamiliar. Jay grabbed her waist and brought it closer so she could feel him on her stomach. Their tongues started going back and forth as if they were in an Ultimate Fighting Championship battle. He finally pulled away from her, but he still held her bottom lip with his mouth, as if he didn't want it to end. Melissa was standing next to them shaking her head.

Jay grabbed Sarah again, pulled her towards him and whispered in her ear. "I want you. More than you ever can imagine. I want to show you. It's your birthday. This special day means that you deserve to be pampered. Let me have the honor of doing that for you for the rest of the night."

"What do you want me to tell my sister? She drove me here and all of my stuff is in her car."

"You don't need any of it. Just come. You're worrying too much. You'll be fine. Tell her I'll take you home in the morning."

"You better take care of me. My sister will kill you if you don't. She's already going to be mad at me," Sarah said, looking him straight in his eyes.

"I got you. I promise." Jay kissed her on the forehead.

Sarah turned to her sister. Melissa stood with her arms crossed, listening to Sarah explain herself. "I'm about to go sis."

"Whatever. I'm not coming to pick you up. And what are you going to do about your stuff?"

"He'll drop me off to come get it later. Thank you for the night sis! I love you!" Sarah hugged her. Melissa barely hugged back while looking at Jay. He winked at her and grinned. Melissa rolled her eyes.

"Call me if you need anything! You better be good too!" Melissa said, while holding Sarah's shoulders and looking her square in the face.

"I will. I'm always good!" Sarah said, smiling.

Melissa turned to Jay. "Take care of my sister, or I'll track you down and kill you."

"She's in good hands with me," Jay said, grabbing Sarah's pelvis and pulling her closer.

Jay escorted Sarah into the house. She walked in front of him trying to keep her balance. She flopped down on the bed like it was hers.

"This is so bad! Why am I here with you? I feel so bad. Do you think we should tell Terrance about what we're doing?" Sarah asked, slurring her words a little.

"Don't tell him. What will it solve? He has moved on. He probably doesn't even care to know. I will tell him once I feel like he needs to know."

"Okay. But you don't feel bad?"

"Hell no! The only thing I feel bad about is not making you mine first. Terrance may feel bad after he sees what he was missing out on by not recognizing your true worth."

Sarah said nothing. She sat up on the side of the bed. Jay walked in front of her, grabbed her arm and pulled her so that she was standing. He grabbed her chin so that she would look him in the eyes.

"Stop worrying. One man's trash is another man's treasure. When I find treasure, I hold on to it because I know its value, no matter who walked past it without knowing that it was precious."

Sarah took a deep breath. Jay moved her hair from in front of her face. She put it behind her ear. He grabbed her face and pulled her towards him. Their lips gently touched.

Jay reached for the zipper to her dress. He slowly unzipped it. She didn't resist. As he finished unzipping, he grabbed her shoulder and continued to pull her dress down and off of her body. She assisted. They fully undressed each other.

Jay got on top and slowly went inside of her, skin to skin. Her eyes were wide and she was in a trance, as if she had just witnessed Jesus himself. She said nothing, but stared into his eyes. She was breathing with her mouth wide open, looking as if Jay had answered every question that she ever had about life. Jay tried to avoid looking her in her eyes. He closed his eyes and started kissing her. After that, he placed his face on the side of hers and continued in and out of her.

Jay had an orgasm. He immediately pushed away from Sarah and out of her, and then laid down to catch his breath and fell asleep. The periodic, unfamiliar snores woke him. His eyes opened to the back of a frizzed-up weave halfway under the cover. A mixture of burned hair, worn-out perfume, along with strands of weave tickling the inside of his nose made him sneeze. The entire room was the after smell of two warm and sweaty bodies that had been rubbing and pounding together all night. He was super dizzy, like he had just gotten off of a spinning rollercoaster ride right before puking. His mouth was as dry as sand in the Sahara desert. He laid awake and shifted positions under the covers. Sarah's body heat under the sheets made his legs sweat.

Five minutes had gone by and Jay laid still in bed. He was wide-awake, but his eyes were closed. He felt Sarah moving in the bed. He rolled his eyes. She changed positions and was now facing him. Jay's eyes were still closed. Sarah inhaled and exhaled in Jay' face. He opened his eyes. Some of her makeup had rubbed off, uncovering two different tones of brown skin. She was almost unrecognizable from the night before. He was ready for her to leave.

"Hey, you up?" Jay whispered in a raspy voice.

Sarah's eyes opened. They were red. Her eyes quickly scanned around the room to remind her of her location. They then returned to Jay. She lazily stretched her arms and yawned. Her eyes then closed again. Jay rolled his eyes.

"Hello sleepy head, rise and shine," he continued.

Sarah moaned as if she was aggravated. "Just twenty more minutes, please!" Sarah begged, with her eyes closed.

"I'm sorry. I have to be somewhere soon and I'm already late."

Sarah opened her eyes. "Be somewhere?"

"Yes. I have to go to work soon, like I have to be there in twenty minutes."

Sarah sat up. "But how am I going to get home? You promised that you would take me home in the morning."

"I know. But I overslept. Can you see if your sister is up? She can come get you."

"You're joking right? I told her that you would take care of me. I'm not calling her."

"Well, I have to go like ASAP. And I can't leave you here alone. Do you have Uber? Or we can call a taxi."

Sarah closed her eyes. She took a deep breath. She said nothing for a moment, and then opened her eyes.

95

"My momma always told me, God rest her soul, that if I can't say something nice, don't say anything at all. So I will not speak my mind right now. But just know that you make sure that you delete my number out of your phone and delete whatever image of me last night out of your head."

Jay shrugged. "As you wish. There isn't much to remember anyway. It was all a blur."

Sarah rolled her eyes, threw the covers off of her and stood up out of the bed. She tried her best to hide her private parts with her arms and hands. Her full attention was on the floor, with her head held down searching for her abandoned pair of panties, dress, and high heels. She found what she was looking for and began dressing herself. While she got dressed, she began talking to herself out loud, as if Jay wasn't there.

"This is your fault Sarah. You knew better. You should've listened to your sister. When will you learn, Sarah? I am disgusted with you."

Jay yawned. He moved around freely under the sheets. He eventually sat up from under the covers and watched her halfway naked body finish getting dressed. He grinned.

"You okay over there? I don't want you to hate me now. I'm really not trying to burn any bridges between us."

Sarah paused from getting dressed. She rolled her eyes. Then she shut them. She inhaled deeply and then exhaled. "Jesus, please forgive me if I have to have one of your children hurt and possibly sent to you." She then looked at Jay. "Please don't say anything right now. Like seriously, I'm not bullshitting with you. Please don't say another word, or else I promise you, that you will wish that you never did." Sarah continued getting dressed, then picked up her phone.

"Okay, okay, I'll shut up."

After Sarah was fully dressed, without saying another word, she rushed out the bedroom. Seconds later, the front door slammed. Jay chuckled to himself. He laid back down to go back to sleep. It didn't work. He decided to get up and be productive.

Jay got up and went straight to the refrigerator to get his hands on a cold gallon of water to quench his thirst. After doing so, he walked over to his window, carefully grabbed his black drapes and moved them to the side, making a peep hole large enough so that he could clearly see out, but small enough that no one could see that he was looking. He looked around. Sarah was still outside. He could faintly see her walking down the sidewalk; it looked as if she was on the phone. Even though she was far, he could see that her hair was frizzed up and matted from the heat, as if she had a mini afro. Sarah's face was balled up and shriveled up with anger. He chuckled, shook his head and closed the blinds.

The next day, Jay woke up. He picked up his phone and made a call to Sarah. The phone rang, but he was sent to the voicemail. He called again. No answer. He then sent a text.

Hey. I know you're mad at me, but this is an emergency. Please answer.

A minute later, Jay had an incoming call from Sarah.

"Hello," Jay answered.

"What?"

"What what?"

"What's the emergency? What do you want?"

"Oh. I just needed to hear your voice. I wanted to make sure you were okay. That was the emergency."

"I swear to God! Please delete my number from your phone! I do not want to talk to you at all, ever! What part of that don't you understand?"

"Calm down! Sheesh! I was just calling to apologize. I know I was wrong. I owe you big time. I want to make it up to you. How can I make it up?"

"Well, you can start by deleting my damn number and leaving me the hell alone. Do not call or text me again. Or I will send someone for you! I am so serious."

"Okay. I'll try to leave you alone… but I won't be content until you at least let me take you out to lunch. I think we should start over."

Sarah hung up and Jay heard the dial tone. He chuckled, shrugged his shoulders and laid back down.

Solo, Not a Duet

I was sitting on my couch, bored on my computer and decided to check Grace's progress on her singing career. I looked at her online profile. I was in awe! I hadn't had the opportunity to see Grace much because both she and I had been busy. I was busy with work like always. She was busy with her singing obligations. However, she did periodically send me pictures and event notifications where she would be performing. I was looking at her YouTube page. Unbelievable. She now had over 50,000 subscribers. Last time I looked, which was about a couple months ago, she had like a couple hundred. Then I checked out her Instagram page—75,000 followers. Amazing! She was making major moves! See, I told Fred and Jay about Grace's potential and they didn't listen. Man I couldn't wait to show them her profile on Friday. I wanted to hear Jay's response, since he belittled her the most last time I brought her up.

Fun Friday

"Yo, Jay. Remember the last time you was downplaying Grace? Saying that her singing was only a pipe dream?"

"Who, the basic Burger King chick? Yeah, why?"

"Well, she's been doing her thing lately. She got 75,000 followers on Instagram now. And she has 50,000 YouTube subscribers, just from her singing videos."

"Wow, that's impressive," Fred acknowledged nodding.

Jay nodded too. "Oh okay. She's social media famous? That's good for her. She still work at Burger King?"

"Nah. She actually gets paid to do events now. She's making a good amount of money too."

"That's good. Because being famous alone won't pay no bills."

"Oh yeah, she's fine. Can you admit that you were wrong about her? That girl is going places man, and she is a super hard worker."

Jay chuckled. "I admit I may have downplayed her abilities. I know that's your crush, so I'll watch my mouth from here on out. You sensitive about that little chick."

"When can we meet her?" Fred asked. "All this time y'all have been talking and we still haven't had the opportunity to meet her."

"I have to admit that I didn't want to bring her around y'all at first. I had to make sure she was worth it. Bringing a girl around my friends is almost like introducing a chick to my mama; that's serious. Plus, you know how Jay can get with the slick remarks."

"I know how to behave in front of company. Let us meet her. Stop hiding her from us."

"Does she meet your standards now? Is she good enough to meet the crew?"

"You upgraded her. She has met the requirements, but if I find out that she still works at Burger King then you will get a piece of my mind."

"Bring her next time," Fred suggested.

"So did Terrance officially find his new boo now? Is that bae?" Jay jokingly asked.

"I like her. She's feeling me. So we'll see what happens."

Ha! I made Jay bite his tongue! That's very hard to do! I knew there was something special about Grace a long time ago. She was destined for greatness. Now Fred and Jay could at least respect her talent. I was going to invite her to our next Fun Friday outing. Fun Friday was every other Friday, so I needed to let her know ahead of time so that she could schedule accordingly. I knew she was really busy. If she had no availability, then I'd just have to schedule something around her time. Man, there was no feeling like seeing Grace's progression. I loved the fact that I was a part of the spark that she needed to embrace her dreams. I was ready to take our friendship to the next level. And we needed a title other than friendship. I wanted her to be my girlfriend. I could proudly say that now. I admitted that I wasn't ready at first. She wasn't ready either though. We weren't ready for each other. She needed to experience some personal growth and embrace her passion and her talent. I needed to see her whole picture. I had to look past my surface level perception and not judge her based off of her circumstances. I grabbed my phone to call her and schedule a meet up.

"Hey, Terrance!"

"Ms. Grace Jameson, how are you?"

"Terrance, you know I'm walking on air right now. Everything has been just falling in place for me. I can't thank God enough; He's been so good. I thank you for being a part of it."

"Anything for you, darling! I told you you were destined for it. The reason I called was because I wanted to know what you had planned next Friday."

"Oh, I didn't tell you? I'm in L.A right now."

"L.A? What do you have going on out there?"

"I got signed to a label, Terrance! Destiny and I moved to L.A a couple of days ago."

"What? Why didn't you tell me?"

"I thought I told you! I put it all over my Instagram and YouTube. I thought everyone knew."

I was livid. "Damn, so you just up and left! You didn't even come over to say bye."

"I know, I know. Terrance, I'm sorry! Everything happened so fast. Once I got the call, they told me to pack my bags and get on the next flight to California. So I did just that."

"What about us?" I asked.

"Us? As in you and I?"

"Yes us! Like how will we work this out between us?" I continued.

"Oh! Terrance, we can definitely keep in touch. We will still be friends. This phone number will probably be turned off though since so many people have it. My manager will be handling my calendar now too. I will give you his number so maybe one day you can schedule a visit. And if you need to get in contact with me, just call him."

I was silent.

"Terrance, aren't you happy for me? This is what you wanted, for me to chase my dreams. Why are you so quiet?"

"I'm very proud of you, Grace. I'm so happy that I'm at a loss for words. It's all seams surreal. Just trying to take it all in at once can be a little overwhelming."

100

"I know, Terrance. Thank you for being there for me! You changed my life forever. I will never forget about you, and definitely keep in touch!"

"I will. Keep shooting for the sky."

I was inches from throwing my phone across the room. I needed to sit down to cool off. I flopped down on the couch. Did that really just happen? Talk about being caught off guard! She just twirled the hell out of me. I had a plan on making this chick mine. She was like a seed that I had planted, watched grow and blossom, only to disappear when it was time to enjoy the harvest. I knew I should've been more proactive! Why the hell did I not hit her up more often? Why didn't I go to support her at some of her singing engagements? It was my fault. I didn't even give her hints that I wanted us to become more. Part of it is from listening to Fred and Jay. Why did I let them get in my head? I was guilty of waiting for her to appear as an acceptable catch to them before seriously pursuing her. I blame myself.

Fun Friday – STK Peachtree Street, Atlanta GA

"I'm blaming myself. It's my fault," I said, taking a sip.

"Blaming yourself for what? How is it your fault?" Fred asked.

"I listened to y'all, that's why it's my fault. I really liked her, but I didn't admit it because I was ashamed. I was beating around the bush with her."

Jay was shaking his head. "You are pathetic. Pull yourself together! How many times am I going to tell you this? You didn't really like that girl; you liked her potential! If you really liked her, you would've claimed her a long time ago, but something told you that she wasn't good enough. It wasn't just us; deep down inside you thought the same thing."

"Man, it's just weird. I feel like I should have at least told her how I felt."

Fred looked up as if he was thinking. "Honestly. I think you still should. As a matter of fact, I think you should do what it takes to let her know how you really feel. If you have to go to L.A to do that, then so be it. Think about how you would feel if you never do. If you really care, you would. Plus, I don't think you should let another special person walk out of your life like Lisa did."

Jay looked at Fred confused. "Are you smoking crack? That makes no sense! This girl is not Lisa; he doesn't even love her." He leaned forward and looked at me. "Don't listen to that Disney Channel fantasy shit that Fred is feeding you right now. Don't chase that girl! She didn't invite you to L.A with her for a reason. She didn't see you in her future."

"You're right. I think that's another hard pill for me to swallow. She might not have even wanted to take me serious either. She was too focused on making her dreams come true."

Jay patted me on the back. "Exactly. She dodged you for a reason. If she wanted you, she would've had you. Maybe that was the best thing that could've happened to both of y'all. At least you can always say that you tapped that!"

I ignored him.

Losing Grace only made me realize that I didn't need her all along. She was like a snack, something that we may crave and it may taste good, but you know that it's not good for you in the grand scheme of things. It's a serving of temporary satisfaction that cannot replace what's really healthy for you. Lisa was really what I needed. I was back at square one. Alone. I knew I didn't love Grace. I just liked her a lot. Lisa was still my only love. Now that's a fact. I knew that Lisa still loved me, no matter how far away she was. I hoped she thought about me as much as I thought about her. *I miss the hell out of her!* Why am I suddenly back missing her? Because no matter what new woman comes into my life, there's only one woman that has constantly stayed on my mind. You may say that I need to get over her. How? Ha! I wish it were that easy.

I went home and went straight to my laptop. I needed to reach out to her again to tell her how I felt.

Dear Lisa,

I know you're busy. I just wanted to reach out to you again. I received your mail before and I understand everything. I'm so proud to know that my woman is traveling the world and changing lives. Yes, I said MY

WOMAN. Because I still believe that we're soul mates that'll eventually get back together. I know you're learning so much from the many people you meet and your experiences. I have to admit that I'm learning a lot as well. I'm learning that you're still the one for me. I've had my run in with other women to try to fill your void, but it has only left more empty space in my heart. My love for you is stronger than ever. I know there's no one out here that could ever compare to what you and I had. No woman is good enough. I'm not rushing you to get back to Atlanta, because I know that you're following your dream. God knows that we're supposed to be together and I'm praying that you still know this as well. I don't want to take too much of your time so I'm going to let you go. God bless you and I love you!

Love, Your Fiancé

Chapter 13: Pity-Fool

My alarm clock went off and interrupted my dream. The dream seemed so real! Lisa was in it. That's all I could remember though. But it was a good dream, whatever it was about. After sending that email, I went to sleep thinking about her and woke up thinking about her some more. I placed my feet on the floor and sat on the side of the bed for a minute. I got up and went straight to my computer to check and see if Lisa had responded. She did. That was quick. My heart rate sped up as I clicked on the message.

Terrance,

How adorable. I love you too! As far as my journey is concerned, you're right, I'm learning so much. I've learned that we all were put on earth to serve each other in some capacity. Whatever your profession, occupation, or passion is, it's linked to serve others. Finding your passion is the most liberating thing. As far as us being together, I still feel as if it's not the time. Yes I still love you, but my calling is pointing me in another direction right now. If it's God's will, we will definitely end up together. Be good!

Love you,

Lisa

She said a lot of nothing in that email, which didn't help me. We were no closer. She keeps beating around the bush. I'm not some duck, sitting on my hands and waiting for her to return! Damn! See, this is what I'm talking about. If she wanted me to just move on with my life and forget about her, then she needed to be upfront with me! I decided to call Fred.

"What's up?" he answered

"I emailed Lisa and she emailed me back."

"And? What did she say?"

"She basically told me the same thing as before. That we're not going to be together anytime soon. She's so into her passion that I don't even think she realizes that she's shooting me down so hard."

"Damn. Well…"

"I think it's a sign, Fred. I have to move on and never look back."

"Maybe, maybe not. If that's the case and if she does want you to move on, I know it's going to be hard for you, but I believe you can do it."

"Yeah. I just never thought this would be me, you know. Not me."

"You can do it. Focus more on your career just like she is, that's what will help."

"I will do that."

"Ay, let's have another guys' night out. Both you and I need it."

"Agreed!"

Fun Friday

It was early but the bar was filled with beautiful women. It was as if everyone at the bar needed to blow steam off too. The women were feeling me. The DJ played great music. I had three cups of Remy and it had me feeling good. And it was just Fred and I. Both of us were three drinks in and feeling good. Jay was running late, but he said he was on the way. I didn't know if it was the liquor, but it felt like every chick was eyeing me down as they walked by. I was about to be on drink number four. I even bought a chick at the bar a drink. I usually wouldn't do that, but she was standing around the bar looking thirsty, plus she was cute, so I was just being a gentleman.

"Well, well, well!" Jay said, walking up to the table to join us.

Fred and I sat at the table laughing, with drinks in our hand.

"So this is the first time I don't have to schedule a guys' night out. See what women will do to you? My two best friends are having women problems. One thing about me, I got 99 problems and a bitch ain't one!" Jay said, smiling.

"Shut up and have a drink man!" I chuckled and pointed towards the empty seat across from me. Jay continued talking without sitting.

"You know what, let's not call today Fun Friday. Let's call it 'Fuck her Friday'. Fuck these chicks! They're poison to us, brothers!"

"Are you done?" I said.

Jay took his seat with a grin. "But seriously brothers! How ironic is that? I'm the single one who's supposed to be miserable and lonely, but somehow, I'm the only one not stressing. Isn't that interesting?"

"No one is stressing; we just wanted to come and kick back," I assured him.

"Yeah whatever!" Jay said, looking around. "Looks like y'all found a good time to come to the bar! It's some sexy bitches in here!"

"What do you consider sexy," Fred asked, looking around "because there's nothing in here that seems attractive to me?"

"You don't have good taste, Fred! You don't know what sexy is."

"Oh. Maybe you're referring to these skanks with the high, tight dresses, 7-inch heels, and their cleavage showing. Yeah, how classy?" Fred responded.

Jay looked at me and pointed to Fred. "Where did we find this guy?" He looked back at Fred. "So Fred, what type of women do you like? What do you prefer?"

"Nothing in here, that's for sure." Fred took a sip of his drink.

"Where, Fred, in church? You want to find a Godly girl? Those girls are skanks too. Or maybe you want a geek or a librarian? She's probably a skank too. They're all the same to me, I don't trust any," Jay rambled.

"You guys definitely keep me entertained," I said, reaching out and patting both Fred and Jay on their backs.

"You wanna know what type of women I like? I like a woman with a beautiful face, petite figure and a nice ass. And of course a beautiful smile," Jay explained.

"All physical attributes, huh?" Fred noted.

"I wasn't done! As long as she's real with what she wants, then we're cool."

"Cool for what? Then they're good enough to be your woman?" I asked.

"Nope! They're good enough to be one of my women!" Jay said, laughing.

"I think Jay would cheat on his wife, even if it was Beyoncé," Fred blurted.

"I just might! It don't matter how beautiful they are. You know there's nothing like new pussy! Come on, Fred. Something new just excites me."

Fred shook his head.

"Come on! Look at Robin Thicke! Paula Patton is the baddest thing walking and he still wanted something new. Naturally, we want to try new things, it's in our blood. That's why men hate being faithful now," Jay continued, taking a sip.

"Not all men want to cheat," Fred stated.

"You right! Men like you don't want to cheat because y'all don't get women like that. I've been having sex since I was in middle school. These women flock to me. You'll never understand."

"Okay, I might not be prince charming, I can see that, but what about Terrance? Terrance isn't like you, and he ain't trying to stick his penis in everything walking. He can easily get women. But he still doesn't want to cheat."

Jay looked at Terrance and grabbed his shoulder, then looked back at Fred. "See, Terrance is struggling too. He won't admit it to you though. He loves these women just like me, ain't that right? Don't lie, Terrance!"

I said nothing. I just put my head down.

"Tell me, Terrance! Did you not ever think about the old days sometimes when you were with Lisa? I know you thought about the times when we were smashing a couple of chicks each week in college? Sex was plentiful."

Fred looked at me. I sat back and rubbed my chin.

"Honestly, sometimes I would think about those times. I thought about what I was missing out on sexually. But thinking about cheating meant losing my baby. And that was worth more to me than any new piece of sex that I would ever get."

"See, it's possible. He knew his woman's worth." Fred supported me, nodding and leaning back in his chair.

Jay frowned. "Terrance wants to get all mushy on me. I guess he found someone worth his time. Maybe if I would've found someone that was worthy of my time, I would be able to think differently. But that has yet to come. To me, these hoes ain't loyal, and they never will be. But hell, look at us now. Back at square one. Trying to figure out this thing called love.

To me, love brings heartache, old age, stress, and some badass kids. Being single keeps me young and happy."

"You forgot lonely," Fred stated, taking a sip.

"Ha! No, you're the lonely one! When I need company, I call a chick over to show me a good time. If it's sex, then I have someone for that. If it's a conversation, then I have a chick for that. If I need someone to cook, then I have a chick for that too. They know their place. And if they ever step out of place, that's when I go to recruit. It's very simple," Jay explained.

"Okay, so you're the black Hugh Hefner?" I asked.

"Call me what you want."

"Man as much as I love sex, one thing that I learned is to try to think about my mom. A lot of these women that we abuse mentally, physically, and sexually are other people's moms, sisters and aunts. I couldn't fathom someone abusing my mother in anyway. That helps me to control myself a bit," I elaborated.

"Thank you, Terrance!" Fred clapped his hands.

"That's why I try not to call these women bitches and hoes," I continued.

"Preach!" Fred cheered me on.

"Right. I agree. But there's still bitches and hoes out here. They don't act like women. So, you can't get mad at me for treating them as such." Jay attempted to defend his ideals.

"I would educate them instead of exploiting them and using them; try to understand them," I said.

Jay laughed. "I don't have time for that. You and Fred can do that for me. And plus some of these women don't want to be helped."

"Well..."

"Let me make the toast tonight," Jay volunteered. Fred and I looked at each other. Jay held up his cup. "No seriously, we deserve it! This toast is for us to realize that no matter what; we won't let these women ruin us. We will not let women make us forget our true worth. And most importantly, we will never let these women ruin our friendship."

Fred and I looked at each other and nodded in agreement. We all held up our cups in the air and said our creed.

"Let thy cup runneth over with blessings." We tapped our glasses and chugged our drinks.

Chapter 14:

Boy Meets Woman

The gym is like my sanctuary. I love it. It's the perfect remedy when you're going through tough times. Not only does it help me stay in shape, but it also helps me release the frustration and the built-up tension from my woman not coming back to me. I figured that I would at least have a nice body if I did find another woman worth my time.

I'd just finished working out at the local gym. I wiped the sweat off my face with my workout towel and opened my locker. I grabbed my phone, wallet and keys. Two missed calls from Jay. I hoped nothing was wrong. I called him back.

"Yo! What are you doing tonight?" Jay asked.

"Nothing, why what's up?"

"My job is having this gala tonight at 8. It's some big names from the banking industry that will be speaking and I think it would be good for the both of us."

"Sounds like a plan. What's the attire?"

"Business professional. Duh, it's a gala! Come looking fresh man, we will meet some important people," Jay informed me.

"There it is. I will be there."

Jay and I arrived at the gala at 7:55 p.m. We wanted to be there early so that we could mingle. We were both wearing tailored suits. Everyone in the room looked at us in admiration.

"Boy we look good! When people see young black men looking this fresh, they may get intimidated. We have so much unrealized power," Jay said, taking a sip of his sweet tea.

I panned the room and saw everybody talking and mingling.

"Sheesh, it looks like we're the only black people in here. I don't know if that's a good or bad thing," he said. We both laughed. "That means we have a lot of work to do."

110

Seconds later, I saw my boss. He was sitting by himself. He had a glass of wine. He was not speaking to anyone at the time. I tapped Jay on the shoulder.

"You were right. I guess there are some movers and shakers here. Look, my boss is even here." I pointed to him.

"Do you want me to go tell him to kiss your black ass?"

"No! Why? My boss is cool. He looks just like that white soccer player David Beckham. And he's like a mentor to me. As a matter of fact, I'll be back. I'm about to go speak to him."

I walked over to Mr. Hinson and tapped him on the shoulder. He turned around and was surprised to see me.

"Terrance Hill! What are you doing here?" he said as he stood up to shake my hand. He looked very relaxed.

"A friend of mine invited me. He said that this would be a great networking event to meet some leaders in the banking industry in Atlanta."

"That's smart of you to be here. I admire that about you, Terrance. You're always looking for ways to better yourself. Even outside of work. That's impressive. And yes, there are definitely some powerful people in attendance," Mr. Hinson responded, looking around. "Make sure you meet some folks and gather some business cards."

"I will. How'd you hear about this event? Who'd you come with?"

"A good lady friend of mine invited me. I'm here supporting her."

"Hmmm. Lady friend huh? I forgot you were single. Where is she?" I asked.

"Umm. She's around here somewhere mingling. I didn't want to interfere with her work."

"Oh, it's one of those situations. I understand. So you're saying the relationship is what I like to call *complicated*?"

Mr. Hinson grinned and agreed. "Yea somewhat. We give each other space. Still working out the kinks."

"Is she going to be Mrs. Hinson?"

"Umm, we've been on and off for a while. Who knows what the future may bring, Terrance? I just take things as they come. If it's meant to be, it will. We're just good friends right now. It's nothing serious at all."

111

"Alright, Mr. Hinson. Well, I'm going to let you get on with your night. It was good seeing you outside of work. I'll see you at the office." I walked back to Jay.

"I promise that my boss is the smoothest white guy I know." Jay was looking towards the front of the room.

"Who cares about your stupid boss? I don't. But check this out, it looks like we're not the only black people here after all." Jay pointed to the front of the stage. A light-skinned woman with a petite frame entered the room. Many heads turned. She grabbed the attention of the whole room as she walked up. She looked as if she was the youngest in the crowd. She stood about 5'8" with her 5-inch heels on. Her skin appeared smooth and flawless, and her smile was mesmerizing. People began to gravitate towards her. She shook hands as everyone approached. It wasn't long until she was surrounded and I could no longer see her. I turned back to Jay.

"Who the hell is that?" I asked.

"Oh, her? That, my friend, is Cindy Baker," Jay said, putting his hand on my shoulder.

"Damn! Could she get any more fine?" My eyes were focused in.

"Actually, she probably could, if I told you what she does."

"Please tell me," I said, with my eyes still locked on her.

"Well, she's the Vice President of Marketing for the entire firm. Not to mention that she's only 30 and she's single," Jay replied, while looking on with me.

"You're lying!"

"I swear to God. But you can stop drooling. She's too much to handle. We don't have a chance with her. She's almost untouchable."

"What does that mean?"

"Meaning, I tried to see what was up with her and she wasn't about nothing, that's what. She ain't even trying to converse if you ain't making at least seven figures."

"Damn."

"But she is some nice eye candy though, huh?" Jay patted me on the back. "Let's go take a seat. The gala is about to start. She'll be one of the speakers tonight."

It was time for the event to start, so everyone returned to their seats. The gala commenced. At this point, I was really trying not to keep looking at this chick, but I couldn't help it! Throughout the event, I occasionally glanced over at her. Thank God her chair was turned towards the front, because she would've caught me looking at her a couple of times already. Eventually, the program reached the time where she was to speak. I positioned myself in my chair so that my whole body was in the direction of the podium.

Good evening everyone. I hope you all have enjoyed the festivities thus far. If you don't already know who I am, my name is Cindy Baker and I serve as the Vice President of Marketing for Wilson Bank. "We never know how high we are 'til we are called to rise; and then, if we are true to plan, our statures touch the skies." This quote by Emily Dickinson is one that has inspired me to reach high heights and never settle for anything other than the best...

She had all of my attention. I don't think I blinked. I didn't want to miss a word she said. There's nothing like a woman with substance. In the corner of my eye, I could see Jay frowning at me.

"Ay. You got that look in your eye, Terrance. I'm telling you that she is not the one to try. I know some other freaks that you'd love."

I ignored him. I was still focused on Cindy. She finished her speech. Everyone began to leave their seats. At that moment I had a decision to make. I had two options. Either I leave the event right now with my mind on this chick Cindy, wondering if she would've given me the time of day and listening to Jay tell me why she wouldn't ever talk to either of us. Or I could find out for myself by walking over and letting her know how I would love to get to know her on a personal level. I chose the latter and started walking her way.

"Terrance!" Jay yelled once he realized I was walking in the direction of Cindy. I heard him, but continued. Jay mumbled under his breath and followed me.

After weaving through groups of people, banquet tables, and chairs I made it to her. I walked up while she was speaking with some other guy. I didn't want to be rude. Nor did I want to stand around awkwardly while I

113

was in her sight. So I just stood behind the guy as if there was a line. It made sense because I didn't want someone to hop in after this guy and take my turn to talk to her. I waited patiently until they were done. The man eventually walked away. Then, I stepped up to speak.

"Cindy," I said, as I held my hand out for a shake. She looked at my hand for a second, and then looked up at me once she grabbed it.

"Hello, Sir. What is your name?" she asked with a smile.

"Terrance, Terrance Hill. I came over to let you know that I loved your speech."

"Well thank you! I worked very hard on it." Cindy nodded her head and smiled showing her pearly white teeth.

"You define success. I wish a lot of Black women had heard that speech. It was truly liberating."

"Thank you. I try. So do you work for Wilson Bank? I've never seen you around here before."

"No, I don't. I'm actually a Financial Analyst for Harrison Asset Management."

"Oh really? I love what you all do with your marketing over there. I know some people at your firm. I'm a big fan."

"Thanks. I would love to have lunch with you sometime. I know you're a busy person, but do you think that it can happen?"

Cindy looked perplexed. "Excuse me?"

"I wanted to know if we could do lunch sometime?" I repeated.

"Ummm… Are you serious?"

"Why wouldn't I be serious?" I asked.

"I mean, are you really asking me out here at this formal event?"

"Is that a problem?"

Cindy paused, looked away and laughed. "No. There's nothing wrong with it. Mr. Terrance, how do you know that I'm not in a relationship?" Cindy asked, folding her arms.

"Well, judging from the fact that you sat by yourself while other executives sat with their significant others, on top of the fact that you don't have a wedding ring on, I made a ballpark assumption. Was I wrong?"

"No, you were not," she responded, with her arms still crossed as she looked down at her ring finger.

114

"So, is that a yes or a no?"

Cindy appeared aggravated. She leaned in and lowered her voice. "Look, this ceremony is not some speed dating event where people get to walk around and hook up. I am appalled that you would even attempt to try such a thing at such an event of this stature. That was such a distasteful act in my eyes, and you should be ashamed of yourself," Cindy said to me, as she reached for her clutch.

My eyes widened. I was embarrassed. "Well, I apologize Ms. Baker."

Cindy opened her clutch and pulled out a business card. "Bye, Mr. Hill." She held out the card. I stood still for a second. I was in shock. I snapped out of it and grabbed the card. Cindy walked away a couple steps, until someone else grabbed her and began to speak. I stood stationary for a moment with my eyes still on her. Then I looked down at the card. It had both her cell number and her office number. Jay walked up and he looked down at the card too. His mouth was wide open.

"I cannot believe what the hell just happened!" he said. "You are the luckiest man I have ever met. I think we need to play the lottery tonight. Damn!"

"Wow. My heart is beating like hell right now," I said, still looking at the card.

"You do not know the magnitude of what just happened!" Jay grabbed my shoulders and stood in front of me. "Terrance! Cindy Baker is Beyoncé, Michelle Obama, and Meagan Good all mixed in one! No one has ever had the opportunity to converse with her as long as you did, let alone get her number. Damn, I'm jealous!"

"What happened when you tried to get at her?" I asked.

"Not a damn thing! I barely got the opportunity to ask her for her number! I asked for her card and she told me to contact her secretary, who will direct you to her Assistant if you're lucky."

"Man. Well I'm surely glad I came!"

"Of course you are, you lucky bastard!" Jay said, playfully punching me in the arm.

I walked in the house and placed Cindy's card on my dresser. I plopped down on my bed and took my shoes off. My mind started running wild. I thought about all that I had gone through with Lisa. The signs were becoming more evident that Lisa was over me. Maybe God finally wanted me to let it go. What if this was supposed to happen? What if I was supposed to meet Cindy? What if this is the breakthrough that I was yearning for?

Maybe this could be the chick that was sent to replace Lisa? If this is true, then I was more than ready to move forward. I'd been waiting for her for too long. Would I finally experience love again? When it comes to this love thing, I don't believe in love at first sight, but there was a glow that Cindy had that I just couldn't ignore. But this glow was different from when I first saw Grace. She seemed so elegant; a trait that a lot of other women just didn't have. She stood strong, tall. It was as if she knew exactly who she was and exactly what she deserved.

During her speech, I visualized her as an Egyptian queen. The podium represented her throne, as she addressed the people of her land. As she spoke, the people in the crowd either looked up to her with respect and honor, or had hearts filled with hate, envy, and wanted her dethroned. All that was missing was a crown, and of course a king. How did I know she carried herself as if she was royalty? Because I had to elevate my mind to think like a king before even approaching her and expressing my interest.

Chapter 15:

Impatiently Waiting

It was 5:30 p.m. and I pushed open the doors as I walked out of the office building. During my shift, my mind was on Cindy, which made the day go by faster. What if this chick was actually feeling me? Boy, she would be the perfect remedy for letting go of the past. Hell, I've been looking at my past for so long that my neck hurts. I was looking forward to contacting her. Speaking of the past, I wonder if Fred's okay. He's just like me; he thinks too much. I know he's probably still thinking about Michelle, what went wrong with them, and if he could've avoided it. He may even be thinking of how to get her back. I called him to check up on him.

"Fred! What's going on man? I haven't heard from you in a while. Everything okay?"

"I'm getting by."

"What do you mean getting by?"

"I'm not happy, Terrance. There's a lot on my mind."

"It's not easy for anyone after a breakup, so I understand."

"No, Terrance, you don't understand. I went to pick up my stuff from Michelle and she had all of the stuff packed up in boxes in front of the yard. Then I wanted to try to speak to her, but she wasn't there."

"Let me guess, Keith was there."

"Keith and his friends were there. Some of them were gambling, throwing dice in front of the house. Some were inside of the house. They watched me as I put my stuff in the car. It was embarrassing."

"Michelle must've been at work."

"Of course she was! She wouldn't allow that! It just makes me feel terrible. I don't like Keith at all, Terrance."

"You shouldn't have beef with neither him nor her; it's time to move on."

"This is my first and only love, Terrance. I know Keith begged her to live there. She doesn't want him."

"Look, none of that matters, Fred. Even if he begged, the fact that she chose to let him move in and move you out should be enough. You deserve better. She deserves him."

"But, Terrance, I can't even imagine starting over. I've never been more in love. I just want my baby back."

I shook my head in frustration. "Well either you move on now, or it's going to be more of a mess in the future. You decide."

'You're right. I can do better."

I got home from work and changed into more comfortable clothes. I fixed myself a small dinner and sat on my couch to watch some television. I probably looked at my clock on the wall twenty times within a thirty-minute span. I sat with the phone in my hand waiting until 7 p.m. when Cindy gets off from work to give her a call. I know that she'd probably be busy if I had called her anytime earlier. I wanted her to be free from all of her day's obligations before I spoke with her. When the clock finally hit 7 p.m., I dialed her number.

"This is Cindy speaking." She answered on the second ring.

"Yes. Hi, Cindy. This is Terrance."

"Terrance? Terrance who?"

"Terrance Hill from the gala. You gave me your business card."

"Hmmm. Terrance... Terrance. I don't recall."

"I told you I work for Harrison Asset Management as an analyst."

"Oh, Terrance! Right! I remember. How are you?"

"I'm great! I wanted to check and see if you were available for lunch anytime soon."

"Ummm. I have a little time on Saturday."

"Saturday is good. How's 2 p.m.?"

"Sounds like a plan. I have another call on the other line that I have to take. But see you soon!"

Buckhead Diner 2:30 p.m.

118

My table was close to the window so the cars zooming by were the only things that kept my attention. My afternoon coffee had turned cold. It was 2:30 p.m. The waiter had come to the table to check on me twice already. I told her that I was waiting on my guest to join me. I looked down at my watch again. I was starting to think that I had been stood up. She should have at least given me some type of notice that she would be running late. I'm sure she was busy but damn! That goes to show where I was at on her priority list. I didn't want to call her, but this was ridiculous. I texted her.

Hey I'm here. Everything okay?

Sorry, Terrance. I was running a little late due to a meeting that went over time. I'm en route now.

Okay. No worries, I'll see you soon.

While waiting, I decided to call Jay.

"Cindy is 30 minutes late bro!"

"Seriously? Damn. Did you speak to her?"

"Yeah, she said she was running late from a meeting that went over. I already know I won't be able to deal with this foolishness."

"Relax brother! This woman probably makes over 200 grand a year. She is always on the go and her business comes first. Hell, I would wait three hours to have a date with her. There are plenty of guys that would love to be in your place. Calm down, she'll be there soon."

I looked up at the front door. "Speaking of the devil, she's walking in now. I'll call you back."

While I was placing my phone on the table, Cindy walked in. My stomach dropped. She walked in graciously. Wow. Beauty and elegance at its finest. She had on a black dress that hugged her petite physique. She favored Halle Berry, but with a lighter skin tone. She smiled when she saw me, and walked my way. Without trying, or even thinking about it, I licked my lips and changed up my posture in my chair. Everyone looked at her when she walked in. I stood up, as she got closer.

"Sorry I'm late again," she said. We hugged.

"It's fine. I didn't mind the wait. I have all the time in the world," I said sarcastically.

The waitress approached Cindy as she prepared to sit. "Ma'am, what would you like to drink?"

119

"A cup of green tea would be fine, thank you."

We sat and talked, while enjoying the complimentary bread that the waitress brought.

"So, Mr. Terrance, you should know that I'm a bit different from other women," Cindy said, taking a sip of her tea.

"I can see that."

"Well, I don't want to scare you with what I'm about to say."

"Let's hope it doesn't."

"Okay. Well, there's a reason why I accepted your offer to go on a date with you. From the start, I saw value in you. Ninety-nine point eight percent of the time if someone comes to me and asks me out in a professional setting, I would say no."

I laughed.

Cindy continued, "But in this case, I knew that there was something about you. And honestly, I don't like to waste time. I don't have time for any games. I am very straightforward and blunt, and some men cannot handle that. That's why I'm single."

"I can see how some men can be intimidated by a strong and ambitious woman. But I am intrigued by it. I love it."

Cindy nodded. "Okay. I need you to be one hundred percent honest with me. Is there anyone that you are seeing now?"

"No, I'm single. Just like you," I rebutted.

"And why is that? What happened with your last relationship?"

"Ummm, that's a very long story." I shook my head and looked down as if I didn't want to expand on it. I looked up and her eyes were beaming through my forehead.

"Well I need you to be the storyteller."

"What if I don't feel comfortable talking about it?"

"Then I won't feel comfortable moving forward with getting to know you," Cindy said, sipping more of her tea.

I sighed. "Well, long story short, my ex and I were college sweethearts. After college, everything was fine and dandy. We were living together, enjoying life, and living the American dream. We had a small debacle that led us to taking a break from each other. During that break she had relations with an NBA ball player. Allegedly, someone recorded him and her during sex. It got released onto the Internet and I eventually

120

found out. We were back together at the time and we were progressing. I had proposed to her right before I found out."

"Wow. That sounds like a movie. What type of girls do you attract?" Cindy asked.

"She wasn't a bad girl. She just got caught up in the wrong situation, that's all."

"Poor thing. At least you will never have to worry about me chasing a man just because he has a little status."

"What do you mean by that?"

"I mean I make more than you. That's no secret. Money is no issue over here. No guy with huge pockets or with any type of star power will make my knees buckle like they may do other women. It just takes more. Women that don't believe in their ability to make a lot of money will sleep with a man just because he has a lot of it. I know my worth, it takes more," Cindy explained.

I was shocked and amused. "So, am I supposed to be mad at what you said or am I supposed to be inspired?"

Cindy giggled. "Did that make you feel some type of way?"

"I just see that you are very confident. I am too. I am going to be on your level soon. They love me at my firm. I'm one of the top Financial Analysts."

"Yeah, about that. What are your long-term goals with your company?"

"My goal is to become the Chief Financial Analyst there soon. I just have to keep working my ass off."

"That's great! Keep working. It will happen! I believe in you. I want to help you get there. If there's any woman that knows about lofty goals, it's me."

"I'm sure you do. So what about you? What are your goals? It seems like you've accomplished so much, what else is there for you to do?"

"Oh no. There's much more that I want to do. Not only with the company but also in life. As an executive, my goal is to help this company become the number one choice for bankers in the Atlanta area. Period. It will be an uphill battle, but we're taking it one step at a time. In regards to personal endeavors outside of the company, I will promote women empowerment and achievement all across the nation through conventions,

121

workshops, and things like that. It gets a little deeper but that's just a high level answer. It's a lot more to it."

"Cool. It sounds like we have a lot in common. I'm excited to learn more. Maybe we can support each other. We can be like accountability partners and build together."

"We'll see," Cindy said, taking a sip of her tea.

The lunch went great! I felt more confident. I admit that I was a little nervous before sitting down with her. The conversation flowed; it was natural. The idea of me actually being her man seemed more realistic than before. I could actually see it happening. What's a king without a worthy queen anyway? My life is complicated and hard to solve, just like a puzzle. The missing piece of my life was previously Lisa, but it seemed like she didn't want to play a part in it anymore. That's fine, because the good news is that Cindy could possibly be an even stronger, better fit, and the piece that completed my puzzle.

Fun Friday, Twin Peaks 11:15 p.m.

The aroma of chicken and beer filled the room. The bar was fairly dead for it to be a Friday night. So dead that some of the bar's waitresses had been sent home from their shift. However, Jay, Fred, and I were far from dead. We were alive—especially me. I was the most turned up out of the three of us. Fred and Jay were a little surprised. They were probably most intrigued by the fact that I put all the drinks on my tab. Jay always says that I'm the cheapest person that he's ever met. I don't like the word cheap, I just like to say that I know the difference between price and value.

"Bro, she is so cutthroat! And I love it!" I said.

"What do you mean cutthroat?" Jay asked.

"I mean she is all about business. She doesn't waste time and she speaks her mind."

"Yeah, I can see that. You think she feeling you?" Jay asked.

"Feeling me? She mentioned us becoming a couple. She's the one that is moving. I'm with it!"

"I'm so jealous man. How did I let her slip by me?" Jay shook his head and looked to the sky.

122

"She likes chocolate brothers, light-skinned dudes are played out son," I said, patting Jay on the back.

"So what's the deal with Lisa? Are you going to give up?" Fred inquired.

"Uhhhh, no I'm not. I'm going to write her again soon."

"I agree, keep trying with Lisa. I think y'all will eventually work it out."

Jay shouted, "The hell with Lisa right now! This woman Cindy challenges Terrance's mind and supports his dreams, and not to mention she exemplifies success. Terrance, I need you to look at the big picture; this woman was sent from heaven. She is the one!"

"I'm going to play my cards right. I love Lisa so I'm going to continue to reach out to her, but I will definitely keep looking forward. Cindy is amazing. In fact, we have another date soon. She isn't wasting any time, but I don't mind. I'm on cloud nine right now. I'm just excited to see where this will take us."

Jay chuckled. "You're such a damn lover boy! My goodness! But I'd rather see you happy than miserably waiting for your girl Lisa to return. Let's make a toast to Terrance possibly finding someone that will make him get over Lisa!" Jay said, holding up his glass.

"Wait. I don't know about this toast. Let me clear this up. I love Lisa, but I'm not waiting miserably on anyone. I'm just excited for new possibilities. This is not about getting over Lisa. This has nothing to do with Lisa actually."

Jay still had his cup up. "Okay, correction! This toast is strictly for the possibilities of new beginnings. And specifically for my boy Terrance to possibly having the finest chick in Atlanta under his wing." I nodded in agreement and held my cup up. Fred followed.

"Let thy cup runneth over with blessings," we said simultaneously as we tapped our glasses together and took our shots. I briefly looked at Fred. He looked as if he was bothered by something.

"Fred. You okay brother?" I asked.

"Yea I'm good?"

"Come on brother, as long as I been knowing you. I know when something is wrong. Talk to me."

123

"Nothing man. I'm just happy for you. It seems like you bounce back quick. You upgraded. Me on the other hand, I'm not as lucky as you."

I flipped. "What? First of all, nothing is official with Cindy and I. I'm just ambitious and excited about the possibilities. Second, your time is coming brother. All of these women in Atlanta are waiting to meet Fred Brown. You just have to be patient. And plus, like Jay said, sometimes you need to be happy single, love life. "

"Yea, stop acting like a little bitch!" blurted Jay.

Fred took a sip of his drink and said nothing. He had me a bit angry. It seemed like he was feeling sorry for himself. No one was going to throw him a pity party. He's a grown man. That's my friend, but I won't hesitate to speak my mind.

Wednesday Night, 8:00 p.m. Baltimore Crab and Seafood, Cascade Road

Cindy and I were on our second date. This time, I could tell that she was a bit more relaxed. A bit more open. I was too.

"I told you about all of my dirt with my ex, but you never told me anything about your past relationship," I said to her.

The dim lighting made our date a bit more romantic. I liked it! I didn't mind looking into her hazel eyes. It gave me a tingle inside. I wondered if she felt the same way when she looked into mine. She probably didn't. I was just happy to be there with her. Her pearl earrings sparkled in the light. She reminded me of a princess straight from a Disney film.

Cindy smiled. "You're right. I would eventually have to tell you that, huh?"

"Yep!"

"My last man didn't work out because he didn't appreciate me."

"What do you mean?"

"We were talking for a while and he just did not want to commit. I guess he just didn't see a future in me."

124

"Interesting. That's hard to believe. Who wouldn't want to be with a person like you?"

"A person that is selfish and full of themself."

"What did he do for work?"

"He is a very successful businessman, I'll give him that. But it all came down to me wanting him way more than he wanted me. I'll admit that I was madly in love with him."

"So do you all still talk?"

"I'm moving on like a big girl should. I learned my lesson. One day he'll realize what he is missing and it will hurt more than ever."

'Our stories sound very similar," I rebutted.

"Yeah, well I'm done talking about him, let's move on to a new topic."

"I agree."

"Do you think you can appreciate a woman like myself?" Cindy asked, sipping on her drink while keeping her eyes on me.

I hesitated for a moment, and then cleared my throat. "Of course I can."

Cindy put her glass down. "We'll see."

"You deserve someone like me who will do whatever it takes to keep you happy," I said, looking directly into Cindy's eyes.

Cindy giggled and grabbed one of my cheeks. "You're so cute. We'll see."

Sunday Afternoon, My House

I was expecting company from Lisa's old friend, Wanda. A while ago, I reached out to her. This was when I was really depressed. I was missing Lisa and I was mad. I needed answers, so I called Wanda. I don't remember much about this Wanda chick, but what I do remember is that she could be a bit loud and obnoxious. Even though I'm fine now and I'm not stressing like before, I wanted to see what she knows about Lisa's current situation. I wouldn't mind a bit of clarity. Wanda was out of town when I first reached out to her, so she promised to pay me a visit once she got back.

I looked through the peephole and saw a wide-framed woman with big clothes. I unlocked and opened the door, "Hey Wanda. Nice to see you."

"Terrance, I am happier to see you! I thought you didn't like me!" Wanda yelled as she entered.

"Didn't like you? What do you mean?"

"Lisa told me you didn't like me, you know. We talked about everything."

"I didn't even know you like that," I said. "Have a seat." I pointed towards the couch.

Wanda walked over and plopped down. She pulled a bag of Cheetos out of her pocket and opened it.

"Why would she say such a thing?" I took a seat across from her.

"Ummm... She just said that you thought I was a loose cannon and I was off the chain. There's some validity to that, that's why I'm not mad at you for it."

"I definitely didn't mean anything by that."

"Anywho! What's up? I know something is up since you invited me here," Wanda said as she began munching on her chips.

"Well Wanda, I know you were best friends with Lisa, and I know if there's anyone that knows Lisa other than me, it would be you."

Wanda laughed. "Yes, we were best friends. We are not close anymore due to the sex tape situation, you know."

"Yeah about that, I just want a little clarity. So, you were the one who recorded it?"

"No, I did not. My cousin did. It was a big mix-up. I hate talking about it honestly. I lost one of my best friends because of it. Lisa didn't deserve that."

I nodded. "I understand that, I just want to know if there's a way for me to get her back. She seemed very distant since the last time we spoke. I can't wait forever."

"Wait? Get her back? Weren't you the one who ended the relationship, after you found out about the tape?"

"Yes, but it was only because I was more shocked than anything. It was off of straight impulse and panic. I mean if you see your fiancé on a sex tape with a celebrity you would probably break up with them too!"

"So you still love her despite what she did?" Wanda asked crunching loudly on the Cheetos.

126

I leaned forward. "Wanda, I love Lisa. She made a mistake, and had to pay for it. I know she's my soul mate, despite everything that happened. I don't care. I really want her back."

"Well, what have you done? Have you reached out to her?"

"Yes! I reached out by writing her. She basically told me that God wanted her to continue her journey. And now I'm here just wondering, does she not want to be with me? Is it over forever?"

"Honestly Terrance, I don't know. She's really on to something now. I don't think she's ever been happier."

"You think she has another man?"

"Lisa probably doesn't even have time to be dealing with another man. She's on another spiritual level right now. In order to get on her level, you need to be like best friends with Jesus or something," Wanda said.

"So you're telling me that Lisa is too good for me now?"

"Are you best friends with Jesus?" I hesitated before I spoke, but Wanda interrupted me.

"I didn't think so, Terrance. Give her some time, and maybe you should get your life together before you go back to her."

"Are you trying to say that I'm no good or something, Wanda? You know I'm a good man, right?"

"I can see it in your eyes, Terrance. You're a good man, but I just don't want to mess up what Lisa has going on. She's pure and she's uplifting people and changing lives. She's on a God-driven journey," Wanda said before holding the bag up and dumping the crumbs in her mouth. "That doesn't mean not to write her. You all should definitely keep in touch."

"Okay. Thank you for coming, Wanda."

I escorted Wanda out of the house. I shouldn't have let her come over. Now she had me thinking there was a possibility that I would never see Lisa again, which was insane. Yes, I was getting to know a wonderful woman named Cindy and moving on, but damn. Lisa will always be my baby... my best friend... my back bone.

I went into my room, sat at my desk and began typing.

Lisa,

It's so crazy. Still can't believe I'm writing you. You should be here. I really miss you. I know we're going to get back together sooner or later, but I do understand that you have a lot going on. I've been talking to God a lot, too. I'm on a spiritual journey just like you. I just pray that my journey gets me back to my best friend. By the way, I talked to Wanda. She's really sorry for what she did to you. I definitely look at her differently than before. Seems like she's growing as a woman. Other than that, all is well over here. Don't hesitate to hit me up anytime.

Love you to death!

Terrance

Chapter 16: Break Fast or Stay for Breakfast?

The Ivy, 11:35 p.m.

Another Fun Friday with the fellas was needed.

"So now I'm asking God is Cindy the one that He has sent me to replace Lisa?"

Jay smacked the table. "Hell yeah, Cindy is the angel that you prayed for! Right after you saw Lisa's sex tape, I know you asked God for answers and another woman. Cindy is that woman!"

I looked at Fred.

Fred put his hand on my shoulder. "Look, go with your heart. If you feel like Lisa is who you truly love, no one can replace her."

Jay shook his head. "Are you serious? Hell no! Shut up, Fred! Terrance, look who you're getting advice from! Another guy that can't get over his ex-lover even though she wants to move on."

Fred leaned over and pointed. "Watch your mouth, Jay!"

"Terrance, I'm telling you man. Look at the God-given omens. The woman of your dreams just somehow fell in your lap! She's gorgeous, rich, single, and she is into you. Not me, you! What's wrong with Cindy? What more could you ask for? It's not rocket science. Lisa has moved on. She's probably a born-again virgin that practices abstinence and never wants to have sex or some shit. She's moved on, now it's time for you to do the same," Jay continued.

I sighed. "You're right. It may be time for me to move on. The thing is, once I move on, I'm not looking back. Plus, I love the fact that Cindy motivates the hell out of me."

"Exactly. That's what you wanted! I'm telling you, she's an angel! And, Terrance, you know I ain't the one to promote being a one-woman man, but dammit, this time I want you to hold on tight and never let go!" Jay said, slapping the counter and sitting back in his seat. Fred and I laughed.

129

"Don't ignore the signs, Terrance. Cindy looks so good, she don't even have to wear makeup!"

"Yeah, I noticed that," I said, sipping my beer.

"Man. I wish Michelle didn't wear as much makeup sometimes," Fred interjected.

"Don't you hate that? With some of these women I just want to grab a napkin and do them a favor. They look so fake with all that damn paint on their face," Jay complained.

"Some women need it though," I replied.

"Hell yeah, or else they look like Freddy Krueger."

"I believe that most women don't though. They're just so used to it now, that they can't leave the house without it. I've seen so many women without makeup that just shined from within. It's a beautiful thing," I said.

"Makeup to make them appear prettier, 6-inch heels to make them taller, push-up bras to make their boobs bigger, weave to make their hair longer, butt shots to make their butts bigger... And they call us the liars," Jay clarified.

I laughed. "You got a point."

"I'm not going to be surprised when I eventually see some of these hoes with damn masks on," Jay said jokingly as Fred and I laughed.

"That's exactly why I don't trust them! They don't trust me and I don't trust them," Jay continued, sipping his beer.

"You'll find your match!" I replied.

"No time soon! I'm a bachelor for life! I don't love these hoes like y'all!"

Fred shook his head and looked at me. "I hate when he calls them hoes."

I laughed right before my phone went off. It was a text message from Cindy.

What are you doing at this moment?

I looked at my phone, contemplating on what to say.

"Uh oh? Who is that?" Jay asked.

"It's Cindy. She asked what I'm doing at this moment."

"Damn, you lucky bastard!" Jay exclaimed.

"What should I say?"

Jay smacked the table. "Are you serious? You say you're doing absolutely nothing!"

I looked at Fred. Fred shrugged.

"But shouldn't I make it seem like I'm a busy man or something. Women don't want a man that has too much time on his hands, right?"

"No! When Cindy Baker asks you what you're doing, at that moment you are doing absolutely nothing! Why is that? Because nothing is more important than what Cindy Baker has to offer. Her presence is a gift. Would you tell Beyoncé you were busy?"

"Okay, okay, I get it." I picked up my phone and texted her back.

I'm not doing anything right now. Why what's up?

"Seems like you have all the answers, huh Jay?" Fred observed.

"You damn right. It looks like I might have to school Terrance. You lost your touch with the ladies, Terrance? I need you to shake off the lameness and get back with the program. I like the old Terrance that could talk a girl out of her underwear in 10 minutes."

"Whatever man. I still have a little talk game. Relax."

My phone buzzed again.

Ok. Get dressed for a classy occasion and meet me at this address in 45 minutes:

722 Paces Ferry Rd.

"Damn," I said.

"What'd she say?" Fred asked.

"She said she wants me to get dressed and meet her at this event in 45 minutes."

"Well… What are you waiting for, get your ass up and go. She's inviting you to an upscale event, and if you do right this will probably be an easy way to get in those panties!"

"Is that all you think about? Sex?" I asked.

"Nope. Sex and money," Jay responded, taking a sip of his beer.

Fred shook his head and looked my way. "Are you fine to drive?"

"Yeah I'm fine. I didn't drink much." I stood up.

"Alright. Make us proud son!" Jay rooted me on.

I got in my car and zoomed home. I sifted through my closet, looking for the best combination of clothing. Right before flipping the light switch

131

and leaving, I saw the mess I'd left. My room looked like a hurricane. Suit jackets, hangers, neckties, and pants were scattered across my bed and on the floor. I had no time to straighten up though.

I got in the car, entered the address in my GPS and put the pedal to the medal. The directions took me to a private property in Buckhead with a gated entrance. It looked like something that I would never go to, because I would never be invited. The gate entrance was open and I followed the cars as they all went through. They drove in a line to the front of a mansion where I saw valet men taking the guest cars and driving them to another location. Now I was worried, wondering how much this was going to cost me. Valet? Wealthy folks? I'm not broke by a long shot, but this valet guy may be expecting something that I'm not willing to pay. If I needed to, I'd park my car on my own. I picked up my phone and dialed Cindy. She didn't answer. It wasn't long until I was next in the line of vehicles. I was ready to hear a ridiculous number. I pulled up and the man dressed in a black and white tuxedo signaled me to roll my window down. I pressed the button.

"Hello, how much are the valet services?"

"They're free sir, we're only taking tips," he said.

"Oh okay. Can I tip you once I leave?"

"Yes sir, you can."

That's exactly what I needed to hear. I put the car in park and hopped out, then grabbed my phone to call Cindy. I stood there, with the phone to my ear, waiting. I didn't want to walk anywhere looking lost. Cindy answered on the second ring.

"I'm pulling up now. I'm third in the valet line. Stay there, I can see you," she directed.

A brand new black Bentley pulled up. It was Cindy. She got out of the car. I was impressed. I couldn't do anything but respect her. Talk about representing for women. She was a boss. Just watching her get out of her Bentley gave me the shivers. She smiled at the valet man and handed her keys to him.

"Thank you, Ms. Baker," he said.

As Cindy walked towards me, I visualized her in a wedding dress. I blinked quickly and shook my head slightly to make the image go away. That was my problem. I always started planning ahead like I had the answers. But I did thank God for that moment. I was a lucky guy. I knew other guys would die to be in my shoes.

I caught the valet guy looking at her backside as she walked up.

"You look nice!" Cindy said, walking up and smiling.

"You look..." I was practically speechless as I continued to shake my head, still in awe.

"Breathtaking?" Cindy filled in the blank as she threw her hair back with her hand. "Just kidding. I sound conceited."

I waved my index finger and nodded. "That's the word, breathtaking. Flawless, all of that."

"Why thank you! I'm sorry it was so last minute. I meant to ask you to come sooner, but it slipped my mind." Cindy grabbed my arm and started walking towards the mansion.

"It's fine. So what's the occasion? This place is amazing," I said, looking up as we walked inside the mansion.

"Well it's really just a little wine tasting gathering that the CEO of my company, Bobby White, is putting on, so it's almost certain that I have to be here to show my face."

"Okay. What made you invite me?" I asked.

Cindy laughed. "You want me to be 100% honest with you? Although I am a Chief Officer for my firm and I'm always speaking to people of very high ranks around the industry, when I'm in a social setting, it really gets annoying and boring talking to them."

"Oh really? Why is that?"

"It's mainly because we don't have much in common. We come from drastically different backgrounds. It can get really awkward at times. The only real thing we have in common is our high ranks so all I can really talk about is things that relate to our business and the industry, and I don't like talking about that 24/7."

"It makes sense. Thanks for being honest," I said.

"So I'm dragging you along with me so you and I can talk most of the time and I can avoid them."

"So you're using me?" I asked.

"That's exactly what I'm doing. But trust me, it would be in your best interest to just go with the flow," Cindy said, as she threw her hand behind me and hit me on the butt. I jumped forward.

133

She looked me in the eyes. "Is that okay with you?"

"I don't think I have a choice. Let's get something to drink," I replied.

We walked up to the open bar together. The bartenders handed out wine glasses. I grabbed one for her and I. I didn't know the type of wine we were drinking, but whatever it was, it was delicious. We drank them fairly quick. I grabbed two more for us.

"I'm tipsy," Cindy confessed.

"Are you serious? This is nothing."

"I barely drink, Terrance. Like almost never. You're like a bad influence on me," she said, looking me in the eyes.

"What? Why didn't you tell me? Why don't you drink?" I asked.

"I'm usually always tied up with work and I have no time to wind down. It's work, work and work for me. Been like that since I was younger."

"Wow. No wonder you've accomplished so much. But sometimes people can run themselves in the ground. I feel like I have to enjoy myself. You know," I said taking a sip.

"Well my father was an alcoholic as well. That's why I choose not to drink much because I feel like it's in my genes to become one too."

"Oh, I'm sorry to hear that. I had no idea."

"No it's fine! I have nothing against my dad! He helped me become the woman I am today. He would preach to me the importance of going the extra mile and working hard at all times. He wanted me to chase my dreams and to never settle for anything lower then what I wanted. He instilled it in me at a young age, because he never got to live his dreams. That's why he would try to drink the pain away. By being so into my school work at all times, it helped me block out my dad and his drunken antics around the house."

"That's interesting. It explains so much. So you only stayed with your father?"

"Yes, my mom was heavily on drugs. My dad had custody of me. Although he was an alcoholic, he had a steady job working at the bank and he had enough sense to raise me."

"Wow, you have an amazing story, Cindy."

She lightly shoved me in the chest. "You know, I have never told anyone my story."

134

"Why is that? It's inspiring! You can move people with it," I replied.

She paused, looked away and shook her head. "I was scared that people would look at my past and determine that I wouldn't be fit to be an executive of a firm."

"Never be ashamed of your past. It molded you into the person that you are today. I feel like if they knew your backstory, they would respect you even more," I said, grabbing her hand.

"So what about you? How were your parents?" asked Cindy.

"My mom was my everything. She raised me. I'm pretty much a momma's boy. But that's mostly because my dad refused to be in my life. For what reason, I don't know."

"Sorry to hear that. You turned out to be a pretty good guy without him."

"Yeah, I did. I always wanted to know why he left my mama and me. But I definitely told myself that I would be a better father than he was because I always yearned for his presence."

Cindy looked away, and then looked back at me. "I want you to meet the CEO, Bobby White. He's over there." Cindy pointed in his direction. "After he sees that I came, we can get out of here."

"That's fine with me," I said, beginning to walk in that direction.

Cindy grabbed my arm. "Wait, let's have another drink first."

"Cindy, are you sure?"

Cindy looked me in the eye. "Does it look like I'm sure?"

My eyes widened. "Okay then, one more."

We both got our drinks and finished them before we walked over to Bobby White. As soon as we approached Mr. White yelled, "Cindy! I am so glad you came!"

"Bobby! Thanks for inviting me!" They hugged.

Mr. White looked about 70 years old and was about 5'9" with pale skin and a big belly.

"Can I get you anything? Have you had some wine?" he asked, pointing to a waitress.

"I'm fine, Bobby. I just came from the bar," Cindy told him.

Bobby looked to me, and then held his hand out for a handshake. "Oh I'm so sorry, Bobby White."

"No problem. I'm Terrance Hill and it's a pleasure to meet you." I reached out and shook his hand.

"I apologize. How rude of me, Mr. White. This is my boyfriend, Terrance. Terrance, this is my boss and the CEO of the firm Mr. White," Cindy said, looking at us both.

My nerves jumped. Did she really just say boyfriend? It caught me off guard.

"Well, Mr. Terrance, you have a very special woman there. Make sure you take great care of her," Mr. White said as he leaned down and winked.

"Oh most definitely, Mr. White. I know she's special and I will do my best to take care of her," I responded.

"Now that's what I want to hear! You look like a fine young man yourself. You all look terrific together. I know you'll do a fine job."

Cindy smiled. "Well Bobby, we're going to head out. Thank you again for the invite and the event was amazing!"

"Any time, Cindy! You all make it home safely! And it was nice meeting you, Terrance."

"It was my pleasure, Mr. White," I said, walking away.

Cindy grabbed my arm and wrapped it around hers. She then began walking to the exit, pulling me along. I was looking as I was walking at all of the people drinking and having a good time. I tilted my head up at the high ceilings and saw the large dangling chandeliers sparkling from the light. My eyes shifted down to the walls with the fancy colorful paintings. The furniture looked like antiques that were probably from the 1800s.

"So this is what real wealth looks like," I said.

Cindy looked at me as we walked. "You're going to see a lot of this when you're with me."

"I don't mind. I just didn't know that I was your boyfriend now. You learn something new every day."

Cindy smiled. "Come on. It just sounds better if I say 'boyfriend' rather than 'friend' around him. Just makes it easier for him you know. He was going to assume something anyway."

"I was just a little surprised, that's all."

"My boss really liked you for some reason."

"Why do you say that?"

"Because he's never that friendly to anyone he first meets. He automatically sizes everyone up the first time he meets them and I think you impressed him."

"Real recognizes real, I guess."

Cindy giggled and rolled her eyes. We approached the front of the mansion by valet. I gave Cindy a long hug.

"Well, I really enjoyed the night. I definitely saw a different side to you. I feel like I know so much more about you now," I said.

"What are you about to do?" Cindy asked, looking into my eyes.

I hesitated. "Ummm, I don't know. I didn't have anything planned."

"You should follow me home, just to make sure I get there safely," Cindy suggested, before she winked.

I nodded. "Okay, I can do that."

I was still thinking it was a dream; this was definitely too good to be true. She winked at me! What did she mean? The night had turned even more interesting.

Cindy led the way as we drove to her house. We pulled into a long, oval driveway in front of a two-story house with three garages. There was no way she lived in this place alone. She had to be renting rooms out to people or something. I parked next to her, sat in the car and waited. She walked over to my driver's side window.

"So you stay here by yourself?"

"Yep," she said, looking at the house and then looking back at me.

"That's crazy. I don't know how you do it."

"You want to see the inside?"

"You sure?"

"Get out of the car, Terrance," she demanded.

"Okay," I said, while opening the door.

I walked into the house. There was a couch directly in front of me so I sat down. Cindy went into a cabinet in her kitchen. I could hear cabinet doors opening and closing. She walked out of the kitchen with two wine glasses and a bottle of wine.

"This bottle of wine is so old," she said as she sat next to me on the couch and popped it open. She sat the glasses on the coffee table and then poured.

"I thought you didn't drink much," I stated, watching her fill the cups.

137

"Which explains why I said this bottle is so old," Cindy replied, as she concentrated on pouring.

"So why drink now?"

"Because it's a special occasion." Cindy picked up a glass and began to drink.

"Oh really? What's so special about this?"

Cindy said nothing as she held the cup to her mouth and continued drinking until the glass was empty.

"Excuse me, Ms. Cindy. Answer my question... what's special about this occasion?"

Cindy leaned closer to me and whispered, "This."

She grabbed my chin and pulled me closer. Yep, it was happening. This was real. Her lips were just as soft as they looked. Time stopped. It was as if I was the star in a romantic movie with the most gorgeous actress in the industry as my lover. The love scene that every guy would dream of. Usually I'd be jealous of that actor, but this time, at this moment, it was me. Dammit I was lucky. But I was cautious. I needed to not mess this moment up. So I followed her lead. She was in charge. She was the master; I was her slave. I was her property. She could use me to her liking. I didn't want to make any sudden moves that would fall out of line with her plan. There was no way that I would risk ruining the moment.

She reached for my shirt and began to unbutton it. I let her. Her neck looked like it needed to be kissed, so I caressed it gently. She lifted her chin up and began to moan. Her moan got to me. This was really happening. The same Cindy that I had hoped to accept me as an associate was now moaning from the touch of my tongue. She began to kiss on my chest. She reached for my zipper. *Damn!* I remembered that I didn't have any protection.

"I don't have a condom," I said abruptly.

"Don't worry, I have some," Cindy said as she continued to unzip.

"Well, where is it?" I asked.

"Hold on." Cindy hopped up and ran upstairs like she was on a mission.

"Should I come up there?"

"No! Stay down there!" Cindy yelled as she went up.

I sat on the couch with my zipper halfway down and my shirt unbuttoned with no shoes on. My emotions were all over the place. I was confused, horny, amazed, and in awe at the same time. But my mind was on one thing: Cindy Baker. I was still nervous. Everything was moving fast. I didn't want to disappoint her. After sitting for two minutes, I heard steps coming from the stairs. I looked up. Cindy walked down the staircase. She was half naked with only a black bed robe on. She held two Magnums in her hand. I took a deep breath. She threw the condoms and they landed on my lap.

"Get to work," she said.

I didn't hesitate. I got naked and slipped on a condom. Cindy took off her robe. My heart pounded so hard that I figured I was inches away from a heart attack. She sat on top of me and began kissing me again. Her robe was off. Her breasts sat perfectly on her chest. I leaned forward and began sucking. My tongue caressed her nipples gently. She winced. I had to get the most out of this moment. It was as if a Victoria Secret Model was on top of me. My hands rubbed up and down her thighs and waist, like a kid rubbing on a tightly wrapped Christmas present trying to guess what was inside. Her skin was smooth and soft. Just like her lips. I couldn't have her sitting on top of me for long without going inside of her, so I slid in smoothly and quietly like someone late to a staff meeting. It was official. I'd entered into a queen's temple and I didn't want to leave. She started slowly thrusting back and forth. My lap turned wet as if I had just jumped into a pool. She moaned so loud that I almost shushed her to quiet down. I forgot that we were the only ones in the huge house - her house. That would be disrespectful to give orders in the house that she had paid for. So I just went harder. I glanced up at her. Her eyes were closed. She was biting her bottom lip. She had the sexiest facial expression that I had ever seen. We continued our session for forty-five minutes until we both finished. She fell asleep on top of me.

The smell of eggs, pancakes, and turkey bacon filled my nostrils. I woke up. There goes another good dream that I couldn't remember. I checked my watch: 6:00 a.m. I looked around. Nothing looked familiar. Then it dawned on me. Last night wasn't a dream. It was real. As real as could be. *If Cindy is up cooking breakfast for me, I'm probably going to just melt. It might be too much for me to handle at one time.* I rubbed my

139

eyes to wipe the crust out and wiped my mouth to make sure I hadn't drooled. Cindy walked out the kitchen in her bedroom robe with a large plate of steaming breakfast. She sat the plate on the table in front of me.

"Do you want orange juice or apple juice?" she asked.

"Good morning to you too, sheesh," I said smiling.

"Good morning, Terrance. Would you like orange juice or apple juice?"

"Orange juice would be fine."

The smell of the breakfast in the morning made me happy. It really made me feel some type of way. I hadn't woken up to the smell of breakfast since living with Lisa. Prepared breakfast made me feel like royalty. Cindy knew what she was doing.

The food was scrumptious. I felt like I was being spoiled. While I sat stuffing my stomach, my mind was moving. I contemplated on how to approach the conversation that I knew Cindy and I had to have. There was a lot of uncertainty in the air. A lot of questions needed to be answered. I liked Cindy. A lot. She was a dream girl. However, I had to come down to reality to admit that a lot had happened in a short time frame. Things moved faster than I expected them to. Don't get me wrong; I'm not saying that I was opposed to moving forward with this relationship. I just didn't know what was going through her head. What if she didn't want anything but sex from me? What if she's just some kinky chick that just has sex with random guys? I doubt that.

But either way, I wanted to know where she and I stood. Where was she intending on taking this relationship, especially after last night. There's nothing like being on two different pages. One side is in lust. One side is in love. The pages turn, but no one usually lives happily ever after. There's no fairy-tale ending. I knew I had to address the situation immediately.

"You didn't have to do all of this," I said.

"It's nothing. I always cook breakfast. I'm going to head into the office in a little bit. Are you going to stay here or are you going to leave?"

"You go into the office on Saturdays?" I asked.

"Always. While my competitors are relaxing on the weekends I'm working."

"Right. I get it."

It was silent for a moment until I decided to inquire about our relationship.

"Hey, so I don't want to rush anything, but I kind of need to know where we stand."

"What do you mean?"

"I mean when I do things with people I like to have clarity. I just want to know what last night meant."

"What did it mean to you, Terrance?"

"I asked you first."

"Stop with the games, Terrance. I want to know what you think last night meant."

"Honestly Cindy, I really feel like we have a connection. I'm really into you and I want to see where it can take us. I think you're a special person. It's all up to you though of course."

Cindy smirked as she began to wash dishes. "Terrance I knew exactly what I was doing last night. I don't think it would hurt for us to take it one step further."

"Great! That's all I needed was clarity. With that being said, I'm going to head home and let you get to work."

I made sure I had all of my stuff before I left. I kissed Cindy on the cheek goodbye before walking out the door. While driving home, all I could smell was her sweet perfume. Images of the night before kept flashing in my mind. My tastes buds still remembered her lips. A month or so ago I would've been excited with the thought of her bumping into me accidentally and touching me. I went from that to being as deep inside of her as a sunken ship in the depths of the Arctic Ocean. Although I was on cloud nine, the question still loomed over my head. We were moving too fast. I was moving at her pace. I couldn't be mad at the fact that she wanted to cut the crap and get to business. She's a straightforward person. She doesn't have time to beat around the bush. She gets what she wants with no questions asked. Sometimes you can't wait. The chemistry was there, so why waste time? I felt like one of the luckiest men on earth. Fred and Jay weren't going to believe this.

141

Chapter 17:

Hooked on Ex-stasy

Fun Friday 11:30 p.m. Local Brewery

"Bruh, I don't know what to think. Everything is just moving so fast," I said.

"So, basically you asked her out? So, you and her are like… officially dating now?" Jay inquired.

"Yep."

"Congratulations! I don't see what the problem is." Jay patted me on the back.

"You don't think it was smart, huh? I can see it in your face." Fred jumped in, squinting at me.

"Do you not like her or something? Was the sex terrible? I'm so confused," Jay said, holding his arms up in frustration.

"Everything was great! The sex was amazing. She's gorgeous; it just feels so different. I'm sort of still in disbelief." I looked down at my cup while twirling the drinking straw around. I looked back up. "Maybe I didn't expect it to happen this fast. It took a while for Lisa and I to establish a relationship, let alone have sex."

"So, you're basically saying that she gave it up too quick?" Fred asked.

I continued looking down at my cup and twirling my straw. "Maybe. Usually if a woman gave in to sex that quick, I would look at them differently and sometimes even lose interest." I looked back up at Fred. "But not Cindy. I even respected her and I wanted her even more after, which explains why I basically wanted to make it official."

"Damn, the sex was that good huh?" Jay said, leaning in.

"But Jay it ain't all about the sex. That's not even the half. It has to be more. It just felt like I wanted to have her to myself after what happened. I just felt so lucky to have a woman like her. You know, lucky to have someone so strong, so driven, so elegant—a trophy piece. I'm proud."

Jay leaned back. "Yep! She got you sprung! I told you she was God sent! She's going to upgrade you too," Jay said, waving and pointing his finger at me.

"So, what about Lisa? Are you giving up on that?" Fred asked.

Jay snapped. "The hell with Lisa, Fred! I'm tired of you bringing up Lisa! Don't you see that this man is doing his best to get over his past, unlike you! Cindy wants Terrance right now! This is what Terrance prayed for! She's perfect for him. It doesn't get any better than this."

I looked at Fred. "I love Lisa. And I will still try to keep in touch. Lisa is still my friend, but I just have to look forward now and see what the future has to bring. But I'm not going to lie, the future looks bright as hell with Cindy."

"That's my boy!" Jay said, grabbing my shoulder and tapping me.

"Do you love Cindy?" Fred asked. Jay and I both paused and looked at Fred.

"I'm not in love yet. I wasn't in love with Lisa at first either. It takes time. But as of now, all I can say is that Cindy is pretty much everything that I can ask for in a woman. She's the woman that I would fantasize about marrying when I was little. But again, we'll see how everything works out."

Fred nodded. "I wish you the best of luck."

Jay looked me square in the eye and pointed towards me. "I'm going to make sure you're faithful this time! No more going out. I don't want you to lose this one."

"Of course. I'm all in this time. I learned from my past mistakes."

Grocery Run

I was hungry, but I didn't feel like cooking. *What should I eat?* I needed something healthy. Something that would fill me up and not leave me hungry in an hour. You know what tastes good? Those Publix subs at the deli! It's the closest I was going to get to a healthy meal, so that would do. I hopped up to head to the grocery store. Once I got there of course there was a long line. So I had to wait. After a few minutes passed, I

143

finally ordered my sandwich. As soon as I exited the line, I looked down at my phone to respond to a text. I wasn't paying attention to where I was going and bam! I ran into someone's grocery cart.

"Sorry ma'am!"

The woman had on large dark shades with a hoodie. I looked closely while apologizing before realizing who she was.

"Michelle, is that you?"

Michelle glanced at me, waved slightly and tried to walk away.

"Wait, I wanted to talk with you for a minute about Fred," I said, following her.

"What you want, Terrance?" Michelle said, looking down to hide her face.

I looked closely at her face and recognized a dark scar right below her shades.

"Why do you have shades on in Publix, Michelle?" I asked, standing directly in front of her buggy.

"Damn, Terrance, because I want to! You got any more questions for me?" Michelle snarled, trying to go around me.

"I'm sorry, I'm just trying to figure out why the hell you're acting so funny."

Michelle stopped moving, stood there, and said nothing.

"Take off the shades, Michelle." She proceeded to walk away and ignore me.

I grabbed the buggy. "Michelle, please take off the shades. Or I'll make a scene in here. I want to see your eyes."

Michelle stopped moving and stood with her head down. She pulled her shades off quickly and then tried to put them back on before I grabbed her arm in the process. Her right eye was swollen shut with a cut directly over her eyebrow.

"Stop, Terrance!" Michelle said as she struggled to put them back on.

"Michelle, who did that to you?" I asked, letting her arm go. Michelle said nothing and put the shades back on. "Was it Keith?"

"This is none of your business, Terrance! Why the hell are you even worried about it?"

"This is my business when all my best friend does is talk about you 24/7! Believe me, if I could shut him up when he talks about you, I would.

144

He loves you still, in spite of how you did him. I wish you could see value in him, more than what you see in this Keith guy."

"It ain't that simple, Terrance. You don't know what you're talking about. You just know what Fred told you," Michelle said with her arms folded.

"Well enlighten me please. I need to help my friend somehow," I said, grabbing on the buggy again.

"Me telling you something will do nothing but worsen the situation. Do not tell Fred you saw me like this!" Michelle screamed, looking me square in the eye and pointing at me.

"Ok I won't," I said, backing up.

"No, promise me you will not, Terrance! I swear to God, I am not Fred's business anymore! This has nothing to do with him," Michelle stated, still looking at me squarely with her finger out.

"I promise I will not tell Fred," I said, holding my hands up. Michelle fixed herself and walked off. "One more thing, Michelle." I grabbed my business card and held it out. I stood in front of her, looked directly into the dark shades and touched both of her shoulders. "This is my number if you feel like you need someone to talk to about this." Michelle paused, then took the card and walked off.

The automatic doors opened for me while I was walking out of the store. I was pissed. I needed to tell someone. I pulled out my phone and I was about to dial Fred, but I stopped. *Think Terrance. Is that a good idea right now?* Plus, I promised Michelle that I wouldn't tell him. *I'll keep my promise for now.* Fred probably wouldn't be able to handle the situation anyway. I honestly don't know. How could I help her? I felt powerless. I thought Jay might be able to help me with this one. I called him instead.

"Bruh, I need help," I said into the phone while walking through the parking lot.

"What happened?"

"I just saw Michelle in Publix with her eye swollen shut."

"Are you serious?"

"Serious as a heart attack. She looked like she was losing weight too."

"Damn! So Keith is beating her ass?"

"That's what it looks like," I said while sitting in the car.

"I feel sorry for her, but what does that have to do with us?" Jay asked.

145

"She made me promise not to tell Fred. But I feel some type of way by not telling him, you know. What should I do?"

"Hell no! Don't tell Fred! He would go crazy. Listen to her. She knows what she's talking about."

I sighed. "Okay. I won't tell him."

"She's stupid anyway."

"It seems like it's more to it; there's something deeper that Fred doesn't know about," I said, while driving out of the Publix parking lot.

"It always is. But I would just leave it alone; it's not our business."

Cindy's House 9:35 p.m.

I was glad Cindy invited me over. I needed to relax and clear my mind. The image of Michelle's black eye was still fresh in my head. Domestic abuse really does something to me. Especially when I feel something is out of my hands. I just prayed that everything works out, as it should. I wanted Michelle to be safe and I wanted Keith to be dealt with. It was in God's hands. Anywho, I received a text from Cindy saying that she wanted me to come over for wine around 9:30 p.m. I confirmed and I got there at 9:35 p.m.

"Hey, hun," Cindy said as I walked in.

"What's up?" I replied as I kissed her on the cheek. "How was your day today?" I took my coat off and sat down.

"The day was long and fun," Cindy said while walking to her wine cabinet.

"Long and fun at work? Never heard someone say that."

Cindy grabbed a bottle and two wine glasses as she looked at me. "I love what I do, so it's easy for me to have fun. This is my dream job. I'm a boss. I get to tell people what to do and I set the standards," Cindy explained as she set the bottle and the wine glasses on the table in front of me.

"Makes sense," I said, looking at the table. "So I feel like I'm a bad influence on you now. It seems like you like to sip a lot lately."

"A little wine never hurt anyone, Terrance. I'll be fine. Plus, I just like to relax when we're together. Is that fine with you?" She stood there looking at me with her hand on her hip.

146

"I'm completely fine with that."

"Do you know why I invited you over?"

"Not necessarily. Maybe you just wanted to spend time. I don't know."

Cindy smiled. "Remember I told you that I was a different type of woman?"

"Yeah, I remember."

"Well, since this is our first time hanging out since we decided to take a step forward in our relationship, I thought we should have a little board meeting laying down the ground rules of this relationship. You said you like clarity... well I do too."

I laughed. "Well, I'm all ears."

Cindy sat next to me on the couch. "You understand that there are no other people to be discussed in our relationship. So in essence, I don't want to hear about your ex-girlfriend Lisa, at all, from here on out," she said.

I nodded. "And of course, the same for you as well, no bringing up your ex."

"Correct," Cindy agreed.

"Also, when it comes to my career, I don't want you to have anything to do with it."

I scratched my head. "Huh, what do you mean?"

Cindy grabbed the bottle and began pouring it into the two glasses. "My position as a VP is a high-demand position. So, at times I may need my space because it can get hectic every now and then. I worked hard to get here and anything that has the potential to get in my way of continuing my legacy, I will have a problem with."

"Okay, so how would I possibly mess that up?"

"Ummm, maybe by begging me to go on a cruise with you when I have meetings and conferences to attend, or by showing up to my job with flowers. People at the firm already think that I'm weak and emotional just because I'm a woman, even though I'm the opposite. My corporate image is everything."

"You are very interesting."

"Told you I was different," Cindy said, taking a sip of her glass.

"But I like it! I completely understand. It actually takes pressure off of me to try to flatter you all the time."

147

"Exactly! I'm very simple to please. Simplicity is key." Cindy sat back with the glass in her hand.

"I'm taking notes."

"So, what is your plan with your firm again? What are your long-term goals with them?"

I picked up my glass and took a sip. "My dream is to be the CFO of the company."

"Okay. What are you doing currently to get there?"

"I'm one of the top Financial Analysts at the firm right now and my boss loves me."

"What else? Is that it?" Cindy probed.

"Ummm, yeah, and I'm working my butt off every day pretty much."

"That's good to hear. Especially since that's a problem with our generation now. We don't know what it feels like to truly work for something. However, that's not enough."

"Oh really? What am I doing wrong?"

Cindy sat up in her seat. "Looks like I'm going to have to school you, because you can't be with a person like me with a mediocre work ethic."

I laughed and put my glass on the table. "Mediocre! Wow! You're the only person that has ever told me I was mediocre."

"Because those other people weren't being truthful with you. If you really want to be the CFO of the firm, you have to be the first choice that comes to anyone's mind when the position opens. You said that you were one of the top Financial Analysts at the firm; in my opinion you need to be number one. You need to be able to do more than everyone else. You need to study the current CFO's agenda thoroughly. You need to know and develop solid relationships with all the board members of the firm or whoever appoints the CFO. You need to study all of the past CFOs of the firm and know how they got there. If they're available, get in touch with them and ask them to become your mentors."

"You're right; I have to tighten up. I'm guessing you did some of these things to get your current position."

"There was no denying me of this position. I worked my ass off to get here. So when you tell me your dreams, don't tell me unless you're 100% serious about accomplishing them, because I know what it takes," she said, leaning back in her seat.

"Wow, I will definitely make sure I do what it takes."

"Oh don't worry, people tend to do better when they have others holding them accountable. Believe me I will be watching you," Cindy said, with a grin and a wink.

"I'm down for it. Damn, I love this! This is how a relationship is supposed to be, I love the motivation!"

Cindy sighed and looked up at the ceiling. "There's nothing that'll make me happier than seeing you as the CFO of your firm, and by that time I would probably be a CEO. Talk about a power couple! Jay-Z and Beyoncé might have to watch out," she said looking back at me.

I smiled. "You know what, let's make a toast to this. Cindy Baker, I'm ready to go on this journey with you!" I said holding up his glass. Cindy smiled and held up her glass too.

"Okay, say this with me, *let thy cup runneth over with blessings.*"

"Ummm... Okay, where did you get that from?"

"It's like a ritual that me and my friends say whenever we toast. It means that we hope that God continues to provide us with more blessings than we could ever imagine... *thy cup runneth.*"

Cindy shook her head. "I guess."

"*Let thy cup runneth over with blessings!*" we both said as we tapped glasses and began to drink.

Okay. So this is how it feels to be a part of a power couple. When you and your partner are on a mission to build and mold the future together to your liking. A power couple's relationship is not just about loving each other; it's bigger than that. It's about motivating each other to maximize their potential and to strive for nothing but the best. We work on each other's weaknesses. We sharpen each other's strengths. We don't scold or bring each other down. We support one another. We look at each other as a bonus, not a burden. When one fails, the other encourages them to fight forward. When one wins, we both win, and we celebrate with two glasses of wine. Neither of us are victims, but we're both striving to become victorious. None of us are a suspect, but we're both searching for success. We're a team that wants to accomplish goals, together. We're not competitors. I love it. I love the feeling. Cindy speaks with conviction. I knew that she was serious. She didn't just talk the talk; she walked the walk. I listened. I was ready to apply it. Since I was a child, I'd always had

149

big dreams. I remembered motivating myself to always do better. Cindy had ignited a fire in me again. She was the spark that I needed. She's a great accountability partner. It feels good to know that someone as successful as her saw so much potential in me.

Fun Friday 11:00 p.m.

"She's so corporate minded! And I love it! We had a meeting about our relationship and she basically told me that I need to work harder if I want to become a CFO," I said.

Jay pointed at me. "What did I tell you? I told you she was going to upgrade you! That's what you need, Terrance. I should be cupid. It feels so good to know that I hooked y'all up!"

"You didn't hook us up. You told me she was out of my league. I'm the one who made the move. Remember?"

"Sounds to me like she's the man of the relationship. She seems very demanding," Fred observed.

Jay sighed and threw his hands up. "Again look who's talking—a guy that couldn't take control of his relationship and who had his girl walk out on him for a gangsta! Terrance don't take advice from Fred; he doesn't know what it means to have a strong black woman in his corner."

"I'm sick of your mouth man!" Fred pointed his finger at Jay and stood up.

"Sit down!" I said, looking at Fred and pointing to his chair. "I'm not taking relationship advice from either of y'all! I'm just riding this wave to see where it takes me."

"Well, whatever you do, make sure you listen to her. She can wear the pants in the relationship because she makes over 250k a year. She is a legit boss! She has her own. She don't need you," Jay stated.

"That's actually a good feeling. To have a chick that kind of doesn't need you because she has a lot of her own. I swear it just does something to me, so sexy," I said.

"Yeah! You don't want none of these broke down chicks that want to sit around, do nothing, and spend all of your money. Talking about buy me a Birkin bag... Bitch, go buy your own bag! Find a real career!" Jay yelled.

150

Fred and I laughed.

Sunday Night

I was slouched on my couch with house slippers on and a white tank top, locked in on the television watching Sunday Night Football. The Falcons were losing by 15 points. Pathetic! We had to do better. We needed to win this important game. My phone rang from the coffee table and it was an unknown number. I reached over to pick it up, with my eyes still on the screen.

"Hello."

"Hey, can I speak with Terrance?" said a woman in a low voice.

"Yes, this is Terrance. Who is this?" I asked, still looking at the screen.

"It's Michelle."

"Michelle?"

"Yeah, you got a minute to talk?" she asked.

"Ummm... yeah, what's going on?"

There was short period of silence before Michelle spoke. "Well you said to call you if I need someone to talk to about my situation. So I decided to go ahead and reach out to you."

"Yeah, I'm all ears. What happened?" I inquired, reaching over to turn off the television.

Michelle sighed. "Keith put his hands on me again and I can't take it anymore."

"Why were you taking it in the first place? You chose to put up with him Michelle! You had a man that loved you to death and that would take a bullet for you."

"I know, Terrance, I know. But it's complicated. Keith was my first love. I ran away from home when I was 17. My dad used to beat my mom so bad and she would say absolutely nothing to him. And she told me not to tell anyone. She used to say, 'Sometimes being in love hurts,' or she would say, 'I deserve to be hit.' Keith was my boyfriend at the time. He was 22 and I was 17. He had his own place so I just moved in with him. That's when I lost my virginity. He was the sweetest person that I had ever

151

met. I knew he was a drug dealer, but I ignored it. Mainly because he would buy anything that I wanted or needed. I stayed with him for two years until I went off to college. Since I was going to college, he told me to promise him that I would not become too successful and forget about him. I would promise him all the time. He bought me a car and he paid for me to live in a nice dorm. It wasn't until my sophomore year that he got arrested. I was devastated. I would write him and tell him how I was doing, and he would tell me to stay on top of my studies and to get straight A's. After a while, I started to get lonely and that's when I became good friends with Fred. Of course Fred wasn't the best looking, but he was such a nice guy. He was probably too nice of a guy. He really appreciated me. I loved Fred, but I was never in love with him. I would still write Keith all the time. I even told him about Fred. Keith told me that it was okay for me to be entertained until he got out. The more time I spent with Fred, the more I realized that we probably wouldn't last. I just never knew the right time to break him the news. It was just such a coincidence that Keith got out of jail around the same time Fred tried to propose. So, of course I decided to move Keith in with me."

"You said a mouthful. But it still doesn't change how I feel."

"Terrance, I'm not a bad person, I promise. I just didn't know how to deal with everything. I felt obligated to give Keith a chance to get his life back together."

"You felt obligated; however, I think you were in love too. Weren't you?"

"Yes, I was in love. But I don't think I love him anymore."

"Oh you think? Did you decide before or after he gave you a black eye?"

"Terrance, stop! I feel like you're judging me right now! It took me a while to realize that I had matured so much faster than him. I used to look up to him as if he was my father. But now, all he does is have his old friends that don't do shit at the house, smoking and selling weed. All they do is roll dice, watch TV, and eat up all of the food."

"So, I'm guessing you said something and that's when he hit you?"

Michelle hesitated. "After the first time I told him that he would not be able to stay with me if he continued to act up, he took me in the back room and punched me in the face. He told me that he couldn't believe that I had the audacity to try him like that, after all he's done for me."

"So did you call the police?" Michelle grew silent.

"I thought so. Michelle you have to call the police. You have to walk out on faith."

"I can't send him to jail. Not because I love him, but because he would come out and kill me. Or if he doesn't get out, he would get his friends to do something to me. I just know it."

"So you're afraid?" I asked.

"Hell yeah! He's crazy. It's even deeper than me being afraid though. Keith has no one but me. He has no family here. All of his other friends are in the streets just like him. I'm the only thing that he tries to cling to for stability," Michelle continued.

"Michelle, the only advice I can give you is to look out for yourself by being smart. If not, somebody is going to get hurt. Get a restraining order on him or something."

"Terrance, take the police out of it. It's not happening. I just can't put him behind bars."

"Well, I don't have any other suggestions Michelle. There's nothing I can do."

"Just pray for me, Terrance."

"I will do that, Michelle."

I was fed up and inches away from calling Fred immediately, but I stopped myself again. Calling Fred could possibly put Michelle in even more danger. Plus, I still had a promise to keep. I would stand by my word. Again, I felt helpless. *Damn!* I hate woman beaters. I wish I could confront Keith myself, but that wouldn't end well since he's a shooter and not a fighter. And, he had nothing to lose. He also looks like he loves drama. He wanted someone to come for him. I just hoped that Michelle was smart enough to figure things out on her own. My hands were tied.

Chapter 18: Poor Me? No, I Said Pour Me a Drink

Fun Friday – Suite Lounge, Atlanta GA

"I know women like the back of my hand!" Jay yelled.

"Really? You know everything about women?" I asked.

"Hell yeah! I know them. There's different species of women," Jay said, before sipping on his glass.

Fred laughed and nudged me. "Species, huh? What are the different species?"

"Light-skinned women and dark-skinned women, two different species," Jay said, after sitting his cup down.

Fred and I threw our hands up laughing. "Ahhh man."

"Really Jay? Light-skinned and dark-skinned?" I asked.

"Terrance, let him finish. This will be interesting coming from a light-skinned brother himself," Fred interjected.

"You see, I love light-skinned women! They are just sexy! I don't know why; they're just naturally sexier. But I could never be in a relationship with one," Jay explained.

"And why is that?" I asked.

"Are you serious? Because they are too arrogant! They're full of themselves. They rely too much on their looks for everything. They are spoiled rotten." Fred and I laughed.

"They play too many games! It's like rocket science to get them to come over my house man!" Jay said, shaking his head.

"So, why do you still pursue them?" Fred asked.

"Because I'm addicted to them. I'm just like a coke addict that knows he has a problem. I know they're not good for me, but I just like going back."

"So, what about dark-skinned women? What's your break down on them?" I inquired.

"Oh, see dark-skinned women are less attractive, so they are more humble," Jay explained further while sipping on his drink.

"I disagree, but continue," I said.

"No they are! They're nicer. They're easier to talk to. I'm just not really attracted to them. They try too hard. And they hate light-skinned women."

Fred and I looked at each other and shook our heads.

"Jay, I think you're going to end up marrying a light-skinned chick. Because, in that case, both of y'all would be crazy, spoiled, and made for each other," I told him.

"Terrance, I'm never getting married. You know that."

"I can see it now, you'll marry that random light-skinned chick that's famous on Instagram and has over 20,000 followers. All of her pictures look professional and most of them are half naked." I replied. Fred laughed.

"And usually no one knows what they do as a career," I continued.

"Or her occupation is showing up to clubs around the world and hosting twerking contests," Fred added.

Jay held his middle finger up at both of us. We continued drinking. Out of the corner of my eye I saw Wanda, Lisa's old friend.

"Hey, Terrance!" she said, approaching the table.

"Oh what's up, Wanda? What are you doing here?" I asked.

"I actually just wanted to get out of the house today and get my drink on. I had a long week, you know."

"Oh. I apologize, these are my friends, Jay and Fred," I said pointing at them.

"Nice to meet you both." Wanda held out her hand.

"So, who did you come with?" I asked.

"I came alone. You know how girls are sometimes. I'd rather hang out with men; y'all have less drama," Wanda confessed.

I nodded. "Well ummm, I guess you can vibe with us," I said, looking at Fred then Jay.

Jay stared at me with a confused face. And subliminally shook his head without Wanda noticing.

"I mean, if it's fine with Jay and Fred." I looked at them, grinning.

"I don't mind." Fred shrugged.

155

Jay turned to Wanda. "We call this time Fun Friday. It's our men's night out, so the conversation may make you feel a little... uncomfortable."

Wanda sighed. "Oh please! I grew up in a house full of brothers. Believe me, there's nothing that I haven't heard," she said as she pulled out a chair to sit. Jay rolled his eyes.

"Well, I guess you can join our conversation then. Jay is like anti-marriage; he wants to live the single life forever. So we love hearing his crazy theories about women."

"And why is that?" Wanda asked as she shifted in her seat.

Fred chimed in. "Because he's never witnessed real love before."

"You don't know what I've witnessed, lover boy!" Jay yelled, "I just look at things differently. Some people wish to get married, have a couple kids, get a dog, and grow old. I don't."

"What's wrong with living happily ever after and raising a family?" Wanda continued to probe.

"Nothing. I think people get married thinking that's what's going to happen and it's like the total opposite. It's usually a mess... a big divorce waiting to happen! Kids running around with step fathers and step mothers, custody battles, financial disputes, just a big mess."

"How can you go into it looking at the negatives, Jay? That's not always the case," I said.

"No, Terrance, I have too many nightmares about this stuff. See this is how I envision it going. I'm going to find this gorgeous woman that I think can be my wife, right? I'm going to marry her. Then I find out that she's crazy. She's always an emotional wreck and wants to vent to me about everything. Then I have to pretend like I care. Then we have a kid. Then she gets comfortable and starts getting fat." Jay paused then looked at Wanda. "No offense."

Wanda leaned back with her hand on her chest. "So you basically just called me fat in my face?"

"I'm so sorry! I didn't mean it like that. I just..."

"Please excuse him, Wanda," I said, trying to clear things up. "He's had too many drinks and he has no filter to what he says."

"It's okay. People like you don't deserve a good woman anyway. The Bible says that when a man finds a wife, he finds a good thing. You'll just never get to witness that good thing."

"See, Wanda, I'm fine with that. I don't mind. I can live single. I love the single life! I don't want to have to answer to anybody."

"So you want to just be lonely all your life?"

"No, I'm going to be far from lonely! I'm going to be like Hugh Hefner. Plenty of women will be around me."

I put my face down in embarrassment.

"So, Terrance, you mean to tell me that you won't feel trapped if you get married? All of these beautiful women in the world and you want to be limited to one for the rest of your life?"

I nodded. "Yep. All the women in the world aren't for me. I just want to give my all to one woman and spoil her with all of my love instead of trying to spread myself thin to so many others."

Jay shook his head. "That's such a lover boy answer."

"You know what, Jay? I can't even be mad at you. Because I used to think the same way before I actually fell in love. When I fell in love with Lisa, it changed my perspective on everything," I said.

"Yeah whatever, and here you are with another woman now," Jay said.

Wanda turned to me. "Oh. You found someone else now?"

"Yes, currently I'm with someone else, Wanda. You know Lisa is still doing her thing around the country."

Wanda nodded. "Okay. I didn't know that. Just hard to imagine you with anyone other than Lisa."

"Yep. That's why I can't trust women; maybe I'm just scared to get my heart broken again," Jay informed us.

"I honestly can say that I have never seen someone so against relationships. I'm going to have to pray for you Jay," Wanda responded.

"Ain't nothing wrong with me! The closest I'll ever get to marriage is if I get to have multiple wives. They'll all serve different purposes in my life."

"And why would you need multiple wives?"

"Glad you asked, Fred! I would need them for multiple reasons. Of course all of them would be gorgeous—nothing but dime pieces. However, they'll all look completely different, so that they'll satisfy all of

157

my sexual preferences. They'll all play specific roles in my life. One would be the chef; she'll be able to cook anything I want. One would be a sports fanatic, so we can watch ESPN together and she can know what she's talking about and not ask stupid questions. One would be an intellectual so we can have thought-provoking conversations. And they'll all be great at sex."

Fred scratched his head. "You know, Jay? I think I see the problem here. When you're looking for love from so many different women as if one isn't enough, it's usually because you perceive flaws in each one as if one is lacking something while the other makes up for it. However, what you fail to realize is that each and every woman is an intricately crafted, and precious work of art from God. Art can never be inadequate, because it's perfect as is. Therefore, this equates to each and every woman being flawless. The man that recognizes this, and takes his time to love one can experience a love so powerful that it's infinite; more than he could ever imagine. Do you agree with this, Wanda?"

Wanda nodded and smiled. "That is so true! You get it!"

"Fred, shut the hell up. You can't walk in my shoes, so you really would never understand where I'm coming from. You only had one woman, so of course you're going to think that one woman is enough. I've been with many different women, and I'm happier that way. Plus, that's every man's secret desire! You all just don't want to admit it," Jay rebutted. "Plus, there are men living like that somewhere in the world. So I'm not as crazy as y'all think. It exists."

I looked to Wanda. "See what we have to deal with?"

"I understand. He just has a little boy's mindset. Real men don't think like this," she replied.

Jay threw up his hands. "Ha! Now I'm not a man? Please tell me more!"

"A real man realizes that he only needs one queen. And although she's not perfect, he still continues to learn how to love and to give her the world," Wanda elaborated.

"And let me guess? You're single?"

"Yes, I am."

Jay nodded. "Thought so. You should hook up with Fred."

I looked at Fred as he was looking at Jay with a frown.

Jay shrugged. "I'm just saying, Fred! Don't look at me like that. We need you to get over Michelle some way or another. And, Wanda, you need to get with a real man like Fred. He ain't gon' cheat and he's a man of God. Hallelujah!"

"I'm fine, thank you. I'm not looking for anyone right now," Wanda claimed.

Jay shrugged. "Your loss."

Fred looked at Jay, still frowning and shaking his head.

"You know what. Now that I think about it, I might have someone that Fred could talk to. She just dumped her boyfriend because he was a compulsive liar and a cheater," Wanda remembered.

Jay leaned forward. "Who? She better not be ugly! My boy Fred needs another boo thing right now."

"Wanda, I'm not miserable. Jay is making it seem like I'm a desperate and lonely human being. I'm fine."

"You sure about that?" Jay inquired with a smirk as he picked up his drink to sip.

"No, Fred. My friend is really pretty. Her name is Ebony. She's a sweetheart. Believe me, I would not hook her up with just anyone. She needs someone who is loyal and caring. She's done with busters. You seem like a respectable guy, so I think y'all would look cute together."

"Do you have a picture of her?" I asked on Fred's behalf.

"I actually do." Wanda took out her phone, found a picture, and gave her phone to me.

I looked closely. "Oh, she is fine! Fred, she's a winner man," I said with a thumbs up.

Jay snatched the phone from me. "Let me see." He looked closely at the picture. "Oh hell nah! Forget Fred, Wanda you need to hook me up with Ebony! She looks too good for Fred."

Wanda snatched the phone from Jay. "Nope! I wouldn't dare let you get close to her. You don't deserve her. And she's humble; it's not all about looks with her. If you have a good heart, she'll talk to you," Wanda told him as she handed the phone to Fred.

"Yeah, she looks really good. She actually looks better than Michelle."

"I'll put in a good word for you," Wanda said, smiling.

159

I patted Fred on the back. "See. I told you your time is coming,"

"Fred can't handle a woman like that." Jay was pushing it.

Fred frowned and popped out of his chair. "I'm going to head out. I'm getting tired."

"Wait, what? You're leaving?" I asked.

"I'm out. I'll see y'all later," Fred stated, walking off.

"What's his problem?" Wanda asked, looking at me.

I looked at Jay. "See what you did? Come on man!"

"He'll be fine! He needs to get out of his feelings; he's so sensitive."

I shifted my seat towards Wanda. "Now Wanda, since you're a matchmaker tonight and you're giving all of this valuable relationship advice, I'm curious to know, how's your love life?"

"Why do you ask?" she replied.

"Ummm, no reason, is that a bad thing to ask?" I rebutted.

Wanda took a moment to answer. "Well, since you asked, I'm not into men anymore," she said Wanda taking a sip.

Jay and I looked at each other, then looked back at Wanda.

"You don't like men? As in you like women now?" I asked.

"I'm just living. Trying different things, that's all."

"What made you go gay?" Jay asked rudely.

"Men like you," Wanda replied, pointing at him.

"Seriously?" I asked.

"I just wasn't happy with men. Over and over, I've been disappointed. They've broken me down to this point. So I decided to just be free."

"You just wasn't getting no dick, that's all!"

"Shut up!" I blurted to Jay. "Wanda, that can't be it. Men aren't that bad. Are they?"

"Honestly, Terrance, I don't want to talk about it."

"Wait, one last thing!" Jay yelled.

"What?" Wanda rolled her eyes.

Jay leaned in. "If you have some gay girl friends that are bad, do you think they'll be interested in a ménage à trois with me?" Jay asked, winking.

Wanda shook her head. "Never in a million years. Bye, Terrance, I'm going home," she said as she grabbed her coat and walked out the door.

"Looks like we're making everybody mad tonight," I said.

"Hope she didn't think I was talking about a ménage à trois with her. I was talking about two of her friends. I don't want her ass," Jay said, sipping his drink.

"You know you have issues right?"

"I just say what comes to mind brother."

"But seriously though, take it easy on Fred man. You know that he's sensitive. Don't be surprised if he flips on you one day and tries to swing at you. I can't be the mediator all the time, everyone has their tipping point."

"Fred knows he's chubby and ugly. What's the use of babying him? He has no chance with that chick, Terrance! Be honest with yourself. Be honest with him. He's better off chasing Michelle. He's going to get his feelings hurt again. Watch."

"If that's the case, then let it happen on its own. Stop making him feel like shit before he even meets the girl. Confidence is everything. You know he needs it. He needs that support from us."

"Well you're going to have to give it to him. I can't do that. I can only be brutally honest, or else I'll just have to shut up."

"Okay. I'll just have to remind you to shut up then," I said.

Fred's Residence

The next morning Fred slept in. Saturday was his rest day. He woke up at 12:00 p.m. while wiping the cold out of his eyes. Fred got up and took his phone off the charger and saw that he had two text messages. Rubbing his eyes again, he had to squint to make sure he wasn't seeing things. The messages were from unsaved numbers at 9:35 a.m. and 9:45 a.m.

Fred, this is Wanda. I told Ebony about you. I gave her your number. She should be hitting you up. I put in a good word for you so don't let me down. :)

Hey Fred, this is Ebony Wanda's friend. How are you?

While wondering what to reply he was mad that he didn't hear his phone ring while asleep. The text was sent two hours ago. He pictured her sitting there and waiting to respond, so he decided to call.

"Hello," a woman answered.

"Yes, may I speak to Ebony?"

161

"This is Ebony."

"Ebony, this is Fred. I apologize for not responding to your text message. I didn't hear my phone."

"No need to apologize, I understand. How are you?"

"I'm doing well. I can't complain. How about you?"

"I'm fine. Just leaving my aunt's house."

There was a slight pause in conversation. Fred was stuck. He had no idea what to say next. He really had no real objective on why he called her.

"Did I call you at a bad time?"

"Not at all."

"Okay. What do you have planned today?"

"Nothing really, a couple of errands and that's all. Why do you ask?"

"Well, if you're free sometime today, maybe we can meet up to speak in person."

"That sounds good to me. Where and what time?"

"Good question. I'll get back with you on the place. But how about 7 p.m. for the time?"

Ebony giggled. "Okay. Just let me know."

Fred hung up and did a little shuffle dance. While he danced, he picked up his phone to send her a text.

Do you like The Cheesecake Factory?

*OMG! Are you kidding?! That's my favorite restaurant! LOL. I would love that! ^_^*

Great! See you then!

Fred did the same shuffle dance he had done before and went into the bathroom to face the mirror. He saw that he was overdue for a haircut. Looking down at the bathroom counter, he realized that his cologne bottles were empty. Immediately, Fred hopped in the car and headed to Lenox Square Mall to buy some Kenneth Cole cologne. He stopped by Macy's and bought a nice suit as well. After the mall trip, he went to get a haircut. He spent $650 in four hours.

It was already 5:30 p.m. when Fred started getting dressed. The date had been on his mind all day. Fred saved a list of talking points in his

162

phone so that he wouldn't run out of things to say. He wanted to be as prepared as possible.

Fred got to The Cheesecake Factory at 6:35 p.m. to ensure that he would arrive earlier than Ebony. It was just him and a few others in the waiting area. After a couple of minutes, he started sweating bullets. His body felt moist because of his three-piece suit. He grabbed a menu off the host stand and began to fan himself. Fred then got up and went to the bathroom to grab some paper towels from the dispenser. He stood in front of the mirror. There were beads of water dripping from his forehead. He wiped his forehead and the back of his neck. Afterwards, he stayed in front of the mirror to double-check himself. Satisfied with what he saw, he went back to the waiting area.

It was 7:02 p.m. when Ebony walked in. She had on a tight red dress. Fred smiled as he saw her. She was dark-skinned with long black hair and voluptuous. Fred stood up and greeted her.

"Ebony?"

"Hey Fred! Nice to meet you!" she said, holding her hand out.

They shook hands. The greeters then came over and guided both of them to their table. They both sat down and looked over the menu for a couple minutes, then they ordered. The waitress came back with their drinks and took the menus.

"So, what do you like to do in your spare time?" Fred asked.

"I'm a very simple girl. I just like to read, shop a little, and watch Netflix. How about you?"

"Um, I'm simple too. I don't do much. Just hang with my friends here and there."

"Okay. Yeah, Wanda told me that you were a pretty cool guy. That says a lot because she hates men now."

"Really? Hope they were positive things. What did she tell you?"

"She just said that you were a bit different from others. She said you very respectful and you didn't see women as a piece of meat like others do. She said you were a good guy."

"I try. What do you look for in men?"

Ebony sighed. "Well, I used to be all about a guy being tall dark, handsome, with a nice smile, but those were just physical attributes that

163

didn't matter in the long haul. I got my heart broken so many times. So now, I think my new preference is a guy with a great heart, that is loyal, trustworthy, caring, and that can make me happy. That's it."

Fred chuckled. "Heart broken? Is that what happened with your last boyfriend?"

Ebony rolled her eyes and shook her head. "My last guy was the biggest liar. He had so many side chicks that I couldn't count them on two hands. But the worst part of it was that I put up with it for the longest. I ignored it and played the fool. When I was confronted by one of his side chicks at the gas station, that's when I became fed up."

"Confronted? I'm scared to ask, but what did she say?"

"Oh she was very nice. She just told me that my boyfriend was cheating on me with her. And she said that she stopped talking to him because she found out that he was messing with another chick that I didn't know about. She showed me pictures for proof."

"Ouch. Well, I'm sorry to hear that."

"Oh, I'm fine. I'm free now from the foolishness. You shouldn't be sorry because I'm here with you."

Fred smiled. "I guess so. Well as far as being loyal and all that stuff you said, that's never been a problem with me. If I'm with someone, I'm as loyal as can be. Not to sound cliché but that's just the truth."

"I hope so. You look like you're very sincere."

"It's just crazy how some women don't see that. They'd rather be with someone who treats them like crap. I understand that I'm a heavier guy, but for women to choose guys with a better body that doesn't even appreciate them like that; it just doesn't make sense. I love hard."

"You make a great point. You deserve a woman who appreciates that. Like I said, I look past the physical now; I used to be one of those girls."

They continued talking as they finished their meals. The waitress came to their table.

"How was everything?" she asked.

"It was amazing!" Fred exclaimed.

"I'm glad you enjoyed it. Will you all be having dessert tonight?"

Fred looked at Ebony. "No thank you. I am so full," she said, rubbing her stomach.

164

Fred looked back at the waitress. "You can bring the check."

"Everything on one ticket?" the waitress asked.

"Yes, all on one," Fred replied.

"I really enjoyed this, Fred. I'm glad Wanda introduced me to you."

"I enjoyed you too, Ebony. We have to hang out again soon. I love your conversation."

"Oh we definitely will," Ebony said, smiling.

Fred smiled back. The waitress came and dropped the ticket on the table. Fred picked it up and saw that the bill was $43.00. He reached into his right pocket to grab his wallet. It wasn't in that pocket. He switched and checked the left pocket. That pocket was empty too. He then checked every opening on his suit. He began sweating again.

"Ummm... I don't have my wallet."

"Uh oh. When was the last time you saw it?" Ebony asked as she started looking around as well.

"Uhhhh. I don't remember," Fred stated as he kept sweating and looking.

"If you can't find it, don't worry about it. I can pay," Ebony offered, reaching for her purse.

"No! I'm going to find it, maybe I left it in the car." Fred stood up.

"Fred, it's fine. Relax! I got it. You can pay for our next date," Ebony said laying her card on the ticket and winking.

Fred sighed. "Okay. I guess."

Ebony paid for the meals. Fred was livid, but didn't show it. They both walked out of the restaurant together and he walked her to her car.

"Man I still can't believe I can't find my wallet."

"I'm sure it's in your car or on your dresser somewhere. Don't worry about it."

They stopped at Ebony's car. Ebony turned and faced Fred.

"Well this was an amazing night, Fred. Thank you for everything!"

"No, thank you for coming. I really enjoyed you. Definitely keep in touch."

Ebony took a step towards Fred, grabbed his chin, and gave him a quick kiss on his lips. "I will!" Fred was shocked. Ebony got into her car and pulled off.

On the way to his car, Fred continued checking his pockets, still searching for his wallet. He opened the driver side door and got inside. He looked over and the wallet was right there in his face. Right there in the passenger's seat. He sat in the car and reflected on the date. He was relieved, but still disappointed. He decided to call Wanda, to let her know how the date went.

"Wanda. I like your friend!"

"Really?! I knew you would."

"Yep. She and I just went on a little dinner date together. The vibe was perfect."

"Yes, Fred. You know she already told me this. She really enjoyed it. You know us girls talk."

"Yep. She probably told you that I left my wallet, didn't she?"

"No, she didn't."

"Oh. Well Wanda, I was so embarrassed! That's a must that the guy should pay for the meal. I had lost my wallet, and she didn't even hesitate to take care of the bill. She was so cool about it. My old fiancé, Michelle, is the type that wouldn't even bring her wallet to dinner, let alone pay for anything."

"Ha! Ebony has her own money and plenty of it. Darling you would never have to worry about her doing something like that."

"Well, I thank you for introducing me to her. I can see already that she's a special girl. We'll see how all of this plays out. I will keep you updated on everything."

Fred was finally looking forward to waking up in the mornings. He had more of pep in his step. Ebony and Fred talked every day. He texted her phone every morning saying things like, *Good morning, beautiful.* She responded back with messages like, *Thank you handsome, hope you have a great day.* Every response from her warmed his heart. He loved the fact that she always responded to him. Sometimes when she didn't respond immediately he worried a little. However, even when it took a while, she apologized and stated her reason for not responding right away. It showed him that she cared, and to him that meant a lot.

Michelle, on the other hand, sometimes would never respond and pretend as if she didn't get the messages. He admitted that he would sweep

166

t under the table back then, but now he could see it clearly; it made more ense why she didn't. At night if he didn't get to talk to Ebony on the phone, he would always still text her good night. Sometimes, he would go through all of Ebony's pictures on Facebook and Instagram. For one, he wanted to learn more about her. He wanted to see her progression through life. He wanted to see her timeline, so he could get a mental picture of how she developed to become the woman she is now. His second reason for going through her pictures was simply to admire her beauty. It was fun wrapping his head around the fact that Ebony could possibly be his in the future. He even looked at the pictures that she had up with her ex-boyfriend. From what he saw, she didn't look happy.

He saw her smiles as if they were masks that served to cover her unhappiness. Fred believed that he was there to turn her smile into something genuine, something real; a smile that would last.

It had only been a little over a couple of weeks since Fred and Ebony had their first date, but to him, it felt like a lifetime. Fred decided that he was going to invite her over for dinner and a movie. At first he was a little hesitant about asking her to come over. He was worried that she would say no or just straight up decline the offer. He thought about Jay and how confident he was when it came to inviting women over. After that thought, he sent Ebony a text message and waited patiently.

Ebony, what are you doing later on tonight around 7? I was thinking that we could have a dinner and a movie night at my place.

I would love that! I don't have anything planned as of now. So you're going to cook for little ole me?

Of course I am. Plus, I owe you since you took care of the tab at The Cheesecake Factory.

Oh yeah! You do owe me :) Well I'll be there. Just text me your address whenever it gets closer to that time.

Ok.

As soon as he sent that last text, Fred got up and started cleaning. The vacuum vroomed across the carpet. His sink looked like a mountain full of dishes but he washed them all thoroughly. His bed was made as neatly as a hotel room's bed. He scrubbed down the bathroom and sprayed every bit of odor-eliminating fragrance he could find. After cleaning, he hopped in the car and went to Publix, gathering all of what he needed to make dinner.

It was 4:30 when he started cooking. Boyz II Men was playing on his laptop. He sang along to the song like he was a member of the group. The music reminded him of something important. He immediately picked up his phone to call Jay.

"Jay! You got a minute?"

"You sound excited. Yeah I'm chilling, what's going on?"

"So the chick Ebony is coming to my place for dinner and a movie. I got the dinner down pat, but I don't know what movie to show. I need something that's going to set the mood just right for... you know... a great night. I thought you'd be the right person to call for that."

"Word! You got her coming to your crib? You been putting in work huh? How'd you get her to come?"

Fred laughed. "Man we went out to eat, and since then, everything has been cool. We've been talking every day."

"Watch *The Notebook*! It's the perfect chick flick. It's a love story that'll have her in her feelings, and you'll probably be in your feelings too. She's going to be ready to do whatever. It's going to be easy to get in them drawers after that. If you can't get her naked after watching *The Notebook*, you ain't never going to be able to get her naked," Jay suggested.

Fred laughed. "Okay. Yeah, I never heard of that. But *The Notebook* it is."

"Aight, good luck man! I'm rooting for you."

It was 6:30 p.m. and the house was spotless. The food was prepared and the wine was chilled. Fred lit the candles and cued the movie up. He had been sipping on a little wine already. He was feeling good. Before Ebony appeared he bowed his head for a prayer.

God, I know this is a weird thing to pray about. But please let this night go well. Don't let me screw it up. I don't know if Ebony's the one for me, but if she is, the last thing I want is for me to screw up something good tonight. Let your will be done. Amen.

Ebony arrived at 7:06 p.m. He greeted her with a long hug at the door.

She looked around the apartment. "Look at you! You're fancy, huh? This is a nice set up! You did not have to do this," she said smiling.

Fred smiled back. "Whatever, you deserve it."

He led Ebony towards the counter where dinner was set up. He had the silverware placed around the plate like a five-star restaurant. They said their grace and started eating. They talked about the highlights of their week and sipped on wine while they ate.

"The food was amazing, Fred! You're a true chef. Who taught you how to cook like this?"

"Well, my mom and grandma were always in the kitchen cooking. Since I was the only child, I had no brothers and sisters to play with. So I would just sit in the kitchen and watch them. I was always the taste tester. They would give me a sample of everything, and I would tell them if it was good or not. Which pretty much explains why I ended up a little hefty."

"Well, your grandma and mama taught you well! I cleaned my plate!" Ebony said, pointing at her empty plate.

"I'm glad you liked it. I love cooking. This is where time stops for me, and the world seems simpler."

"But seriously Fred, have you ever considered pursuing a career as a chef? This meal was scary good."

Fred sighed. "I thought about it. But starting off, chefs don't make much. I guess I just never took the time to take it seriously. I've always been scared for my food to be judged. I'm so sensitive about my food. My specialty is soul food. But really, if you put a recipe in front of me, no matter what the dish, I can make magic. And I love learning and experimenting," he said chuckling.

"You need to share your talent with the world. Fred, that was hands down the best meal that I ever had. You need to seriously consider cooking as a career. Or at least a side hustle, especially if it's your passion," Ebony encouraged him.

"You're right. Cooking was always my escape from the real world. I have never told anyone this about me. But I love the fact that I can create something that will make someone feel good—from the time they smell it to the time it enters their mouth to the time that it hits their stomach and makes them satisfied. I remember envisioning myself as a famous chef

169

known for spreading love through my dishes. I envisioned having a white chef's hat on while I worked magic in a huge, clean kitchen. The customers at the restaurant would always ask to see the chef so that they could thank him for such a magnificent eating experience. That would be a dream come true. One day, I will look into getting back into the groove of cooking and taking it more serious."

"Promise me you will," Ebony said, grabbing Fred's hand and looking him in his eyes.

Fred smiled. "I promise."

Ebony smiled back. "Good! So what movie do you have me watching tonight?" Ebony inquired as she went to sit on the couch.

"We're watching *The Notebook*. Have you ever seen it?"

"No. I've actually never heard of it."

"Really? Me either. I guess I don't feel as bad now. My friend said it's a must-watch."

They both sat comfortably on the couch. Fred reached over to grab the bottle of wine. He filled both of their glasses up so that they could sip while watching the movie. Ebony sat in front of him, in between his legs. He was able to wrap his arms around her waist. Every time he inhaled, he smelled her sweet scent, savoring every breath. Fred hoped she liked his cologne as much as he liked her perfume. Sitting behind her and out of her sight, he looked up to the ceiling and silently said with his lips, *Thank You God.* He held her a little tighter.

They were well into the movie and Fred heard Ebony sniffle occasionally. He tried to make his sniffles as quiet as possible, but a tear or two did escape. The movie ended, and they wiped their faces. They looked at each other and laughed at the fact that they were both emotional.

"That movie was too much for me!" Ebony said, wiping her face and sniffling. "I'm all in my feelings."

Fred laughed. "I'm with you on that. It made a grown man cry. It's too powerful."

Fred got up and turned on his speaker. Boyz II Men played softly in the background again. Then he went back and sat back down in his position.

"That's that real love right there! These days y'all men don't love that hard," Ebony said.

"I need you to rephrase that. You mean the man in your past relationship didn't love hard," Fred corrected her.

Ebony laughed. "Touché. Yeah, he didn't."

"I don't know why though. Because, if I had you, I would love you so hard, I don't even know if you would be able to handle it," Fred exclaimed.

Ebony chuckled. "Oh really? Why do you think I wouldn't be able to handle it?" Ebony asked, looking at Fred squarely.

"Because you've never experienced a love like this one."

Ebony smirked, licked her lips, and continued looking Fred in the eyes. "A real woman could never have too much love. We're built for it."

The music continued softly in the background. The room was dim and the candles were still lit. Fred looked down at her moist lips. He leaned closer to her for a kiss. Ebony grabbed the side of his face and leaned in with her eyes closed. Slowly. Steadily. Fred pulled her closer and held her tight. He rubbed his hand around her body slowly. She was rubbing his back. They were both kissing as if they had something to prove, as if their desire for each other had to be released. After two minutes, they let go of each other.

"Wow! That was intense!" Ebony said, wiping her lips off.

"I'm sorry about that."

"No, you're good! It takes two to tango. I just had to stop before it went any further. That usually doesn't happen on the second date for me. We're just moving a little fast."

"I agree. I respect everything that you have to say. That was a bit fast. I'm willing to take it slow. I understand."

Ebony nodded. "I'm glad you understand. I can be weak at times so it wouldn't be a good idea for me to continue. I have to head out before I do something I will regret in the morning."

Fred nodded. "Got you."

Fred walked Ebony to her car and opened the door for her. They hugged, kissed again, and she got in and left. He went back inside. The music was still playing softly. He smiled and started doing a two-step to the beat while snapping his fingers. He licked his lips and could still taste

171

Ebony's sweet lip gloss. He took a deep breath and could smell her scent. Back to his room he went, and then sat on his bed. Fred sent Ebony a text, telling her to let him know when she got home safely, but he was asleep before she responded.

Fun Friday

This Fun Friday had a different feel for Fred. This time, Fred had something positive to bring to the table. No more sob stories. He had something to be jolly about, Ebony. Finally. He sat up straight. He was ready for any of Jay's slick comments that he may have about his love life. He welcomed them.

"Fred is the man," I said, patting him on the back. "I'm not going to lie, I thought that you would never get over Michelle, but you seem fine. Ebony seems like a good girl too."

"It wasn't about getting over Michelle. It was just about finding a woman worthy of my time. I needed a woman that I could connect with. I'm feeling her and she's feeling me. Everything seems so natural."

"So you ain't trying to tap that? She was at your crib late night and all y'all did was suck on each other's face all night? Didn't y'all watch *The Notebook*? That's an easy slam dunk into some ass," Jay said.

"Nope. I ain't trying to be like you man. I respect her and her body. I ain't trying to move too fast. It will happen when the time is right."

"That's a typical lame response that a virgin would give. See what I've learned is that you have to take advantage of every opportunity to tap that ass. Because you never know when you'll have another chance, but that's just me," Jay said, shrugging and taking a sip of his drink.

"That's why women don't respect you though, Jay. You just want to take, take, and take; but you never want to give. How about giving her the respect that she deserves? It's not all about you."

I laughed. "Let him know, Fred!"

"So Fred got game now? When the hell did this happen?" Jay asked.

"I just carry myself differently than you."

"You damn right! Because I would've came back telling y'all how I had that ass up in the air! We are two different people."

"We know that, Jay," I replied.

172

While looking at the bar, I did a double take. "Wait a minute... Speaking of the devil. The girl walking in looks just like your chick Ebony, Fred."

"That can't be Ebony because she's with a dude. Is that her?" Jay asked, looking at Fred.

Fred turned that way. He was squinting as if he couldn't see. He recognized that it was Ebony, with another man. He looked confused at first, then embarrassed. He began to sweat.

"Fred, is that Ebony?" I asked.

"Yep, it's her," Fred confirmed, turning back to face the table.

"Damn! So what the hell is she doing with another guy? Ain't y'all dating? " Jay asked.

"Let's not jump to conclusions. That might be her brother or something. Or he might be her gay friend. You never know. Plus, y'all aren't officially a couple anyway, right?" I asked.

Fred said nothing for a moment. He looked back in Ebony's direction then responded.

"I'm about to go speak to her really quick," Fred told us, getting out of his chair.

"You sure bro?" I asked.

"Yeah, I just want to speak." Fred looked towards Ebony and the man.

Jay looked over at Ebony and then back at Fred. "Don't be trying to start no trouble. If you do start trouble, don't get beat up."

Fred walked towards Ebony and the man as they took their seats in a booth in the corner of the restaurant. They sat with their heads down looking at their menus, not paying attention to their surroundings.

"What's up Ebony?" Fred stated.

Ebony looked up from her menu and her eyes got big. She looked to the man and then looked back at Fred. "Hey Fred! What's up?"

"I'm okay. Just came over to speak, to let you know that I saw you over here. Don't be rude, introduce me to your friend," Fred insisted, looking to the guy.

Ebony looked befuddled. "Ummm, sorry. Mark, this is my friend Fred. Fred, this is Mark."

"Nice to meet you," Mark said, holding his hand out.

173

Fred looked down at Mark's hand. Fred's hand didn't move from his side. He then looked at Mark and nodded. "Nice to meet you as well."

Mark chuckled as he pulled his hand back in, then he looked at Ebony. Ebony held her head down in embarrassment.

"Did you need anything brother?" Mark asked.

"Yeah, I want to speak with Ebony in private," Fred stated, looking at Ebony.

"Umm, well that's not going to happen," Mark replied.

"Fred, what are you doing here? Why are you interrupting our dinner?" Ebony asked.

"So, this is who you are, huh? Boy did you have me confused."

"What are you talking about, Fred? You and I are friends! I am not in a relationship with anyone," she said.

"So last week meant absolutely nothing to you?" Fred asked.

Ebony looked at Mark and looked back at Fred. "Fred we had dinner and we watched a movie. I appreciated every bit of it, but that night does not mean I am your property."

Fred chuckled and looked away. Then he looked back at Ebony. "So you mean to tell me that us cuddling and kissing meant nothing to you. Okay, I get the picture."

Ebony shook her head and covered her face with her hands.

Mark looked at Ebony and then looked at Fred. "What the hell is wrong with you? If the woman says that she is single, that means she is single. I don't care what y'all did last week. She is enjoying a night out with someone else. You're doing too much right now."

"Fred, first of all, I am so embarrassed. How dare you stand there and share my personal business with someone else! What I do behind closed doors is my business, and I trusted you to keep that between us. Thank God that it didn't go any further than just a kiss. Second of all, when I say that I am single, I mean it. That means that I can go out on dates with whomever the hell I want, whenever I want, wherever I want, without answering to anyone. I did not expect this from you at all."

"What part of that do you not understand?" Mark added, looking to Fred.

Fred looked at Ebony. "So this is what you want, huh? The funny thing is that this guy Mark is probably going to treat you just like your ex. I'm sure he doesn't give a damn about you either."

"Okay, Fred. Please leave our table before I call security and tell them you're harassing us. Better yet, I think we should go find somewhere else to eat Mark. Let's go." Ebony grabbed her clutch and walked past Fred. Mark stopped and looked back at him.

"The worst thing about this situation is that Ebony and I have been friends since middle school. I just invited her to dinner since I hadn't seen her in forever. It was nothing serious at all. But the fact that she knows what type of dude you really are now is serious, because you can kiss her goodbye. You fucked up this whole situation by yourself... big man," he said, as he looked Fred up and down while shaking his head and walking off.

Fred stood at the table even after they had left. The waitress walked up behind him. "Where did they go? What happened?"

"I scared them away," Fred said solemnly.

Fred turned around to return to our table. Jay held his head down; he had turned red trying to hold his laughter in. I was trying to remove the smirk off of my face from laughing at Jay's antics, not Fred. The fact that we were drinking made everything a joke, but I could tell that Fred was deeply disturbed. Fred pulled out the chair and sat down.

"You okay?" I asked.

"Yep, I'm fine." Fred picked up his drink and took a sip.

"So, are you going to tell us what happened?" Jay asked.

"There's nothing to talk about."

"See, I told y'all! Never trust these women! She ain't who you thought she was, is she?"

Fred shrugged.

"By the way, I know that dude she was with. I smashed his chick a while back. She used to always vent to me about how he was so full of shit. How ironic, such a small world," Jay said grinning and sipping his drink.

While we were talking I received a text message. "Ah, damn. Whatever you said Fred you pissed Wanda off. She just sent me a text. She said that Ebony called her and cussed her out. She said that Ebony is

175

so mad that she got a speeding ticket after leaving the restaurant. She wants me to tell you to lose Ebony's number immediately."

"Damn!" Jay said before he busted out laughing. "How did y'all break up before even getting together? That's brutal!"

I looked at Fred with a serious face. "Bruh what in the hell did you do?"

"I don't care about what she has to say. I don't give damn about any of them," Fred blurted angrily.

I nodded. "Okay, I'm just checking."

"As a matter of fact, I'm out of here man. I'll holla at y'all later."

"Ay man, don't get emotional on us! Let's laugh this thing off man!" Jay suggested.

"I'm out." Fred said while pulling his chair and walking away.

Jay replied, "Where you going man? You going to look for Ebony, she ain't coming back man!"

Fred turned around and walked towards Jay. I knew that he was going to try to charge him, so I quickly jumped up and got between the two of them, holding Fred back.

"Jay, today is not the day! I swear to God I will kill you! You keep fucking with me and I will kill you," Fred warned, pointing to Jay as I tried to hold him back.

"Fred! Stop it man! It's not that serious! All of this animosity is over a chick that you haven't even known for a month. Take it easy man!"

Fred stopped his pursuit of Jay and walked towards the exit. I turned to Jay.

"I told you that everybody has their tipping point. If you keep on picking on him then I'm going to let him loose on you. What do you have to say now?"

"That's exactly how someone acts when they don't get no pussy! Dry dick dudes always want to fight! If we found him a prostitute or something to get his dick wet, then he wouldn't be acting a fool like this," Jay said, drinking his drink.

"On that note, I'm going home too." I left Jay sitting there alone.

Chapter 19:
Like Father, Like Son

I was on the couch bored out of my mind. There was nothing to do; so I knew today would be a lazy day. My remote had my thumb hurting from flipping through all of the channels. There was nothing good to watch on television. I needed entertainment, so I grabbed my laptop and logged onto Facebook to see what everyone else was doing. I scrolled down my timeline and noticed a lot of old friends. It's so crazy how this social media stuff came pretty much out of nowhere. It was made for people that had nothing much to do. Because when I'm bored, I log on. Well it's made for nosy people too.

To me, social media is a good and a bad thing. Now, people pay more attention to other people's lives than their own. Sad reality. Now people want attention, love likes, and love to be mentioned. Some people won't admit that they need a certain amount of followers and friend requests to feel relevant and accepted. Now don't get me wrong, I understand it has its benefits. It gives everyone an equal platform to speak his or her mind, and to have a voice. We become aware of worldwide news, special causes, and join social movements that touch us. But a real movement requires more than just moving thumbs. It takes more than just a comment on a trending topic to have an impact. And to tell the truth, if we're really touched by something, we'd do more than tap our touch screens.

It baffles me. I don't know why, but hey, that's my generation. We are the Millennials, the same generation that expects a million dollars in a minute, with just the press of a button. Microwave mindsets expecting doors to be popped open prematurely, without putting the work in. No patience and we want instant gratification. We want things handed to us for free. We don't want to pay the price for what it takes to be great. We won't even pay attention.

Yeah, we may show up to class, but when the professor lectures no one listens. The professor takes attendance, but having us present doesn't mean he has our attention. Instead, heads are tilted down, focused more on reading text messages rather than textbooks. Face down always, but rarely acing a book. We know more apps, but less about applying ourselves for success. That's filling out an application for failure. But I'll stop my rant. I'm just as bad.

I had an unread message in my inbox from a profile that had no picture. A profile named Terry. *Who the hell is Terry? I don't know a Terry. It's probably spam.* I was hesitant to click at first, but I did anyway.

Hey son. I know it's been a while, but I would love to meet up with you. I know you're a busy man. Please let me know when you're free.

I clicked the log off button. It wasn't spam, but it was someone that I didn't know; my father. I hadn't seen or heard from him in 18 years. I didn't care to see him, because he didn't care about me. *He doesn't give a shit about me. We have nothing to talk about.* I don't hate my father; I just don't want anything to do with him. Just like he didn't want anything to do with me as a child. But I get it. I know that in order for my heart to be healed, I have to forgive him. I must move on from this cold heart that I have towards him. Maybe seeing him would warm my heart up. Maybe. I had a lot of questions to ask anyway, so many empty holes that needed to be filled. My father was a clouded memory that was hard to make out. No good memories. No bad memories. I just have faint memories of him appearing like a thief in the night, but disappearing just as quickly as he appeared. He'd leave nothing but a crying mother, and a few random size twelve socks lying around the house. I messaged him back.

I will be free Saturday morning at 10 a.m. Let's meet up at Taproom Coffee.

I got to Taproom Coffee at 9:55 a.m. It was empty. I was glad. I loved meeting new people, but waiting to see my father was the most uncomfortable thing that I could ever imagine. I was meeting up with the man who left my mother alone to raise a child by herself with no support. I was meeting the man who left my mother crying in the dark on so many nights. I was meeting the man who left a little boy to grow up with no man to look up to. I was finally meeting my father.

It was 10:03 a.m. when a dark-skinned man with a grey, clean-shaven beard walked into the café. He stood about 6'2" and had on an all-black baggy suit. The suit looked as if he'd slept in it, hopped out of bed and then left the house without ironing it. He had on a gold watch with three big shiny gold rings on three fingers. He was greeted at the door, pointed towards me and began walking my way. It was him. I cleared my throat and stood up from my chair. He walked towards me with a big smile. I was shocked, disgusted, and amazed at the same time. We had so many similarities that it scared me. I made sure that I didn't get emotional. We shook hands and hugged each other before we took our seats.

"Damn, son! I'm about to get emotional just looking at you! You are one handsome man!" Terry said, taking a seat.

I nodded. "Well, I get all my looks from my mama," I said jokingly.

Terry laughed. "Boy, you crazy! I wish I had a picture of myself when I was your age. You would be shocked."

I nodded. "I'm sure I would."

We continued our small talk. I explained my career, how successful I'd been and what I planned on doing in the future.

"Boy, you are a spitting image of me. You're handsome like me. You're smart like me. You're all about your business like me. How about the ladies? You holding your ground with them?"

"No comment," I replied.

Terry leaned forward. "C'mon, son. You can tell me. I'm your pops. Let me know."

"I did a little damage back in the day," I confessed.

"That's my boy!" Terry said, tapping me on my shoulder. "I knew you had it in you. Because I used to slay these women back in the day."

I picked up my cup of water and took a sip.

Terry stared at me with a grin. "I cannot explain how proud I am to call you my son. To see you running around in a pamper to seeing you now, it's just a dream come true."

I put my head down for a second then back up. "You could've seen way more if you were there."

Terry looked at me. "Pardon me, I didn't hear what you said."

"Where were you? When I did all of this growing, what were you doing?"

"You have every right to ask me that... Me and your mother never were able to work things out."

"So, she was stopping you from being in my life? Did she not want you near me or something?"

"Not necessarily, son. I was just going through a lot at that time."

"Going through a lot of women?"

"Son, please hear me out first."

"Terry, answer this question: Did you love my mother?"

"Excuse me?"

"I have a better question. Did you love me or my mother?"

"Absolutely! I sure did."

"So why didn't you ever show up to tell me that you loved me. Why did you never reach out to help my mother? Why didn't I ever hear you say that you loved me out of your own mouth?"

"I'm telling you now, son. I love you, Terrance."

"I lived my whole life wondering why you didn't want me. I asked my mama that question all the time. I had to learn how to be a man on my own. My mama couldn't teach me that. Do you know that you're a stranger to me, Terry?"

"I know that, Terrance. That's why I'm here now. I'm trying to strengthen our relationship right now."

"You made my mama cry. You left my mama to struggle. You left me hanging. What if I don't want to be friends with you, Terry?"

"I want you to forgive me. Your granddaddy did the same thing to me. I never knew my father nor did I meet him. I didn't know any better at the time. Can you forgive me, Terrance?"

"I forgive you. I'm forgiving you for myself, but don't use that excuse about your father. Because you're the reason why I respect women now. It took me a while to learn a woman's value, but when I felt like I was turning into a spitting image of you, I began to change. I will never leave a woman to raise a child by herself knowing that I'm willing and able to help her, nor will I ever leave my seed feeling like they are not loved by their father. I'm determined to be better than you."

Terry nodded. "Sorry, son."

"I know. Believe me, I know. I knew you were sorry a long time ago. A sorry excuse for a father."

Terry sat silently for a second. "So are you done, son? Are you done venting?"

I nodded. "Yep, I got my 25 years of frustration out."

"Okay. Well it was nice seeing you. Thank you. I enjoyed our time together," Terry said as he got up to leave.

"Likewise."

I watched Terry get up out of his seat and walk out the door. He didn't even look back. It was a walk of shame. He should be ashamed of himself, not me. I sat there. Maybe I said too much for him to handle. Oh well. Words flowed from my mouth like a pipe that bursts from too much pressure. He couldn't handle the pressure. It was an overflow. A flood. He was chest deep but he couldn't swim. There wasn't a life jacket to save him from my tsunami of frustration. He wasn't ready for it. There was no way that I could keep my mouth shut about how I truly felt. It's hard to heal open wounds that have been open for so long. Trying to cover them up won't do much. What did he expect? I forgave him, and that was enough for me. It's not like I needed him in my life anyway. He never needed me. He never wanted me. It was time to taste his own medicine.

Chapter 20:

Oven-Baked Goodies

It was another couch potato day. I was watching some reality show on cable. I always wondered how someone could actually be into this reality TV stuff. If someone is surrounded by a camera crew getting their makeup done, and doing multiple shots of one scene, that's not reality. If cameras surrounded me and I knew millions of people were watching, I'd be on my best behavior. But for the most part, people on these shows were the opposite; they were on their worst behavior. That's always been interesting to me.

My phone started ringing. I looked over and noticed Sarah was calling. *What in the hell does she want?* I ignored it. My eyes went back on the reality TV show, but my phone went off again. This time it was a text message. I looked over again and it read: *Call me ASAP.* My stomach dropped. *What now? Damn!* I called her back.

"Terrance?"

"Yes, Sarah."

"Are you busy?"

"Um, no. What do you need?"

Sarah cleared her throat. "You might be disappointed with what I'm about to tell you, but it's very important."

"What could that possibly be?"

"I'm pregnant, Terrance," Sarah said softly.

It felt as if my heart dropped to my stomach.

"Pregnant from who?" I asked.

"Hello! Who do you think?" she replied.

"How could that possibly be? We only had sex two times Sarah. And I could've sworn I used a condom both times," I replied.

"Terrance you were drunk. You had no idea what you were doing that night."

183

I took a deep breath. "Sarah, I'm not the only person you had sex with, why are you calling me?"

"Terrance, you don't know what I do! You think I just go around and open my legs to anyone? You're the only person I've had sex with recently. Before you, I had been celibate for a year," Sarah explained.

"Sarah... Please don't lie to me. If this is some type of joke, I promise you I don't play games like this."

"Terrance! Why would I play a game with you? I am pregnant!"

I tossed the phone on the bed as I paced back and forth. I could still hear her talking. Her voice was cracking up like she was worried and about to panic. *This shit can't be happening to me right now*, I thought. I reached over and picked the phone back up. "Okay. Okay. Okay. Calm down. So what are you going to do about it?"

"I've been in this position before in high school. I told myself that I would never have an abortion again."

"So what does that mean?" I asked.

"I'm keeping it, Terrance! Don't act stupid!"

I was silent for a second, still trying to collect my thoughts. My mind was all over the place.

"Okay. Sarah, can you please give me some time to get my mind together? This is all a blur right now. I promise I'll give you call back soon."

"You better."

I hung up and my head started spinning. It felt like I was about to throw up. Inhale. Exhale. I was trying to calm my nerves. I was about to lose it. I had to call the only person that could make me feel better. The only person that could bring some sense to this situation. I couldn't sit down. I just kept pacing back and forth around my house.

"Fred!" I yelled.

"What's up?"

"I got a problem. I got a huge problem!"

"What happened now?"

"You remember that one night stand with that girl; the night I went out to vent with Jay?"

184

"Yeah, why?"

"The girl's name is Sarah, and she just called me and said that she's pregnant!"

"What?"

"Yes, Fred! Pregnant!"

"Do you think it's yours?"

"Hell no! That's the point! I feel like she's lying on me!"

"Okay. Calm down. Let's figure this out."

"Fred, what if she's right? Then Cindy would leave me for sure!"

"Let's not jump to conclusions. All you have to do is ask her to take a DNA test."

"You're right. She just needs to take the test. Then I'll be off the hook."

"Yep. So next time you talk to her, let her know."

"What if she wants to take me on Maury or something? This chick is a drama fanatic," I said.

"Shut the hell up, Terrance. You're talking reckless now."

"I wouldn't put it past this chick, she's crazy and loves attention."

"Well you'll just learn not to stick your penis in everything, won't you?"

"Damn! I have to call Jay. I know he's going to clown the hell out me for this."

"At least he'll make you feel better by making you laugh."

"Bye, man."

I was still pacing as I dialed Jay's number. Only God knew what Jay would have to say about it. He can help a situation, but he can damn sure hurt one too. But at this point, I just needed some advice. I needed something.

"Jay, we need to talk man," I said.

"Wait! Wait! Before you speak, I want to confess something," he said.

"What?"

"I know what you want to talk about. That's why I need to confess."

"Ummm, okay speak."

"Me and Sarah messed around."

185

I paused. "Wait, come again?!"

"I'm sorry! We only did it once! I swear, I saw her at the club one month or so ago, and I talked her into coming over to my place. I told her that I wouldn't tell you and that you didn't care."

"No, I don't care about all that Jay! I'm confused because Sarah just called me and said that she was pregnant with my baby!"

"Stop lying!" yelled Jay.

"I swear to God! She told me that I was the only one that she had had sex with since then."

"Ah hell naw! That bitch is crazy!" Jay exclaimed.

"Tell me about it! She's a stone cold liar!"

"So what are we going to do? I'm scared, Terrance!"

"I don't know. She said that I was so drunk that I didn't use a condom. Can you believe that? What about you?"

"You know I never wear condoms!" Jay yelled.

"Ah, man I forgot. This is unbelievable!"

"What if she's pregnant with your baby, Terrance? And she wants to keep it?"

"Then I'm going to take care of the baby," I rebutted.

"What? You're not going to at least try to make her get an abortion?"

"She doesn't want to get one, she already told me. And I wouldn't put that on any woman. Their bodies are sacred and that's not my decision to make."

"You're insane! How are you okay with having a hoe as your baby's mother?"

"Because if I helped to make it, then I can help to raise it. Yeah, I messed up, but that's my fault just as much as it's hers."

"Well if that's my baby, I'm denying it to the day I die! Or I'm going to trick her into getting an abortion. There's no way that girl is having my baby, Terrance."

"Real men take care of their business. Real men take responsibility for their actions. I wouldn't dare try to leave a baby that I made without a father. Nor would I leave a woman to bear that responsibility to raise a child by herself. I don't care how much I don't like the baby's mama."

"Okay. Whatever you say, Terrance."

"I'm going to call her to get to the bottom of this."

"Let's call her on three-way," Jay suggested.

"Let's not be childish, Jay."

"Come on! I want to hear her lie!"

"Okay, just please don't say anything. Mute your phone."

"Okay. Hurry up and call."

The phone rang and Sarah picked up immediately.

"Hello."

"Sarah," I said.

"Yes?"

"So I'm still trying to cope with the fact that you might be pregnant with my baby. Are you sure that it was only me that you had sex with?"

"Yes, Terrance! How many times do I have to tell you?"

"You're a damn lie!" Jay interrupted.

"Who was that?"

"It's Jay! Surprise, surprise!"

"Why would you lie to me, Sarah? Why didn't you tell the truth?"

"I did not have sex with Jay's annoying ass!" she yelled.

"Say you swear to God you didn't have sex with me, Sarah?"

The line was quiet.

"I told you she was a liar, Terrance!"

"Sarah, why couldn't you just tell me the truth?" I asked.

"Because I regret ever having sex with him. It was a mistake. He's an asshole and I hate him. Plus, I would never want him to be my baby's father. Ever."

"Oh believe me! I would never want to be your baby daddy anyway. Never in a million years! I would rather fall off a skyscraper than give you a baby. You're a slut!" Jay insulted her.

"Shut up, Jay! Shut up! Hang up the phone, man, right now!" I yelled.

"Okay, I will. I just can't believe her crazy ass is trying to plant a baby on you, Terrance! Don't let her have that baby! She's trying to ruin your life!"

"You're a sorry excuse for a man and I have something for your ass soon! I hate you! And if it is yours, I will contemplate getting an abortion!" Sarah said right before hanging up.

"Bye! Stupid hoe!" Jay screamed.

187

"Jay, listen to me!" I said, trying to silence him. "Don't ever disrespect a woman like that! What's wrong with you?"

"Are you serious? Are you really sticking up for the crazy bitch? She is bipolar!"

"I don't care how crazy she is. Have some respect for her and don't call her out of her name like that. That's someone's sister, someone's aunt, and someone's future mother. No one deserves to be treated like that. You pretty much embarrassed me just now, and that's not how I operate," I rebutted.

"I forgot you're sensitive as hell. I'm sure she'll be okay; I'll call and apologize."

"Call me whatever you want. Just don't ever talk to a woman like that again in front of me."

The Sarah situation was bad. I had no idea how it would play out. Either way, I just prayed that it wouldn't ruin my future if she were going to have a baby from me. And if that was the case, I might as well just kiss my relationship with Cindy goodbye.

Chapter 21: Matthew 7

I never got off work early. Today was different. We were sent home early because the power went out in our building. So of course, I was going to enjoy the free time. I usually got off work at 5:30 p.m. and it was only 3:00 p.m. Cindy got home around 6:15 p.m., but she gave me a spare key, so I decided to surprise her when she got off.

I drove to her house and let myself in. I looked around at the empty mansion. *Damn, this girl is amazing.* I sat on the couch, grabbed the remote and turned to ESPN. Her 70-inch TV looked way better than my little ole screen back at my place.

I was surprised. Cindy didn't get home until 8:05 p.m. I even had time to take a short nap on the couch in the meantime. The keys jingled outside the front door. I sat up and fixed myself.

"Hey, Queen." I greeted Cindy as she opened the door.

"Hey, honey," she said, closing the door behind her. "What made you come here?"

"Well, I had gotten off work early so I decided to just slide over here."

"What time did you get off?"

"Around 3 o'clock, and right after I just headed over here," I said, with my eyes on the television.

"Oh really, what are you watching?" Cindy asked as she put her coat on the rack to the right.

"ESPN, I don't know if you know Stephen A. Smith, but he is hilarious," I said, pointing at the television with the remote.

"Nope. I don't know him. So tell me this, what have you done today to get you closer to your goal of being CFO?"

"What do you mean?"

"How have you gotten better today?"

"Ummm... I mean I handled business at work as usual."

"See that's your problem, Terrance! You just want to be average. You're sitting here on your ass not doing anything. I don't care if you got off work early. Find some way to be productive! Do something to get you closer to that CFO position that you supposedly want."

"You're right," I said, muting the television.

"You want to know the difference between me and you, Terrance? I don't watch much TV. I don't have time to watch someone else; I don't care who they are. I'm not going to waste my time watching someone else. My life is way too demanding for that. I work when everyone else is relaxing."

"I'm sorry. I'll do better."

"No, I don't want to hear it. Show me through actions, not words. Black people have to work three times as hard to get where they want to go!"

I was embarrassed and shocked. I didn't know if she wanted me to stay or leave.

I turned off the television. "Okay, I'm headed home. I'll talk to you later."

"Okay," Cindy responded as she started walking up the stairs.

I walked out the house and closed the door behind me softly. I didn't want her angrier than she already was. I called Jay to vent.

"Brother, guess what just happened."

"What's up?"

"It's about Cindy."

"Oh shit, what happened?"

"Okay. Long story short, I was at her house when she got off from work watching television in her living room, and she pretty much made me feel like a peasant."

"Uh oh. What did she say?"

"She asked me what I had done today to be productive. My answer wasn't good enough, so she basically told me that I needed to get my ass up and be productive. She told me that she doesn't watch television and that if I'm serious about my dreams, I wouldn't either."

Jay was silent. Then he busted out with laughter. "Are you serious? I have never heard anything like this!"

"I don't know how to feel. I don't know if I felt intimidated, insulted or turned on by it all. I'm still in shock."

"I mean, is she wrong? No! Get your ass up and be productive! You're dealing with a woman that ain't about any bullshit! She's powerful for a reason. This is what you asked for; get used to it."

"You're right. I just wasn't expecting that from her. I can't get mad at her for pushing me to be great."

The phone beeped. I looked and saw that Cindy was calling me on the other line.

"Jay, I'm going to have to call you back. This is her on the other line."

I clicked over.

"Hello."

"Hey. I want to apologize for what I said. I had a long day at work. There's just a lot on my mind."

I chuckled. "Sweetheart, no need to apologize for being honest. You were right. If I'm serious about dream chasing, I shouldn't be wasting time like that. I'm going to go home and do more research and get ahead for work."

"I just operate differently. I want the best for you, that's all. I told you that I'm a handful," Cindy explained.

"You're a handful of great things that I'm willing to deal with," I rebutted.

Cindy laughed. "Okay. Well, don't be afraid to come back soon. Didn't mean to scare you away."

"I'll be okay."

One Month Later

My phone went off. A reminder popped up from my calendar. It was a notification. *Damn. I can't believe I almost forgot Jay's birthday.* I had to do something for him, but I had absolutely nothing planned. What would Jay want to do for his birthday? Ha! I had an idea. I called him immediately.

"Happy birthday, fool!" I yelled.

"Much love. I thought you forgot. I'm getting old!"

"What you got planned tonight?"

"Actually, nothing. Why?"

191

"I'm taking you to the strip club. My treat."

"Ha! You know me too well! I'm getting dressed now."

Follies, Atlanta GA

I'm not a strip club person. Some people love it, but it's not my cup of tea. Guys that are thirsty can't live without it. To me, it's just a tease. These chicks don't give a damn about what's in our pants; all they care about is what is in our pockets. Nonetheless, today was not about me; it was about Jay. I brought a couple hundred ones to make sure that my best friend had a good time.

I picked up Jay and we were on our way to this strip club called Follies. We got there and we both sat at a table directly in front of the stage. Marijuana smoke filled the whole club. Girls had only G-strings or with dollars surrounding them. Some had dollar bills in their G-strings, some held their money in their hand. Most of the girls had multiple tattoos and piercings, but they were very attractive. Some guys moved like vultures, congregating and following chicks as they walked by, holding up, waving, and throwing dollar bills as the women came out. It was like they'd never seen a chick naked. Maybe they hadn't. Other guys were cool, calm, and collected. They barely acknowledged the girls, even though they would pull out a couple of dollar bills to hand to a stripper from time to time.

While sitting down, Jay panned the room. "Man I love me some strippers! Damn these girls are bad! Some of them are bad enough to be my girlfriend."

I tapped him. "I'm sure they don't want that, they just want you to throw these ones; they got babies at home to feed."

"Speaking of babies! Have you heard from Sarah?" Jay asked.

"Heavens no! Why do you ask?"

"Man the chick has been blowing me up lately. She's still trying to plant this baby on me. She's saying that she's positive it's mine now. I'm not trying to hear that bullshit!"

"Jay, if it is, you have to handle your business."

"Man it's not mine! She is so crazy! She's threatening me saying that she's going to whoop my ass and she's going send this child support attorney to take everything I got."

"So what are you going to do?" I asked.

"I don't know, Terrance. I don't know. I'm hoping for the best but preparing for the worst. But enough about Sarah, I hate her. Let's just enjoy my birthday," Jay said, looking back at the strippers.

I agreed and took a sip of my drink. The spotlight was center stage and Jay's attention was directed at the next girl coming on.

"Damn, this girl is bad," Jay said, staring.

I looked towards the stage and agreed. The girl's body was impeccable. She had on a red two-piece with 6-inch heels. Men moved closer to the stage and pulled out dollar bills. I looked closer. The chick looked familiar, very familiar. I knew her from somewhere.

"Wait a minute. I know that's not who I think it is," I said.

"You know her?" Jay asked, looking to Terrance.

"That's Latoya!"

"Who the hell is Latoya?"

"That's the chick that I was messing with back in college. Remember? Her text messages were the ones that Lisa found when she kicked me out."

"Damn! That's who you cheated on Lisa with?"

"Yeah, but it was when me and Lisa first made it official, like when I was still young and dumb. You know the story!"

"No, I'm saying, I see why! This girl is fine... look at her body!"

"That's not the point! I just can't believe she's a stripper now. Unbelievable."

"Well believe it! As a matter of fact, since you know her, call her over here and ask if I can get a discount on a dance," Jay said, with his eyes stuck on Latoya.

"No, man! I'm legit concerned about her. I mean she was actually a good student in college. She might've been a freak, but she was still a good student. What the hell happened?"

Jay rolled his eyes. "Ah shit! Here comes save-a-hoe Terrance. I thought you learned your lesson with Grace! Why can't you just sit here

193

and enjoy some ass shaking and titty bouncing with your best friend for his birthday?"

"Because I can see past the ass and titty shaking to see that something is going on with some of these girls deep down inside. Sometimes they can really be struggling to find themselves."

"Please, brother! You think too damn much! Have you ever heard of the naked hustle? Some people just have to survive by any means, Terrance. And some of these girls probably just like dancing for a living. You ever thought about that?"

"I get it. But I'm just going to go talk to her real quick," I said, rising from my seat.

"Don't be lame!" Jay yelled, placing his hand on my shoulder for me to stay seated. "Leave her alone. That's a grown ass woman."

"I'll be right back." I moved Jay's hand and walked off.

I was walking up and I saw that Latoya was on her way to the back dressing room. I then yelled over the music to get her attention.

"Latoya!" I yelled, walking behind her.

She turned around confused after recognizing me.

"Terrance? What are you doing in here?"

"I'm here for my friend's birthday. What are you doing in here?"

"Ummm, I work here," she said, rolling her eyes.

"Man I haven't seen you in forever! You look good!" I looked her up and down.

"I don't even know why I'm talking to you. Your little girlfriend Lisa tried to beat my ass over you a while back."

"Yeah, I heard about that. But I'm not with Lisa anymore unfortunately."

"That's sad to hear," Latoya said, folding her arms.

"But enough about me, Latoya, what's up with you? What's up with this?" I said looking her up and down again. "You know you can talk to me about anything."

Latoya sighed. "Come on, Terrance. What are you talking about? You're trying to give me a lecture while I'm working?"

"No, I'm not. I'm just inquiring about an old friend, that's all."

"Whatever, Terrance. It seems like you're being nosy and trying to judge me."

194

"Really, Latoya? Of course not! I just wanted to ask what made you choose this profession, that's all! Hell, I know you didn't go to school for this."

"Terrance, have your lights ever been cut off on you?"

"No, they haven't."

"Imagine coming home from looking for a job all day to find out that your lights were cut off. I have a two-year-old child, with a deadbeat father that I have to take care of. Imagine your refrigerator empty to the point where you don't even have spoiled food to throw away. I couldn't find a job. I went to school for Public Relations. And when I did have a job, I got laid off."

I nodded.

"I started dancing and everything went up from there. I was able to pay my bills on time. I was able to buy what I wanted. I don't have to work at a shitty job that doesn't want to pay me and that will fire me at the snap of a finger. I make more money in a week than some of y'all make in six months. And I'm happier than ever because I don't care what people like you have to say." Latoya shrugged.

I was silent.

"Is there anything else you need? I have to get to work."

"Latoya, I'm sorry, I wasn't judging you. It just surprised me to see you here. That's all. I didn't mean to offend you, but I respect you and I hope that you make enough money in here to quit this one-day and to build a business empire somewhere. Only because you're smart, talented, and I know there's more to you than the naked eye. No pun intended," I said with a smile and a wink.

Latoya smirked and shook her head. "That's the plan, Terrance, believe me. I'm 10 steps ahead of you."

"Good. See you at the top."

We both hugged, then I went back to my seat.

"What y'all talked about?" Jay asked. "She gon' bust it wide open for you?"

I laughed. "Nah man. I don't want that from her. I just wanted to make sure that she knew that she had more to offer to the world."

Jay looked at me with a side eye. "Why the hell did you tell her that? A dance from her would've been the perfect birthday present! Now I'm scared to ask because she's probably about to be all in her feelings. Thanks a lot, Terrance. By the way, who the hell do you think you are? Fake ass Dr. Phil."

I laughed and took a sip of my drink.

Chapter 22: Rocky

We hadn't had a Fun Friday in over a month. We'd cancelled for various reasons. Fred needed time to himself. For whatever reason, I don't know. I was busy with work and spending more quality time with Cindy. Jay was just out and about. I'm not sure what he had going on. We were past due for hanging out, so we had some catching up to do.

"Guys, I have to tell y'all about my new project!" Jay said excitedly.

"We're all ears," Fred replied.

"We haven't seen each other in a while so a lot has been happening. I'm one of the happiest men on earth right now," Jay continued, taking a sip.

"And why is this?" I said with a raised eyebrow.

"Well this may come by as a surprise. But I'm actually in a relationship now."

"What?" Fred exclaimed.

"It's not April first is it?!" I inquired.

"Nope. I'm serious," Jay confirmed, smiling.

"Wait, so how did this happen? Who is this special female kryptonite for you? Where did y'all meet?

"Well, long story short, about two months ago I'm in Trader Joes on aisle four. Briefly, I see a lady walk up to the right of me to get some frozen foods then walk away. I did a double take. I was like, wait a minute. She looks good, I mean really good. No, she was fine as shit! She had long black hair and she had a grey suit on as if she had just got off work. She had a light caramel skin complexion. When she was done shopping, I was done shopping. I followed her ass right to her car. I tried to get her number, but of course she rejected me. She told me her name was Sony. So I gave her my business card instead. And I told her to promise me that she would use it."

"So she hit you up after that?" I asked.

"Terrance, I swear to you, I had never hoped that a chick followed up before as bad as this time. I usually don't give a shit, but this time, it was

197

something special. I just couldn't put my finger on it. And surely enough, my prayers were answered. Two days later, she texted my phone."

"What is the world coming to? Jay has found someone worth settling down? Tell me more about this chick. She has to be special!"

"Well she's an attorney, her name is Sony Cox. She's been practicing for seven years now and she has her own practice. She's 30. No kids. She lives in Buckhead, in a nice ass Condo."

"And she's feeling you?" I asked.

"Man the first time we hooked up, we clicked. I mean she's so damn smart. She's funny as shit. We both speak our minds. She's like my second self, a female version of me. Man she is as real as they get."

"How's her sex game? I know that's important to you," Fred stated.

"I don't know yet. We haven't done anything yet. At first, I was mad that she wants to try the abstinence thing. Especially since she ain't no virgin. But in all honesty, I don't mind now. When I'm with her I'm usually realizing that sex isn't everything. She's my friend first. I tried once and she was agitated by it. So I just stopped. I'm not trying to mess this up. I do feel like I may have something that's worth keeping. But I know when we get to that point, Lord knows that I'm about to wear her ass out."

"So are you done? Like with all other chicks? Are you going to be a one woman man?" I asked.

Jay laughed. "Hell no! I'm still going to explore. Sony is just going to be my main chick. I still have to have my little side dishes here and there you know."

Fred laughed. "Be careful; karma is a bitch."

Jay snapped. "Shut up, Fred! I ain't doing nothing wrong, stupid. Shit, we ain't married."

Surprisingly, I caught a glance of Sarah across the room. Her belly stuck out like she had an inflated balloon in it. She then headed towards our direction.

"Ah shit. Jay, Look who came to visit," I said.

Jay and Fred looked around. Jay spotted Sarah.

"Damn! How did she find me?"

Sarah continued walking all the way up to our table.

198

"So you thought I wouldn't find you huh!" she said, pointing her finger in Jay's face.

"Please leave me alone before I call the police!"

"You won't answer my phone calls or my text messages! But you can take advantage of me and bust a nut in me on my birthday!"

"Take advantage of you? Bitch please! You knew exactly what you were doing! Don't try me!"

Sarah immediately turned around and swung at Jay twice, landing the first punch on his jaw and missing the second one. Jay's drink spilled on his lap. Fred grabbed Sarah and pulled her away from the table. Everyone in the building looked our way.

"We'll see who the bitch is when I sick these child support lawyers on your ass!" Sarah yelled as Fred let her go. She walked away.

"Go home, Sarah! Get out of here with that foolishness!" I screamed.

Jay stood up out of his chair and grabbed the napkins from the table to dry his lap.

"You alright?" I asked.

Jay looked up. "Am I alright? Hell no! I wish I could've slapped the shit out of her. But I can't because I would've gone to jail. Now I'm just sitting here embarrassed."

"How did she know you were here?" Fred asked.

"I don't know. But one thing I do know is that bitch punches like a man, damn!" Jay stated while massaging his jaw. Fred and I laughed.

"Well, at least Fred and I are not the only ones having women issues anymore," I said laughing.

"Enough with the jokes. Go get me some ice." Jay tried to stretch his jaw.

My pocket vibrated. It was my phone ringing.

"Hey baby." It was Cindy.

"What's up?"

"I want you to come to this gathering tonight with me."

I looked at my watch. "You and these social events! Can you give me about forty five minutes?"

"That's fine. And hey, I can't help that I'm an elitist in Atlanta. I get these invites because people want me at their events," Cindy bragged.

"I get it, sheesh," I said.

199

"You should be happy to attend these events. You get good exposure and you meet people with power and influence. Especially since you're trying to be an executive of your company. Get used to it."

"I am. I'll get dressed and I'll be at your place in forty five minutes."

"Well fellas, this has been an interesting night. I wish I could stay and fellowship with y'all, but I have to go somewhere with my woman," I said, getting up from the table.

"Your woman? Cindy?" Fred asked.

"Yeah, who else would it be?"

"I guess it just sounded weird when you said it. It didn't hit me yet that it's official. You really moved on."

"He sure did. He moved on to something better. He got over the past. Unlike you."

"You better shut the hell up before I call Sarah back," Fred threatened.

"See y'all later," I said as I walked out.

I was glad we picked that bar to hang out at. My house was right around the corner, so I was home in no time. I looked through my closet and threw on a grey fitted blazer and slacks. I looked good as I checked myself out in the mirror. I got in the car and headed to Cindy's. Once I finally arrived, I parked my car and walked up to her front door. Right before I got up close to it, Cindy opened it and came out. She had on a red dress with red lipstick. The dress looked like silk and hugged Cindy's hips and curves gently. She was perfect as always.

I stared as she walked up. "Damn I have to be the luckiest man on earth," I said, as I looked her up and down.

Cindy locked the front door and turned around. "Stop trying to flatter me, Terrance. You were talking like you didn't want to go to this event with me."

"My goodness, I didn't mean I didn't want to go, it just seems like you do a lot of these things. I'm willing to get used to it though. I apologize if it came out the wrong way."

"I'm over it. Don't worry about it," Cindy said walking to her car. She headed towards the passenger side of her Bentley.

"Where you going? You want me to drive your car or something?"

200

"Yep! I need you to drive. It doesn't look right with you in the passenger's seat. I'm supposed to be your date. Plus, you don't mind driving luxury, right?" Cindy asked.

"That's straight with me."

"Good! Here you go!" Cindy tossed me the keys.

We drove to the gathering. The parking lot was flooded with luxury cars. I parked next to a red Lamborghini and a black Maybach. I pulled the keys out of the ignition and turned to Cindy.

"Damn. It seems like the more I'm around you, the more I realize I need to get my shit together."

Cindy laughed. "It's okay baby. It's something you just have to get used to. It's a mindset. You'll be living like this soon if you're with me. Believe me. I still love you for you though, don't get it twisted."

"I hope so. But whose event is this anyway?"

"I believe it's the General Manager for the Atlanta Hawks' house."

I nodded. "Big time, huh? Do you know I'm a big fan of basketball? Maybe I can talk to him about making some changes on the roster so we can win some championships."

"Um, no. Please don't. No business. I'm sure he knows what he's doing," Cindy said with a smile.

"Come on, I was just playing. I would never critique someone on their job. I can't believe you took that statement serious."

"Well you never know. You represent me and I can't have you embarrassing me. I just have to make sure."

"Whatever, let's go."

We got out of the car and walked up to the entrance of the mansion. Our arms were locked together as we entered. I didn't mind it. I was confident that I was walking in that building with the most gorgeous, hardest working woman in our proximity. There was no doubt in my mind. Why be shy about it? Only a man that was ashamed of a woman wouldn't want to hold hands with her in public. I felt liberated walking in with Cindy.

Everyone's head turned. Everyone looked at Cindy first, then me, then back at Cindy. It was hilarious. The bright chandeliers sparkled down on us from the ceiling. The staircase looked like something that would only

201

appear in a magazine. If I knew no one was watching me, I would've taken pictures. It was amazing. This was the life that I deserved. Cindy and I walked over to the bar that was set up to our left.

"Can you get us both a cup of Remy Martin on the rocks please?" she asked.

"Coming right up," the bartender said, wiping off glasses and moving swiftly to fulfill the order.

"Was it me, or did it seem like everyone was looking at us?" I asked.

"Yes, everyone was looking. I have that effect on crowds sometimes you know," Cindy said, winking.

"Yeah, I see that," I said, looking around.

"But they know me. They were probably looking at you, trying to figure out who you were."

"What you trying to say Cindy?" I asked with a raised eyebrow.

"You probably took that the wrong way. Don't get defensive. I meant that to be with someone like me, you have to be a special person," Cindy explained. "They're trying to figure out what your x-factor is."

"Oh. I guess I don't have one," I said shrugging.

Cindy slightly hit me on the side of the arm. "Yes you do! You're the future Chief Financial Officer of your company. Right?"

"Oh yes! Yes, I am."

"Well act like it."

The bartender handed us our drinks. After a while, we walked away from each other. I wanted to explore a bit anyway. I loved the atmosphere. I shook hands and mingled with executives and business leaders that owned major businesses throughout Atlanta. These people were true power players. After a lot of mingling and eavesdropping on a couple of conversations that piqued my interest, I decided to rest my feet. I took a seat on a couch. *One day I'll have a life like this. I'll own a place like this. I'll have events of this stature and invite people like this.* As I fantasized, I saw Cindy walking around out of the corner of my eyes. I shouted her way.

"Cindy, you looking for me?" She walked my way.

"Baby, I've been looking all over for you! Everything okay?"

"I'm fine; I just sat down for a little bit. You needed me?" I asked, grabbing her hand gently looking up at her.

"Yes! You told me that you loved basketball right?"

"Yes, I did."

Cindy smiled. "Well I have a treat for you, come on." Cindy tried to pull me up from my seat.

"Wait, what is it?" I held back and tried to stay seated.

"I got someone that I want you to meet, a great friend of mine," Cindy said.

"I don't like surprises, but okay."

"Just come!"

"And be careful! I'm tipsy!" I said, agreeing to follow her.

Cindy held my hand and we weaved through multiple groups of people. We walked into another room that was quieter. The people in the room looked younger than all of the other guests. It looked like we belonged in there. A super tall, light-skinned gentleman stood taller than everyone in the room. He was turned the opposite way. The guy was conversing with two other women. I couldn't make out who he was from the back. I assumed he was a basketball player since he was so tall.

"Tory!" Cindy yelled as we finally approached him from the back.

The guy turned around. I instantly knew who it was. *Damn. Not him. Out of all people.*

"Terrance this is my good friend, Tory. Tory, this is my boyfriend, Terrance," Cindy said, looking at us both.

Tory stuck his hand out for me to shake. "Tory, Tory Bishop."

I was hesitant at first, but I put my hand out. "Nice to meet you Tory. I'm Terrance."

Cindy smiled. "Yeah Tory, Terrance says he loves basketball so I thought it would be a good idea to introduce you to him."

Tory looked at Cindy. "You assume that I like basketball, huh Cindy?" They both laughed.

"I mean since you're the leading scorer for the Atlanta Hawks, I would make a wild guess that you may like basketball a little."

Tory looked at me. "Cindy and I go way back, she's actually good friends with my big sister. We're like family."

203

Cindy nodded. "Yep! Well let me go speak to my boss really quick. I'll be right back." Cindy walked off.

My palms and armpits were sweating. I was so jittery and I had the cottonmouth. It was him. Tory Bishop was the basketball player that had the leaked sex tape with Lisa. I was standing in front of the only other man that had sex with my past fiancée. This was the guy who played a huge part in my separation from her. The guy that was responsible for a lot of my past hurt. My mind was racing. This wasn't just any race; it was a sprint. Scenes of Tory Bishop and Lisa having sex repeatedly flashed in my head like a movie trailer.

I envisioned Tory grabbing her waist. I pictured him putting his tongue and his dick inside her lips, both sets. My Lisa was being thrusted back and forth, like a rag doll. He was pleasing himself on her behalf, with her permission. *What should I do? What should I say?* I know it was the past, but I couldn't let the moment pass by without properly addressing Tory about his history with my Lisa.

"You enjoying yourself?" Tory asked.

"Ummm, yeah. Definitely a nice vibe."

"That's good man. Yeah, I see you got you a bad one there, huh?"

"Oh yeah. She's definitely a good girl."

"I agree," Tory said, taking a sip of his drink.

"What do you know about her? You got any history with Cindy?" I asked.

Tory laughed. "Oh no. She's good people. She's like family, seriously."

"Yeah, I had to ask man. You just never know with y'all superstars Y'all got women chasing after y'all daily."

Tory laughed. "No pressure. I would probably tell you if I did, I promise. Nothing like that."

I stood there silent for a second. *How can I ask about Lisa in the most appropriate way without coming off as rude or disrespectful? He probably can tell I'm uncomfortable by how much my forehead is sweating and how jittery I am.*

"Ay, Tory, do you by any chance remember someone named Lisa?"

Tory closed his eyes for a moment. "Hmmm. Lisa? I'm not sure."

"She's from Atlanta. She said that she knew you," I continued.

"I'm sorry man, I'm terrible with names. It's not ringing bells. What's her last name?"

"Smith. Lisa Smith," I continued, looking at Tory to follow his expressions.

Tory looked down as he tried to remember. "Lisa, Lisa Smith? From Atlanta? Ohhh! Lisa! Yeah, I remember exactly who she is. What about her?"

I figured that I needed to ask the right questions so that I could get an honest reaction from him. I probed him. "Ay bro, be totally honest with me. A good friend of mine is trying to see what's up with her? What do you think about her?"

Tory laughed. "She a cool girl. What he trying to do with that?"

"I don't know really, he's just asking about her."

"Oh okay. Well me personally, I wouldn't wife her."

"Oh really. Why is that?"

Tory shrugged his shoulder. "I was messing with shorty a little bit. She's bad, but she too emotional for me. And plus, just between me and you..." he leaned forward and whispered, "I hit that ass on the second time we hung out."

"Oh damn. So she was easy, huh?"

"I mean for me she was. I don't know what type of game your friend got. Hell he might have better luck than me."

"Wow."

Tory laughed. His tall frame leaned down closer to me so that others couldn't hear our conversation. "I know right! These hoes are easy. Then she was trying to catch feelings. I smash them and pass them." Tory patted me on the back. "No offense to Cindy though. You hold on to that. She's a keeper. She's wifey material."

I said nothing. I closed my eyes. *Stay calm. Stay calm. Keep your composure Terrance.*

My eyes opened. "Lisa Smith is my ex-fiancée," I said, looking at Tory.

Tory looked confused. "Wait, what? She was your fiancée?"

"Yep. She sure was," I confirmed with a straight face.

205

Tory paused. "Well damn! Sorry to hear that!"

"It's fine man. I'm not with her anymore obviously."

"That's right! You got Cindy Baker now. The rest of these hoes ain't no good. Believe me."

"Lisa wasn't a hoe, brother," I said.

Tory chuckled, "Sorry, brother. Didn't mean to touch a nerve. Can I just say that she was adventurous in bed?"

Frames of Tory going in between Lisa's legs played in my head again. Her naked. Him naked. Their bodies intertwined and tangled under the covers going up and down, in and out, back and forth like a crazy rollercoaster ride at Six Flags. Her screaming out his name instead of mine. I was speechless. Nothing came out of my mouth. I saw one color and it was red. My hands were balled up and I lost it. I turned and shoved Tory. His eyes were wide in surprise as he stumbled and fell down, crashing on a vase. The vase shattered. Pieces of glass and sound waves of the crash rippled throughout the room. Men gasped; women screamed. Cindy immediately ran towards me. She looked confused and terrified. I avoided looking her in the eyes as I stood with my eyes locked on Tory, ready for him to get up and retaliate. Two men gathered around Tory to make sure he didn't respond to my ignorance.

"What's your problem? Are you serious, Terrance?" Cindy asked, holding me and trying to look me in the eye.

"Let's just leave, Cindy! I apologize. Let's just leave," I said walking away and avoiding eye contact.

Tory gathered himself and stood up. "What you mad for nigga? It ain't my fault you can't control your bitch! Cindy, he's just mad because his ex-fiancée was too good in bed for him to handle. She needed me to test it out for him too," Tory said with a wink.

I saw red again and I turned around. I was ready to charge and spear him like a pissed-off linebacker. I was going to kill him. Cindy stood in front of me and blocked me. She was petite, but she shoved me so hard that I jolted back.

She yelled, "Terrance! Stop it! Go to the car! Leave!" She pointed towards the exit. I finally looked in her eyes. They were watery as if she was inches away from breaking down. Seeing her frustrated because of me did something to me. I gained sense again. I immediately stopped and

egan walking towards the exit. I heard Tory still shouting from behind
ne.

"You better be glad I can't touch you! I respect this house too much to
vhoop your ass in front of all these people. I got too much to lose, and you
in't got shit to lose. You broke ass buster! You want my life so bad but
ou can't have it! You a low life! You better walk away!" Tory yelled, as
he men continued to restrain him trying to calm him down.

I was power walking out of there. I wanted to be gone as quickly as
ossible. Cindy was running behind me, her high heels clicking the floor
apidly trying to keep up with my pace. Everyone was looking at me
onfused, wondering who invited me. What made me angry? Who the hell
was? They looked at me as if I didn't belong. I power walked until I got
o the car and went straight to the driver's side.

"Terrance! Give me my keys! You are not driving my car acting like
his!" Cindy yelled as she held her hand out.

I unlocked the driver's door and opened it. "I'm fine Cindy."

"Terrance! Did you hear me? Give me my damn keys or I swear I'll
all the police. Your choice." I gave in and put the keys in Cindy's hand.
Ve both got in the car. I faced forward but I could feel Cindy's eyes
enetrating the side of my face like a laser beam.

"What the hell is wrong with you?" she exclaimed.

I couldn't look at her. "I honestly don't want to talk about it right
ow."

"No! You're going to talk! I swear to God we'll sit in this parking lot
ll night if you don't explain what the hell just happened," Cindy
emanded, shifting her whole body to face the passenger's seat.

I kept looking forward. "Cindy, I apologize. He just said something
hat made me fly over the top. I just lost control."

"About what?"

"I guess you didn't know that Tory Bishop is the one that had the sex
ape with Lisa," I said, looking at Cindy.

Cindy paused then nodded. "Okay. No I didn't know that, sorry. But
vhat's your point? That doesn't give you grounds to do what you did. Are
ou not over her? Do you not have enough sense to control yourself at an
pscale gathering?"

"The hell with this gathering! You must have something going on with him too, huh?" I snapped, turning to Cindy. "Let me know now if he had a piece of you already so I won't be surprised! Let me know if he got a piece of that ass too."

"Negro you must've lost your damn mind! Don't try to drop your insecurities on me! I don't want Tory! Tory is like a baby brother to me! Did you not believe me when I told you that he was like family?"

I placed my forehead in my hands. "Ahhh! I'm sorry, Cindy! I shouldn't have said that."

"Hush up," Cindy interrupted. "I have never been more embarrassed in my life!"

"I feel terrible." I hid my face in my palm.

"You should feel terrible! How selfish of you to act reckless at an event that I invited you to. Everyone is watching me. They already think that we don't belong!" Cindy said, pointing to her skin. "But it seems like you want to reaffirm that huh, Terrance?"

"Well just don't bring me anymore! How about that?" I rebutted.

"Don't make this about me, Terrance! You are the one who is struggling with something. You need to grow the hell up and move on. Your ex-fiancée has moved on! She's out being Mother Teresa somewhere, and you're here trying to beat up someone just because they said something that you didn't like. Grow the hell up and move on!" Cindy shifted herself comfortably back into the driver's seat, started the ignition, and we left the event.

We pulled into Cindy's house. I knew she was mad at me, but I really didn't feel like driving back home. As soon as I had that thought, she turned to me.

"I think you should go back to your place tonight. You need time to yourself to reflect, and I do too."

I agreed. I didn't bother asking her for a goodbye kiss like I usually would. I knew she was pissed at me. Hell, I was disappointed in myself. Once we got out the car, she walked to her front door and didn't look back. *Damn. I can't believe I let her down.* I got in my car and went home. Once I got home, I threw my fist towards my wall and punched a hole right through it. A picture fell from the wall and shattered on the floor.

Shit! I still can't control my anger. I pulled my fist out of the hole. My knuckles were bleeding. I didn't even treat it. I went straight to my bed and flopped on it. I laid there on my back thinking, bloody knuckles behind my head and face to the ceiling... *Lisa, Lisa, Lisa. Why do I still give a damn about Lisa? God, why do I still care about Lisa?* And to make matters worse, I knew Cindy was probably thinking twice about dating me now. There's no telling what she thought about me. I made a fool of myself tonight, all because of the fact that I couldn't handle the truth, and I couldn't accept the past for what it is.

God please, please help me figure this thing out. Help me to mentally move on from Lisa. And please don't let me lose Cindy because of what happened tonight. I'm begging you. I closed my eyes. I wanted this nightmare of a day to end.

Chapter 23: Case Closed

There was no way. I mean absolutely no way that I was going to tel Fred and Jay what I did that night at the gala. I usually tell them everything. But this, this was personal. I was ashamed. I learned my lesson and I was moving on, plain and simple. That night would forever be a distant memory, buried six hundred and sixty six million feet underneath sea level. That night, the devil came out of me, so I won't mention it. This would be just a regular Fun Friday with my boys. Good drinks. Good laughs. Good times.

Fred and I were at the bar. Jay was surprisingly late. He told us he'd be coming though.

"Jay is never this late to a Fun Friday. What do you think is going on?" Fred asked.

"He probably just got caught in some traffic, he'll be here soon." Right after I spoke, Jay walked in the door with a tailored dark blue blazer on and a fresh cut. He had a bright smile. "As a matter of fact, there he is."

"Fellas! I'm sorry I'm late!" Jay said, pulling out his chair to sit.

"You look like you just won the lotto man. What's going on? You're shining tonight," I commented.

"Well gentlemen… to tell the truth, I'm late because I'm coming from a date," Jay confessed.

"A date? With who?" Fred inquired.

"With Sony of course."

"Are you serious about this girl?" Fred asked.

"Serious as a heart attack man," Jay replied.

"Really? I have to meet this special woman."

"Yea you can meet her Terrance, she's cool as shit."

"I Googled her, she seems pretty legit," Fred informed us.

"Pretty legit? That's not even the half! She's the shit! She has her own practice. She makes a shit load of money. I feel like you insulted her with that statement," Jay snapped.

"Who are you and what have you done with my friend Jay? You're actually sticking up for this chick? I love it!" I said.

"I'm sorry. I just feel like she does too much to be underestimated. I really respect her hustle."

"But what is it? How did she manage to get you feeling this way? I never hear you talk like this Jay? Why her?" Fred inquired.

"I mean everything feels so right. I can't even lie. I've never felt like this."

"Wow. Explain man! This is big! You never catch feelings! What has she done to you?" I pressured.

"Okay. Look. Usually when I'm with bitches, I feel like they're stupid. All I want from them is a good time in the bedroom. I hit that ass right, after that I want them to leave. Nothing makes me want to commit, but not Sony. When I'm with her, I just want to talk for hours and hours. We haven't even had sex. She said no and I respect that. Maybe that's why I respect her too. I don't mind cuddling. That says something!"

My eyes widened. "You really do feel something! So are you thinking about committing to this chick?"

Jay shrugged. "I don't know. Maybe. It's about that time that I take something serious, you know. Been doing a lot of thinking lately."

"How do you know this isn't a lust thing, Jay?" Fred asked.

"Man, I don't know. It's kind of like I just don't want her to be with no one else. I can see myself with this girl long-term."

"Well, I hope it all works out brother." I held up my cup. "Cheers to my boy Jay finally finding a girl that he sees a future with."

"Terrance, see what Cindy's schedule is looking like. You, Cindy, Sony and I can go on a double date next week sometime. It won't hurt to get us two power couples together," Jay said, giving me a nudge on the shoulder.

"That sounds like a plan. Let's do it."

"Let thy cup runneth over with blessings!" we said in unison, tapping our cups together before sipping.

Friday 6:30 p.m.

Finally off. I thought I'd never be able to leave. I had a lot of work to do. Never put off tomorrow what you can do today. Now is always the time. I had to stay ahead, especially if I wanted the CFO position. Thank

God I finished though. Anyway, I was going with Jay to pick up his girlfriend from her office. He wanted me to see how official she was, so he decided that we'd all carpool together.

We pulled up to her office. I was impressed. The Law Office of Sony Cox was boldly displayed on the front of the building. Jay and I walked up together. We went inside the office and the secretary greeted us.

"How may I help you gentleman?"

"We're just waiting for Sony. Can you let her know that we're here?" Jay directed.

"Hold on," the secretary responded as she began typing on her computer. "She said that she'll be right out.

After about five minutes of waiting, the back office door opened and out came a short, brown-skinned lady with long hair. She had on glasses with a nice-fitting suit and smiled at the sight of both of us. She was very attractive.

"Hey y'all," Sony said, walking our way waving.

"Sony, this is my best friend Terrance. Terrance, this is Sony." Jay smiled as he introduced us.

"Nice to meet you, Terrance. I've heard a lot of great things about you," Sony said, shaking my hand.

"It's a pleasure, Sony."

"Okay. I'm sorry to have y'all waiting, but one of my new clients will be stopping in any minute now to drop off some paperwork. As soon as I meet with her, we'll be good to go, and I'll be all yours."

"It's no rush. I don't want to mess up your money, handle your business," Jay told her.

"I'm glad you understand," Sony said with a wink as she headed back to her office.

Jay looked at me. "See, I told you. Isn't she a keeper?"

"Hell yea," I said, "but the real question is, are you going to do right so that you can *keep her*?"

"Come on man. I told you, when I'm serious about something, I won't let it go."

During our conversation, the front door swung open and a lady with sunglasses came in. She was obviously pregnant. She went to the front

lesk and took her glasses off. Then, she looked back at the both of us. I
couldn't believe my eyes.

"What the fuck are you doing here?" Sarah yelled.

I looked at Jay and he looked as if he had just seen a ghost. He didn't
say anything.

"This must be some type of joke! So you're trying to defend yourself
or something?" Sarah continued.

"Please, Sarah. Please," Jay said, shaking his head.

The back office door opened and Sony came out. "What's going on
here? Everything okay?"

"Why is he here?" Sarah asked, pointing at Jay. "You didn't tell me
that he was going to be here."

"Jay? You all know each other?" Sony asked, looking confused.

"Know him? He's the one that I'm filing the lawsuit against! The devil
himself!"

Jay looked at Sony shaking his head. Sony looked at Jay.

"Is this true? You're responsible for this?" Sony asked, pointing at
Sarah's stomach.

I had never seen Jay more shook in my life. I could see the
goosebumps on his neck and was anxious to hear his answer.

"Baby, I can explain everything. It's not as bad as it seems. She's just
mad that she doesn't know who her baby daddy is. Yes we did something
together, but she's just confused. Terrance hit too," Jay explained,
pointing towards me.

"What? Come on Jay! You gotta be kidding me, bruh! Don't put me in
this!" I said looking at him.

"See... you're a coward! You can't even own up to your own shit!
Sony, please don't tell me you were dating this low-down, dirty skunk! If
so, I'm warning you... he ain't worth shit," Sarah continued.

Sony shook her head and then looked up to the ceiling. She chuckled
to herself. "Sarah, I'm really sorry about this. As my client, you did not
deserve this surprise. My apology. I had no idea. And no I was not dating
him. As a matter of fact, Jay and Terrance can you all please leave the
premises?"

I was getting out of my seat to leave, and then I looked at Jay. He was still looking at Sony while sitting down. I knew he was angry. His eyes were watery as if he was seconds away from shedding a tear.

"Really, Sony?" he asked.

"Jay, did I stutter? Lose my number, and leave the premises. Or I will call the police."

Jay got up and we walked out the door together.

"Really? You're just going to bring my name up in your shit?" I said looking at Jay as we got into the car.

"Terrance, please! I'm not trying to hear your shit right now. It was the truth, wasn't it? Did I lie? No! What's more important is the fact that I just lost a fine ass chick that was good enough to be my wife for a scum bag bitch."

"Whose fault was that, Jay? You have to stop blaming the world for your fuck ups," I told him.

"Whatever man. Call your girl Cindy and tell her the double date is off. I need a drink and some time to myself. I'm dropping you back off home."

I called Cindy and told her that the double date was off. She and I were still free, so we decided to go out to get a bite together at Mary Macs.

"So what happened? Why did y'all cancel?" Cindy asked.

"Ummm... Let's just say that there was a bit of a mix up," I said.

"What do you mean a mix up?"

"It's actually a funny story, but I'll keep it brief. So Jay used to mess with this one chick. A chick that he now regrets messing with because apparently she is pregnant right now with his baby. He was trying to stay away from her as much as possible. Come to find out, Jay's new chick, who is a family law attorney, was supposed to be representing his old chick by filing a suit on Jay. So today, we all met up on accident at her office. And as you probably already know, it wasn't a good ending."

"I'm not surprised at all. It looks like he got what he deserves. Karma will always find you. I'm surprised that you would even want to hang out with a person that treats women like that."

"I don't get what you're saying?"

214

"This guy Jay is a womanizer. Is that the type of friend that you want to have? I was always taught that birds of a feather flock together."

"Jay has been my friend since middle school. He's always been a ladies' man. But that doesn't mean that he's a bad guy. You have to get to know him before you judge him."

"I'd rather not get to know him. That would be a waste of time on my part and his. But just remember this, Terrance... even though you all were childhood buddies; sometimes we have to grow out of our friendships, especially the friends that don't have the same level of maturity. They need to be the first to go. Just keep that in mind."

As Cindy was finishing her rant, I got a call from an unidentified number.

"Hello?" I answered.

"Terrance, I need you brother."

"Who is this?" I asked.

"It's Jay. I'm in trouble... I'm in Fulton County Jail."

"What? How did you get there?"

"After my little situation with Sony, I went to have a couple of drinks, couple too many. I hit a pole. I fucked up."

"Ahh man. I'm coming. I'll be there soon."

We hung up and I looked to Cindy to explain why I would have to leave her.

"You don't have to explain. I overheard him. I know you have to go bail him out. Now you see what I'm telling you. That's so reckless. He could've killed someone. I don't like you around people like that honestly," Cindy continued.

"I get it. I'll listen to your rant later. Let me go get him," I said.

8:30 a.m.

After scraping up some funds, I had enough to bail Jay out. No matter what Jay could've possibly done, he was my best friend. Even if he was

215

guilty, I would be there for him no matter what. I'd never turn my back on him.

I was waiting in the parking lot. The jailhouse was surrounded by a tall fence and barbed wire. I could see Jay walking out. It was a good feeling seeing him leaving that place. We didn't belong there. He opened the passenger side door and got in.

"You okay man?"

Jay looked at me. "You have no idea how I'm feeling man. My emotions are all over the damn place. I'm so angry with myself."

"Just look at it as a learning experience man. Everyone makes mistakes. It could've been worse, you could've hurt someone, or you could've hurt yourself."

"You're right. I just can't believe I'm losing a chick that I was actually serious about. It's hard on me."

"Ay, if you all are meant to be, she'll be back. You just have to work with her and give her some time," I said.

Jay stared out the window and shook his head in disappointment.

"I ran into a pole. My car is totaled. I got a DUI. All over this chick."

I put my hand on Jay's shoulder. "Don't beat yourself up about it. It's the past, let's move on."

"I know man. I know. It just sucks. Hopefully this doesn't get back to the job. This would be a bad look."

"You should be fine man. Don't worry about nothing like that," I assured him.

Jay looked at me and smiled. "Thank you for being here for me in this awkward situation. I really appreciate you, Terrance."

"Anytime brother."

"And let's keep this between me and you. Don't tell Fred. I don't feel like hearing his damn mouth."

"I got you."

Monday 9:00 a.m.

Boy do I love Mondays! That's not sarcasm. I really don't mind Mondays. Not this Monday though… I was late to work. Once I oversleep it always feels like the rest of the day is a downward spiral. First,

216

ouldn't find anything to wear. I tore my closet up looking for clothes that could've sworn I just saw the day before. Then finally as I was rushing ut the door, every single traffic light wanted to turn red once I got up lose to it. And when I was moving in traffic, it seemed like everyone vanted to drive 10 MPH under the speed limit. They must've wanted to nake my life miserable. I needed to get to work.

I eventually arrived. Paperwork was scattered all over my desk and I lready had fifteen unread emails. *Did I do anything productive on riday?* I thought. I couldn't have because this was ridiculous. I left my lesk a mess. I was probably so ready for the weekend that I just zoomed ut of here. I grabbed papers and began to sort and pile them. I had to nake an attempt to get my life together. I couldn't start my week off vrong.

My phone rang, interrupting my attempt to straighten up my desk. jreat. I made a ruckus stumbling in late already, and now my phone was inging extremely loud just to bring more attention to me. I ignored it mmediately to stop the noise. I looked at the number calling. It was Jay. *'ll call him back. Now is not the time. He can wait.*

I continued straightening my desk. My phone rang loudly again. I orgot to silence it. Damn! How aggravating. It was Jay again. I guess he :ouldn't wait. I got up from my cubicle and went to the bathroom to .nswer.

"Terrance! You won't believe this shit! I go into work, only to find ut that I've been terminated. Terminated!"

I got up and walked into the bathroom. "What? How?"

"What do you think? They said that I wasn't meeting my quotas at vork, but that wasn't it! They fired me because I got arrested! They're just rying to cover it up to make it seem like it wasn't that!"

"Man! This can't be real."

"Some of the co-workers told me that they knew about my situation. Vord on the street is that Cindy was the one who was behind me getting ired. Please tell me that you didn't tell Cindy that I got arrested!"

"It couldn't have been her," I said as I paced back in forth in the >athroom.

"You told her. You told her, didn't you?"

217

"I didn't tell her. I was with her when you called from Fulton County She overheard our conversation."

"Why would you let her hear Terrance? Are you stupid? She's an executive. She has the influence to get me out. You got me fired Terrance! Your bitch fired me!"

"Ay, Jay, come on man, don't disrespect my woman. Call me a bitch not her. I know you're mad, but let's not jump to conclusions here okay."

"No! She's a bitch! Terrance, you know she didn't like me in the firs place!"

"Jay! It's my fault man. I apologize. I should've told you that she was there when you called me from Fulton County. I should've known to walk away or something. I don't want to put this on her."

"Tell her to give me my job back! She's the devil! You better not stay with that bitch after this! Dump her ass!"

"Jay, calm down. I'm going to call her to see if she knows anything."

"I'm telling you that she's the one behind me getting fired! My co workers wouldn't lie! Leave her ass now!"

"I love you to death, but I'm not going to leave my woman, Jay. don't know any details to even make a decision like that. I just can" assume."

"How could you do this to your best friend? I'm the one who introduced you to this bitch! You're going to choose her over me? You're going to choose a hoe over your bro? What happened to the brotherhood' May our cup runneth over with blessings? Do we say that for fun? She': cutting off my blessings! So you should cut her ass off!"

I was silent for a moment. "I'm not going to leave her, Jay."

"Okay. Well consider this your last time ever talking to me. Keep my name out of your damn mouth from here on out. You hear me?"

The call ended. I balled up my fist and punched the bathroom stall. My hand instantly began to hurt. The pain from my hand was nothing compared to my frustration with Jay's situation. I paced back and forth in the bathroom. I had to call Cindy.

"This is Cindy speaking."

"Hey, this is Terrance. Do you know anything about Jay getting fired?"

"Ummm… why do you ask?"

"He told me that you might know something about him getting terminated."

"I can't discuss work related issues outside of work, Terrance."

"Why not? This is my damn best friend, Cindy!"

"I don't care who it is! Whatever happens with the firm is confidential. can't talk about it."

"Can you take your corporate hat off for a second to speak to me? I ust lost my best friend because he believes that I had something to do with getting him fired. Did you tell anybody about him getting arrested?"

"Terrance! What do you want to know, huh? What can you do about he situation? Not a damn thing. It's out of your hands and it's out of my ands! There's way more to the situation than what goes on in your head. There's a fine line between business and our relationship! Do not blur the ines, or you will always be disappointed. I don't make those types of ecisions here. So no, I did not fire him. I'm sorry about what happened to our friend, but what's done is done!"

"Do you have a sympathetic bone in your body? Do you understand why I should be mad?"

"Understanding why you're mad, and sympathizing are two different hings. Jay is not my friend so I'm sorry if I'm not crying on your shoulder with you. He's a grown man, Terrance. I'm sure he will be able to handle his business on his own and find another firm."

"I'll talk to you tomorrow," I said before hanging up.

Chapter 24:

Friends or Foes?

When I got off the phone with Cindy, I was stuck. This all had happened so fast. I guess the messed up part about the whole situation is that I didn't know who to blame. I understood why Jay was frustrated. And as crazy as it may sound, I understood Cindy's stance on it. As for me, hell I was just caught in the middle of it.

It was 10:00 a.m. when I called Fred. I knew he was at work, but needed to talk. I needed some outside insight.

"Hey man. Are you available tonight?" I asked.

"Why what's up?"

"I need to talk to you. I'm in a sticky situation."

"What happened? What do you mean sticky situation?"

"I messed up. And I don't know what to do. I'll have to explain it to you when we meet. Let's meet at the bar," I suggested.

"Okay. Is Jay coming too?"

"Nah man. Just me and you."

"You okay man?"

"Ummm, yeah. I'll explain when I see you."

We met at one of my favorite spots, The Tavern at Phipps Plaza. The bar was packed so Fred pulled up a stool and sat fairly close to me.

"So what's going on man?" You got me worried." Fred initiated the conversation.

"Have you spoken to Jay?" I asked.

"No I haven't."

"Jay hates me right now. Like he is really pissed off. He is so pissed at me that our friendship is in jeopardy."

"Really? What did you do?"

220

"To be honest, I'm not supposed to shares his situation. I'd rather him tell you what happened. He already hates me enough."

"That's ridiculous. Y'all are best friends. Whatever it is, we can all talk about it together. We solve problems like men. Face to face. Why can't you tell me what the problem is?"

"Because he just didn't want me to share. He knows that you would feel some type of way about everything."

"But that's what friends are for, right? I'm going to tell him how I feel. There's nothing wrong with that. As a matter of fact, give him a call. Invite him here."

"Okay. But you'll have to talk to him, because he doesn't want to hear what I have to say right now. You're a great mediator. Here." I handed Fred my phone. He dialed Jay's number and put the phone to his ear.

"Hello. Jay? ... Wow. It looks like he hung up on me. He must be really mad."

"I told you."

Fred kept my phone. "I'll call again to try to leave a voicemail... Wait minute, you have an incoming call."

"Who is it? Is it Jay calling back?" I asked.

"It's... Michelle? Why the hell is Michelle calling you?" Fred looked over at me.

I said nothing. I couldn't think of a legitimate answer on my feet, so Fred answered my phone for me.

"Hello?"

"Hey, Terrance, are you busy?" Michelle asked.

Fred hesitated, trying to hide his voice. "Nah."

"Okay. I need to talk."

"About what?" Fred continued with a disguised voice.

"The same thing that we talked about last time we were together... Can you find a quieter place?"

Fred looked around the bar. "Ummm, no. Just talk. I can hear."

"Wait, is this Terrance?" Michelle asked.

"What do you need with Terrance?" Fred questioned, without hiding his voice.

The phone was silent, and then Michelle hung up. Fred looked back at me.

221

"Terrance! What the fuck is going on? What is Michelle doing calling you?"

"Fred don't panic. It's nothing going on between us, we…"

"Save it! I'm going to call her again. I'm going to get to bottom o this."

Fred called her again and he was sent to the answering machine. Ther he called from his phone and got the same outcome. Fred looked back a me.

"Terrance, I swear to God that it's taking every bone in my body not tc throw you out of this chair right now. What business did you have witl my ex that required you to talk to her behind my back?"

"Please, Fred, calm down and let me tell you why she reached out tc me. It looks bad but it's not what you think," I attempted to explain.

"Calm down? I don't want to hear it, Terrance! What do you have tc say to my ex-girlfriend without me knowing? Huh? Y'all creeping behinc my back?"

"Hell no, Fred!" I grabbed Fred's arms as tightly as possible anc looked at him directly in the eyes. "Fred! Listen to me! Please! Before yot punch me, let me tell you the whole story."

"Why are you touching me, Terrance? Let me go!" Fred said whil looking down at my arms.

"Promise me that you will not swing on me," I requested, looking a Fred in his eyes.

"I won't. Just let me go." I let him go. Fred turned forward and sa silently with a frown on his face.

"Are you listening?"

"Talk!" Fred shouted.

"Okay, first off, to clear things up, there's absolutely nothing going or between Michelle and I, if that's what you were thinking. Not too long ago, I saw Michelle in Publix. She had huge shades on and I asked her tc take them off. Come to find out, she had a black eye. She made me promise her that I would not tell you about it. Unfortunately, I kept my promise and I told her to call me if she needed someone to talk to abou it."

Fred turned his barstool towards me. "So you mean to tell me that Keith is beating Michelle's ass and you thought it was a good idea not to tell me?"

"I apologize, Fred. It wasn't smart of me. I should have told you regardless."

Fred said nothing. I watched him sit still in thought. He put his head in his hands, hiding his face as if he was going to cry. I could only imagine what was going through his head.

"Fred, that's not an easy decision. I love you man and I didn't want you to get caught up with something like that."

To my surprise, Fred turned to me with red, watery eyes and punched me in the jaw. It felt like a 100 MPH fastball had just met my face at full speed. My chair slipped from under me and I hit the floor so hard that I felt like I had cracked a rib. A glass fell and shattered by my face. I closed my eyes and covered my face to block the shards of glass. People gasped. All eyes were on us. Fred's shadow stood over me along with people holding his arms trying to retain him.

"The hell with you, Terrance! There are certain boundaries that you just shouldn't cross. The only woman that I ever loved is getting her ass whooped and you decided not to tell me. I swear, God is the only thing stopping me from strangling you to death."

In awe and in pain, I leaned up from the floor. The stale taste of blood in my mouth led me to spit. "Okay. I may have deserved that. Fred, you can be mad at me, I just don't want you to get involved with that situation. That's something that Michelle and Keith have to work out."

"Shut up, Terrance! I've heard enough! There's nothing you can say right now to soothe the situation. You don't know what the hell you're talking about! What if someone was beating Lisa's ass every night? How would you feel?" Fred yelled.

I said nothing.

"Exactly!" Fred stormed towards the exit, shoving chairs and tables in his path on the way.

I got up off the floor slowly. One of the managers came up to me.

"Sir, are you okay? Do you need first aid or medical attention?"

"No. I'm fine. I'm leaving now."

Chapter 25:

Fatal Attraction

My head was throbbing. Part of it was from being drunk and the other half was from Fred's fist to my jaw. Damn. It was painful. I was hurting physically and mentally. I had to be strong. *Everything will be okay*, I told myself. It's hard to be optimistic, especially when your two best friends both hate your guts. Things were bad. Never in a million years would I believe something like this would happen. Never. I still didn't know how it even came about. It felt like my life was crumbling before my eyes. I was barely able to walk out of the restaurant. I was dazed and felt lost. *What should I do now? Who should I call?*

I called Fred to apologize again. I was sent to the answering machine. I expected that. I then called Michelle. I had to make sure she was okay too. The first call was sent to the voice message. So, I decided to text her.

Hey it's Terrance. Fred just sucker punched me and left already. You can answer the phone.

I looked at my phone and it was a call from Michelle.

"Hey," I answered.

"Are you okay?" Michelle asked.

"Yeah, I'm fine. My chin just hurts a little bit."

"Terrance, please tell me that you know where Fred is."

"No I don't. All I know is that he's furious. Fred is the most peaceful person I know. I've never seen him this angry."

"Oh God, no!"

"What's wrong?"

"Fred called my phone like 10 times and left long text messages about what he is going to do once he saw Keith. Keith had my phone and saw some of the texts and he listened to the voice messages."

"What? Where is Keith now?"

"I don't know, he left. I heard him say that Fred was coming over tonight. I know he'll be back. He's probably around here somewhere waiting for him. Terrance, please! Do not let Fred come over here!"

"Okay, okay. I'm going to call him right now. I'll call you back."

I called Fred five times straight, still no answer. I was close to Fred's house, so I rode past it. Fred's driveway was empty. *Damn.* I hoped he wasn't headed to Michelle's house. If so, I needed to get there to try to intercept him. I knew he was going to do something he'd later regret.

Foot on the gas, I zoomed to Michelle's house. Once I got into the neighborhood, I slowed down and rode through cautiously. I was looking around to see if anything looked suspicious. I saw Michelle's house. It looked peaceful. I decided to park within walking distance from the house and then I called Michelle back.

"Hey! Are you okay?" I asked.

"Yes I'm fine. I'm just sitting here on the couch."

"Okay. Is it just you?"

"Yeah, just me. Keith is still gone."

"Okay. I couldn't get in touch with Fred. I have no idea where he is. He may have just gone to another bar or something. So we may be good."

"Thank God. I want to thank you for your help. And sorry for putting you through this trouble."

"It's okay. I just want to make sure everyone is safe."

Michelle kept talking but I wasn't listening. I was watching a car whip in front of her house. The car's lights were bright. Once the car lights went off, I knew who it was. It was Fred. I immediately hung up. I drove up to the car and parked in front of it. Fred and I got out of our cars at the same time.

"Fred! Get back in the car and go home," I yelled, pointing to Fred's car.

"Why are you here? Michelle told you I was coming too?"

I grabbed Fred and tried to get him back in the car. He shoved me off.

"Get your hands off me! What's wrong with you?"

Michelle overheard Fred and I. She opened the front door enough to yell, "Fred, go home! Please, Fred, go home!"

225

Fred started walking towards the door. "I just want to talk to Keith, that's all! Tell Keith to come out and be a man for once. I swear I'm going to kill him."

An engine revved up on the street and a black Camaro zoomed past my car out of nowhere. It all was happening in the blink of an eye. Fred and I were frozen stiff. The windows rolled down and two men with ski masks propped their arms outside the window with aka-47s. They started firing. The sound of the guns echoed through the air. Michelle screamed and closed the door. Fred tried to drop to the ground but was hit; four times in the chest and twice in the back of the head. He jerked as the bullets ripped through his body like miniature missiles. I dropped to the ground, crawling away from the street, desperately praying for my life to be spared.

I felt sharp pains rip through my stomach and through my back. My attempt to crawl away ceased immediately. I laid on the grass, dormant, in hopes that the shooters would recognize that I'd accepted defeat. The firing stopped and the sound of the engine revved and faintly disappeared into the distance.

Screaming. Crying. More screams. That's all I could hear. I blinked and looked up to the night sky. It looked peaceful, unbothered. *How am I still alive?* I tried to get up but it felt like heated butcher knives were in my stomach and back. My stomach and shirt were soaking wet. I looked to my side and saw blood slowly running through the grass. *Damn.* I was hesitant to look Fred's way. But I did. He was lying on his side, mouth and eyes open. His shirt was red. I couldn't handle any more.

I opened my eyes, but everything was blurry. I could see a light blue ceiling, but I couldn't feel a thing. I couldn't move. I felt some type of bandages on me. Someone was standing to my right. My vision began to clear a bit. It was Cindy with her hands folded.

"You okay?" she asked.

"Never been better," I mumbled, closing my eyes and groaning.

"I'm glad you can finally talk."

I nodded.

"Your friend Jay is with Fred's family right now."

"Fred okay?"

226

She shook her head no. "Fred passed."

My eyes opened and I looked to the sky, gut wrenched. I felt the wet streaks fall down the side of my face. Cindy came closer to the bed.

"No more suffering for Fred," she said.

"This can't be real."

"Stay strong. He'll want you to stay strong." Cindy tried to console me.

I lifted my head. "God, why take such a good person? Fred didn't deserve this! Damn!"

"What type of people are y'all dealing with, Terrance?" Cindy asked.

"Fred was too in love with Michelle... but she didn't love him back." The stream of tears rested on the side of my face.

Cindy leaned over the bed and looked into my eyes. "You have to make smarter decisions. You're a Financial Analyst, Terrance. There's no reason why you should be in the hood dodging bullets. I could've easily lost you along with Fred."

I laid there quietly.

The tall, fair-skinned doctor came in the room with his clipboard. "Terrance, I see you're up. That's a great sign."

I nodded.

"My name is Dr. Lovingston, but you can call me Dr. Lo, for short. While you were resting, Cindy and I were talking and she was telling me how great of a person you are."

I looked over at Cindy and put on half of a smile. "I'm sure she did. I'm glad she's here for me." Cindy smiled while grabbing and holding my hand.

"She also told me how strong of a person you are."

I nodded.

"You're a strong person, right? You're going to be strong no matter what?" Dr. Lo said, nodding, waiting for confirmation.

"Honestly Dr. Lo, I don't know how to feel. I can't believe my best friend is dead. It hasn't hit me yet. I'm all drugged up and my body is numb. This is a nightmare to me right now."

"I heard about your friend, Fred. I'm sorry to hear about your loss. There's another reason why I need you to be strong. As a matter of fact, you and Cindy," Dr. Lo said, turning to Cindy.

227

"Everything okay?" Cindy asked, adjusting in her seat.

"Terrance's body feels numb because one of the bullets hit him in the spine. Terrance may not be able to walk for up to a year."

Cindy threw her face in the palm of her hands.

I looked at the doctor with a blank stare.

The doctor walked over to console Cindy, as she began to sob.

This doctor must be smoking crack. I was dumbfounded, still looking at him to see if he was going to say he was kidding or something. His words just weren't registering with me. Cindy was crying louder. The nurses came with tissues for her. They then helped Cindy out of the room while they wiped her tears. I snapped.

"No! Get me out of here. Y'all don't know what the hell y'all are talking about! I have a career. I have work to do. I'm very important where I work. There's no way that I can be out of work for that long!"

I tried to sit up, but I was attached to all this medical stuff. I started ripping it off and grabbed the side of the bed to try and pull myself up on my feet.

"Terrance, stop! You're going to hurt yourself," one of the nurses warned.

I tried with all of my might. Immediately I felt the sharpest pain, as if someone had stabbed me in the back. I dropped back down in the bed. I began banging on the bed with my fist as tears flowed down my face. "No! Why, God?" I felt the nurse's hand rubbing my arm.

I yelled, "Dr. Lo! You can heal me! I will be able to walk soon!? I can walk? Right?"

"I'll try my best to take good care of you, Terrance. We're going to take this thing one day at a time."

I felt light headed. My eyes rolled to the back of my head.

Chapter 26: Amnesia

I opened my eyes. The hospital room light was dim. The room was old. I tried to move again, but the pain was too drastic. *Father, help me. All I could do was pray...*

"God, help me. Help me understand what's going on. I know you're in control, and you know what's happening to me, but I'm lost. Fred is gone. I can't walk. Please give me the strength. I'm your child, and I'm sorry for everything that I did to make you unhappy. Forgive me please. I know Fred's up there, tell him that I love him and I'm sorry. Please help me keep my mind. Please, God. Amen."

I closed my eyes. I began to think about the times that I had with Fred and Jay. I thought back to college. I remember one time the three of us were walking in the student union together. We saw a random clown doing circus tricks. Fred immediately dropped his bag and ran around the corner, so Jay and I ran behind him. We were terrified. We finally caught up to Fred around the corner. We were bent over with our hands on our knees, gasping for air.

"What happened? What did you see?" Jay asked.

"Man. I hate clowns," Fred exclaimed, catching his breath.

Jay and I looked at each other, and then fell on the floor laughing. We talked about that for months. I was laughing that moment just thinking about it. *Rest in peace brother.* I closed my eyes to rest.

The television woke me up. It was my favorite movie—*Bad Boys*. Will and Martin are fools in this one. A commercial came on as a nurse walked in.

"Good morning, Terrance. Looks like you're in a good mood," she said as she came to my side.

"This is one of my favorite movies. Martin is the funniest man alive."

"Good. Well you're going to be in a better mood. Because you have a visitor here for you."

Cindy walked in the room.

"I'm going to leave you two alone," the nurse said as she walked out.

Damn I was happy to see Cindy. She sat in the chair next to my bed Her makeup had runs below her eyes. I knew she had been crying. She was still beautiful. She sat with her arms folded. I hated that she had to see me like this. I could tell she was struggling to hold it together. But she's a strong person. Hell, she's probably a stronger person than I am.

"Hey baby," I welcomed her.

"How are you doing?" Cindy asked.

"I'm not going to lie, at first I couldn't believe it. I couldn't handle the news. I cursed God in my mind. I just had no idea why He would let this happen to me. But last night, I prayed about it and today I think I'm at peace with the situation. I'm happy to be alive. God has a plan. So, I'm not going to stress. On top of that, it helps to know that I have you here Thank you for being here for me."

Cindy stood up and looked out of the window. She tried to hold back her tears.

"Baby, I know it's hard, but I'm going to be fine. Don't worry about me. We're going to be fine. Stay strong for me." I tried to assure her.

Cindy sniffled and wiped her tears.

"Stop crying. Come here," I said, motioning her over.

"I can't," Cindy responded.

"Yes you can. It's okay, come."

Cindy shook her head no as she looked out the window. "I can't do this, Terrance."

"Can't do what?"

Cindy looked at me. "Us. I can't do us anymore."

"I don't get it. What do you mean?"

"I was wrong, Terrance. I made a huge mistake… I have a confession to make."

"If this is about you firing Jay, I forgive you. I'm over that."

Cindy shook her head. "No. It has nothing to do with that. I used you. I lied to you. I'm really madly in love with someone else…"

"Who?"

"Your Boss, Mr. Hinson… John and I had dated for a while but he dumped me. I cried my eyes out and begged him to stay with me, but he still wouldn't give me a chance. I knew who you were before you knew ne. When John and I were together, he would talk highly of you. He said hat you were like a mentee to him. He said that you were super talented. He dumped me right before the gala started. Right before I met you."

Cindy sighed, and then continued talking while looking out the window.

"It was the perfect opportunity for revenge. At first, I only wanted to have sex with you to get back at him. Then I took it further because I actually liked you as a person. I wanted to help you get the CFO position so that you could rise higher than him, and have me by your side to make him even more jealous. I wanted you to get that position more than you wanted that position for yourself. That was the ultimate way of him feeling my wrath. But now I'll admit that I have taken this too far. I'm guilty. It was all stupid. I'm ashamed."

I sat up. "Cindy, you're not serious, are you?"

"Terrance, the lie is over. I'm sorry."

"Cindy…"

"I'm going to pray for your recovery, Terrance. I'm sorry that I had to tell you at the worst time, but I couldn't hold it in any longer. I have to go now."

Cindy walked out of the room wiping her face. The door slammed behind her.

"Go! I don't need you anyway! I don't need anyone! I can take care of my damn self!"

My lips became dry. I balled my fists and my heart rate increased tremendously. I then felt goosebumps. I planted my face in hands. It was as if I'd just gotten shot in the heart. I wept.

God I hate her. I've never hated anyone. But my heart is now filled with hatred for that woman. Just like that? She just up and walked out on me. While I'm lying in the hospital like a worthless, sick, puppy dog that has rabies or something. She just left me to die. After all we've been through together! I don't get it! I've never felt this empty, abandoned, worthless, and played. *You know what, God, if this is what my life comes down to, then you might as well take me now. I swear I've had enough. I don't give a shit anymore. If you don't give a shit about me, I don't give a shit about me either!*

Four days had passed. I hadn't spoken to anyone. The nurses continuously brought me meals and I hadn't touched them. *They know I'm not eating that shit. I don't want it.* Dr. Lo and the nurses begged me numerous times to talk and to eat. Every time they came in, I closed my eyes. Or I'd look at them like they were stupid until they eventually left me alone. I overheard the nurse say I had lost 10 pounds and it felt like it. I just wanted to be left alone so I could die already. Then I'd be out of their hands.

The door cracked open. When I saw him walk in, I was shocked. It was Jay. I'm guessing the nurses called him. They were probably hoping that I would communicate. Jay tiptoed in and took a seat. Seeing me like this was going to mess with his stomach. I know I looked sickly. My skin was dry and flaky. My eyes were bloodshot red. I could see him getting emotional.

Jay wiped a tear from his eye. "You know, Terrance, I wasn't going to come. I had such an ill feeling for you that I almost still didn't come to see you at the hospital. Can you believe that?"

I lay motionless.

"How selfish of me? I'm sorry for holding the stupidest grudge against you. Man you are the brother that I never had. I always loved how much you respected women. Deep down inside, I wish I was able to respect women and treat them how you would. That's what real gentlemen do.' Jay paused and looked down at the floor.

"The nurse told me that you weren't eating anything and you refused to talk to anybody. I know that I can't feel the pain that you feel right now. And I totally understand why you wouldn't want to talk to me, but I will say this. I don't want to lose another friend. If you starve yourself to death then you'll leave me here alone. I don't know if I can deal with that Terrance. I love you man, don't be selfish."

Jay took a final look at me, tapped the bottom of my bed and proceeded out the door. I'm glad I got to see him one last time. Hours later, the door opened. It was Dr. Lo again. *Ugh. Here he comes with some more bullshit about how I need to eat.* I closed my eyes. I wasn't trying to hear what he had to say. I didn't want to be bothered anymore.

232

"Terrance, I know you can hear me. It's just you and I in here. I'm going to be completely honest with you, I know that this is a tough situation, but the way that you're going about it saddens me. I know you're a tougher person than this. But if you're trying to starve yourself to death, then you're doing a hell of a good job. I don't want you to die, Terrance. That's what I'm here for, to keep you alive and to get you out of here. Please help me get you out of here, Terrance, so you can continue your life."

The hospital door opened and the nurse popped her head inside.

"Dr. Lo, Terrance has a visitor."

"Okay. Just give me another second. What's the visitor's name?"

The nurse looked down at her clipboard. "Her name is Lisa Smith."

I almost choked. I started coughing. My eyes opened and I lost my breath for a second. I had a miniature panic attack. I was not expecting to hear Lisa's name. I was not ready to see her. She came like a thief in the night. Unexpected.

Dr. Lo turned to me. "Mr. Hill, are you okay?"

I nodded my head yes. Still coughing, I fanned myself with my hand. A cup of water was to my right. I grabbed it and gulped it. Some of the water spilled down the middle of my hospital gown and some of it went down the wrong pipe while drinking. I almost drowned in it. I coughed again.

Dr. Lo turned to the nurse and smiled. "Yes! Whoever Lisa Smith is, she can definitely come in! Terrance hasn't responded to anything I said until now!"

I finished the cup. I was trying to stay still, but I started shaking. I closed my eyes.

"I'm going to leave you two alone," Dr. Lo said.

I heard the door close. Silence. I knew she was in the room. I felt her presence.

"Terrance... are you going to ignore me too?"

I remained still. Lisa walked up to the side of the bed and gently grabbed my hand. A tear rolled down my face.

"I'm here now," she said.

I opened my eyes. It was a concerned face. My heart. My rib. My weak spot. My first love stood before me. Lisa. Seeing her again was like

233

the joy of a new season. My heart was warm like springtime, right after having the coldest heart for the longest, loneliest winter ever. The sun was shining bright again and she was hotter than ever! I mean Lisa was as beautiful as she was when she left. Her hair was naturally curled. Her light, brown skin was glowing. Her perfume was the sweetest scent. She illuminated the room. Her big brown eyes met mine, for the first time in a long time. I broke down. All I could do was cry like a baby that had been separated from his mama for too long. With open arms, I reached out for her and we hugged. We held each other, together, as tight as ever. We rocked back and forth, but didn't let go.

"I love you, Terrance," Lisa whispered.

"I love you too."

We let go, but held each other's hand.

"The nurses told me what happened, Terrance. I'm sorry for not making it sooner. I didn't find out until yesterday."

"It's okay," I said with a raspy voice.

"So tell me why you're giving up, Terrance? Why have you not eaten? This isn't the Terrance that I know."

"I feel like I lost it all, Lisa. It all started when I lost you. Ever since you walked out of my life, my world has been incomplete. I've been searching for a love like yours, and it's just led to disappointment. I lost a friend. I lost my ability to walk, and my so-called girlfriend, Cindy walked out on me. She had been using me the whole time. I couldn' handle it. I wanted them to just let me die here. My life had turned for the worst," I filled her in.

Lisa shook her head. "You know what, Terrance, I'm so disappointed in you. You know better."

"Disappointed in me? What are you talking about? I've lost damn near everything and all you can say is that you're disappointed in me?"

"Because you're feeding me all of this negativity. You must've forgot all about *Psalm 23*. Did we not agree that this was our favorite Bible verse? *The LORD is my shepherd; I shall not want.* Why are you yearning to be loved? God has already provided you with everything that you will ever need and more. *Ye, though I walk through the valley of the shadow of death, I will fear no evil: for thou art with me; thy rod and thy staff they comfort me.* You're acting as if God hasn't been right here with you hroughout this journey. *Thou preparest a table before me in the presence of mine enemies: thou anointest my head with oil; my cup runneth over.* Nobody can make you feel incomplete without your permission, not even ne. How can you be incomplete when you're already whole? God's been lessing you this whole time, but you've been too busy looking for omeone to tell you that they love you. To be breathing the breath of life is a blessing in itself. Be appreciative of all that God has done for you to this point. Out of all people, you know that this life brings storms, but you have to be able to smile because you know that God is always there. You re stronger than this. God won't give you more than you can handle. You must've forgotten all of this, because you wouldn't be giving up on me ight now."

"You are right. I admit that I had lost focus. I forgot about His grace."

Lisa shook her head. "So often we forget."

"Yeah, I confessed all that and admitted that you were right, but what bout you? Why are you really here? Tell me the truth, Lisa. How do I now that you're not here temporarily? Are you just here to feel sorry for ne? Are you here to make me feel better by feeding me all this spiritual tuff just to make sure that I don't die? If you're here to do all this only to eave me again like before, then you're no better than Cindy and you can et out of my face. I've had enough temporary folks in my life," I said.

"I'm here because I love you, Terrance. I want to get you back healthy."

"So why now? What took you so long to come back? My messages veren't good enough to bring you back? I had to almost lose my life for ou to come back?"

"I couldn't come back prematurely, Terrance. I had to continue on my ourney and follow God's direction. I needed that spiritual healing. I knew would come back for my love, I just didn't know when."

"So God told you that this was the time for you to come back?" I sked.

"Yep, since you like to forget things, you needed a friendly reminder. You needed some spiritual healing, just as I did when I had hit rock ottom. Dr. Lo can't prescribe you spiritual healing." She was right.

I squeezed her hand and took a deep breath. "I need you by my side nore than ever, Lisa. I missed you like crazy. These other chicks made me realize that you are the one for me. Promise me that you will stay by my side."

Lisa smirked. "First off, I can't make a promise to be your *side* chick, but I will say this... Your memory must really be failing you. Did you forget that technically I am still your fiancé too? That's something that I think you should remember," Lisa said before she winked.

I chuckled. "So you got jokes? As serious as I am right now, you still want to be a comedian?"

"I'm serious too! I just couldn't help it because you set yourself up for that one," Lisa said smiling.

We kissed. And held each other again. She was back like she'd never left.

The End

Let me know what you thought of the book!!!

Email-douglastparker@gmail.com
Connect with me on Instagram and Twitter @TreyParker_

Made in the USA
Charleston, SC
15 March 2016